Praise for the K-9 Rescue series by D.D. Ayres

"*Irresistible Force* is simply fabulous! With exhilarating action and stunning sensuality, Ayres draws you in and doesn't let go."

—Cherry Adair, *New York Times* bestselling author

"Incredible! You'll be on the edge of your seat to see if the heroine can make it out alive."

—Catherine Coulter, *New York Times* bestselling author

"Sexy . . . suspenseful . . . delicious . . . The tension and high-stakes drama help to make this a page-turner. And the sexiness of this couple makes this a memorable keepsake . . . Very enjoyable from beginning to end."

—USAToday.com

"Ayres brings gritty realism and sexy heat to this romantic suspense series." —*Publishers Weekly*

"Intrigue, danger, and romance . . . if you think dogs and romantic suspense are an excellent mix, then this is the series for you!" —*RT Book Reviews*

"Sexy, romantic, and with enough humor to keep the pages turning." —*Cocktails and Books*

"A steamy, exciting, suspense-filled love story."
—*Clever Girls Read*

"A story about a HOT cop and his K-9 partner? I was all in! And boy, did Ayres deliver! I count this book as a DEFINITE read. Cops and canines, two things near and dear to my heart!" —*Charlotte's Book Review*

Also by D.D. Ayres

Irresistible Force
Force of Attraction
Primal Force
Rival Forces
Necessary Force (novella)

EXPLOSIVE FORCES

D.D. Ayres

St. Martin's Paperbacks

This is a work of fiction. All of the characters, organizations, and events portrayed in this novel are either products of the author's imagination or are used fictitiously.

EXPLOSIVE FORCES

Copyright © 2016 by D. D. Ayres.

For information address St. Martin's Press, 175 Fifth Avenue, New York, NY 10010.

ISBN: 978-1-250-08697-6

Our books may be purchased in bulk for promotional, educational, or business use. Please contact your local bookseller or the Macmillan Corporate and Premium Sales Department at 1-800-221-7945, ext. 5442, or by e-mail at MacmillanSpecialMarkets@macmillan.com.

Printed in the United States of America

St. Martin's Paperbacks edition / November 2016

St. Martin's Paperbacks are published by St. Martin's Press, 175 Fifth Avenue, New York, NY 10010.

10 9 8 7 6 5 4 3 2

Brad Thompson, a great teacher, K-9 expert, and dog man. Now a good friend.

CHAPTER ONE

"Hello? Hello? Carly?"

Carly Harrington-Reese shifted her cell phone back to her ear. "I'm here, Aunt Fredda. I thought I heard a dog barking next door. But I don't hear anything now."

"Humph." That was Aunt Fredda's famous sound that, when emitted from the judicial bench where she was a juvenile court judge, stood for unimpressed, doubtful, or dissatisfied. "Didn't I just say it's not a good idea for a young woman to be working alone late at night?"

"I'm about done anyway." Carly put her aunt on speaker before reaching for the sterling silver bell necklace on her front display table. It was the reason she'd popped back into her store tonight. She hadn't meant to leave the signature piece of her first jewelry collection behind when she locked up. "Besides, the space next door is empty."

"Now I don't like the sound of that one bit. Empty spaces are just begging for trouble to walk in."

"It won't be vacant long. The landlord has had interest in turning it into a cupcake shop. I'm thinking people who like to buy individual sweets might also want one-of-a-kind items from my boutique."

"I know that's right. Flawless is going to be a hit. How can it not, with my little supermodel niece large and in charge? I saw the grand opening banner when I drove by this morning."

"You came by?" Carly frowned and laid the necklace on the counter. Whimpering sounds again. Was it a dog? Or her imagination working overtime? "Why didn't you come in?"

"Grand-nephew Frye. He just got his driver's permit and talked me into letting him drive around. I told him if he scratches my Mercedes it's coming out of his future college tuition money. Carly? You're not listening to me, are you? Carly?"

"Now that *was* a dog. I'm sure of it. Right on the other side of this wall." Carly had moved in between the racks of handmade scarves loomed in Ethiopia and the raffia-weave document cases made in Madagascar to press her ear to the eco-friendly wallpaper of the wall she shared with the shop next door.

There were faint noises coming from the other side, all right. Sounds like scratching.

"What are you doing? Is that a door I hear opening? Carly?" Aunt Fredda's husky voice had climbed half an octave. "You're not going over there? Don't be crazy."

"Sorry, Aunt Fredda. I'll call you back in five." Carly pocketed her phone and hurried out her front door.

Four of the five one-floor redbrick storefronts that made up the historically restored building strip at the corner of Lipscomb and Magnolia were dark. Only the large plate glass windows of her corner shop door spilled light onto the sidewalk.

Turning her head, she glanced right and left. It was past eleven o'clock on a Thursday night in March. A couple of cars rolled leisurely down Magnolia Avenue. All the slots in the public bike rental rack on the corner were full. The trendy bars in the next block in either direction were closed. The weekend would be different. But for now only one couple walked arm-in-arm on the other side of the street. No dog in sight anywhere.

Then she was sure she heard sounds again, coming from the store on her left. It was like that faint whimper her dog Cooper used to make when he got into trouble. An enthusiastic but uncoordinated mix of curiosity and poor choices, Cooper had height issues. He would climb up without hesitation onto beds, picnic tables, even the flat-bed of a truck. But anything higher than the sofa had him crying for assistance to get down.

She couldn't stand the idea of anything in trouble, es-pecially an animal. "I should just mind my own business." But she wasn't going to.

She never minded her own business when someone or thing was in trouble. Her mother called it her "Good Samaritan Habit" formed at the age of three. That was after she found Carly in their back yard with a garden snake that had half-swallowed a frog. Holding on to both crea-tures, Carly was trying to pull them apart. Sadly, the frog was a goner. Carly's instinct to help the vulnerable was still very much alive.

Moving in front of one of the dark windows of the shop next door, she pressed her forehead to the cool plate glass and framed her face with her hands to block the streetlight. But there was nothing to see. The windows were covered in paper from the inside.

She moved to try the door handle. It was locked.

She knocked. "Hello! Anybody in there?"

Silence. Not even a whimper this time.

The phone rang in her pocket.

"Tell me you aren't out on the street alone."

"I'm okay, Aunt Fredda."

"Did you find the dog?"

"No."

"That's because there isn't one. No one leaves a dog in a building. It's much more likely you heard mice next door. Or, maybe a squirrel looking for a place to build a nest. You're just nervous about your opening. You want me to come down there? Because I can be there in ten minutes."

"No, no." Carly blew out a give-me-patience breath. "You're probably right. I'm just nervous and jumping at every sound. Why don't you wait and come by tomorrow for the soft opening? You'll get the first pick of everything."

"Now that's an idea I like." Her aunt sounded very pleased. "I got to go. I'm missing *The Late Show*. Call me when you are on your way home."

Carly pocketed her phone and stood a moment longer, straining for sounds from the store behind her. Maybe it was just her nerves turning ordinary noises into ominous sounds. Of course, she could call and report that she heard weird noises coming from a vacant store. But what if Aunt Fredda was right and it was mice, or squirrels? Or rats? No, better not bother the police about rodents.

She turned back to her shop and paused, a smile spreading across her face as she gazed at the sign above the door. FLAWLESS.

Her shop represented so much. A fresh start. A new life. Flawless wasn't just about beauty. Or bling. It was about a woman empowering other women while owning her own style.

The idea for a store had crossed her mind when she was still working as a model. Everyone lauded the designers of the beautiful, sometimes bizarre, clothing she strutted on the catwalk. But only a handful of insiders ever met the talented women who embroidered, made lace, or spent hundreds of hours sewing by hand the sequins, pearls, and crystals that made so many of the couture pieces works of art. Most worked in crowded overseas factories, or locally, from home. Paid minimum wages for their exquisite creations, they never saw a cent of the exorbitant prices their contributions ultimately demanded at the retail level. She wanted to change that. So, she'd returned home, sunk a good bit of her savings into creating a boutique where people could come and touch and examine and buy one-of-a-kind pieces.

Flawless would highlight those yet-to-be-discovered women who deserved to reach an audience. Art wasn't just for the rich or those who didn't have to scramble for a living. There were lots of ways of not being okay in this world. Art was a way to be okay.

Carly took a deep breath as she caught her reflection in the store windows. Her two-tone hairdo was new enough that she paused to study it. A riot of tight blonde-tipped ringlets cascaded over her brow from the crown. The naturally darker sides of her hair had been swept back and pinned to mimic the look of being cropped very close. It was an edgy urban look that turned heads on the streets of Fort Worth.

She fluffed her curls with her fingers and smiled. She'd always pulled herself together on her terms. Now she would be helping other women know the feeling of succeeding on their own terms.

Within minutes, the shop was locked up and she walking to her Mazda, parked in the large lot behind the block of stores.

Security lights on motion detectors brightened the alley like a runway. Arms full of work materials, she pushed her key fob to unlock the hatchback when she heard a noise. No, a bark. Absolutely a bark this time.

She looked back over her shoulder to see the backdoor to the shop next to hers was ajar.

The second bark was louder. A bit high and strained. As if the dog was hurt or in trouble.

"I should mind my own business." She talked to herself when she was nervous. A habit from childhood she'd never lost.

She shoved her armload into the back of her Mazda. "Get in the car, Carly Harrington-Reese. Lock the doors. Call the cops, and go home."

Yes. That was the plan any sensible person would follow. But the dog was whining again, a sound so pathetic she couldn't resist the urge to check out the source. Maybe it had run into the store looking for shelter and got stuck, or something.

She hesitated. The "or something" might be the reason she should just follow plan A and leave.

She pulled out her phone. One wrong sound or weird creak and she was speed-dialing 911.

When she pushed, the door to the empty store opened inward on a space so dark it seemed matt finished in charcoal dust. "Hello?"

Her tentative question was met with silence. "Hi. I'm Carly from next door. Anybody here?"

More silence. So far, she'd kept both feet on the outside of the threshold. She wasn't scared of the dark. She just didn't like being alone in unfamiliar darkness.

She switched on the flashlight of her cell phone and stepped inside.

The first thing she saw several yards into the vacant space was the reflective surface of a pair of shiny shoes. The next thing that registered were the trouser legs attached to those shoes . . . and then the body of a man, lying face down on the concrete floor.

"*Ooh. Ooh.* Dead body." She began backpedaling toward the door. The body shivered. And then it moaned.

"Okay, so maybe not dead. Just mostly dead." Carly slapped a hand across her mouth to stop a bubble of nervous laughter. This was too serious. The man was probably a derelict, passed out from drugs or alcohol, or maybe both. He needed help.

She stabbed the emergency button on her phone.

The questions from the other end of the line came thick and fast after her statement of her problem.

"That's right. Man unconscious in an abandoned store. No, I don't know him. I have no idea. Drunk or drugs?" She made herself glance back at the form. "There's a liquor bottle by his head. And it smells funny in here. Like a gas station, maybe. No, I don't know if he's still breathing, and I'm not touching him to find out. Please send the police. Send an ambulance. Send somebody." She gave her location again.

As she punched to end the call, the arc of her flashlight leaped across the man's body to reflect a pair of eyes shining liquid in the darkness a few feet on the other side. Even as her lungs took in air to scream her brain registered the form. A dog stared at her. A big dog.

"I knew it." Carly moved carefully in a wide arc around the man's body toward the animal. An unfamiliar dog was definitely better company than an unconscious—please don't let him be dying—stranger.

She held up her light so it didn't shine directly into the animal's eyes. He was big, with a black muzzle, golden brown cheeks, and a mostly light body. Yep, definitely a German Shepherd.

That gave her pause. A dog under stress might become aggressive. But this one was whining softly, not growling, and his ears were perked up. "It's okay, big fella. You look like a nice dog."

She moved a little closer, keeping her voice low and

even. "You're a shepherd, aren't you? I had a dog growing up. His name was Cooper. He was part shepherd. Part boxer. But mostly parts unknown."

As she closed the distance, the dog stuck out his muzzle to sniff her tentatively, cold nose dabbing the back of her curled hand. After a moment he ducked his head under her hand and pushed against it, suggesting she pet him.

She stroked down one tall ear a couple of times and then the dog moved his head again and tried to move closer to her body but came to an abrupt halt.

"What's the matter?" She lifted her light. He wore a collar, a thick heavy leather one by the feel of it. It was attached to a leash that had been wound several times around a support post in the unfinished space. "You're stuck. No wonder you were whimpering."

She moved closer to pet him more strongly, feeling the tension coursing through his big body just under his fur. And there with his owner doing a face plant beside them.

Carly shook her head. She knew that some homeless people kept a dog for protection and company. But this guy wasn't doing his canine companion any favors tonight. She rubbed the dog's back. "It's okay. I'll get you out of here. You can come sit with me until the police arrive."

At least she could spare the dog the trauma of the police and EMTs arrival with sirens blaring. If too many of them came in quickly, a tethered and stressed dog might accidently bite someone.

She put her phone back in her pocket so she could use both hands to free the animal. "You shouldn't have to suffer because you have a—"

She glanced at the man. Now that her eyes were becoming accustomed to the light, he looked like a large bundle of clothing on the floor. He was murmuring low but not moving. Did he think she was trying to steal his dog?

The push of nervous energy nudged her and she naturally started talking. "Listen. I don't want any part of what you were doing here. Okay? Just in case you can hear me, I'm only trying to help your dog."

As she worked to loosen the knot in the leash, she kept glancing at the man. "I don't mean to pass judgment. Your situation is not my business. All I'm saying is, if you've got time to polish your shoes, you have a minute to pull your life together. Your priorities are completely—"

It was only a soft whoosh of sound. Just like the noise her gas heater made in her former London flat when it came on. And then she understood why.

The baseboard along the far wall began to glow. She froze, her mind trying to catch up with what her eyes were seeing. Flames, little yellow licks of flickering fire. Along the wall.

Fire.

That made no sense. But fire didn't have to make sense. *Oh my God! Oh my God! Oh my God!* She felt her lips moving, but no sounds emerged. A fire had broken out.

Giving up on the leash, she unlatched the dog's collar from it and gave him a shove. "Go! Go! Out!"

The dog swayed in the middle but didn't move. Heavier than she thought, he apparently wasn't going anywhere. Fine. Someone needed to save herself.

She made three steps toward the door when she looked back and saw the dog was nudging the man on the floor. That's why he remained. The shepherd would stay with his owner, despite the risk. She was sure of it.

As if cued, the video she'd had to watch about fire safety as part of her lease agreement came to mind. It said a person only had only four minutes to escape a fire once it began.

Four minutes! She needed only five more of those two hundred and forty seconds to clear the door.

"Crap."

She ran back, poked the man with her foot. "Hey, you! Get up! Fire. Do you hear me?" She leaned down and yelled near his ear. "Fire! Fire!"

When he didn't respond, she pushed his shoulder hard with both hands. The man beneath the shirt felt solid and warm. Alive. "Wake up! Please! You're going to die!"

She bent to peer down into a face that in the dark seemed to have no features. Not even his eyes opened. Hopeless.

She forced herself not to glance at the flames climbing the far wall. But from the corner of her vision she saw smaller flames making crazy progress across the floor. What could be burning in an empty store?

The dog was whimpering and shaking, running in and licking his owner but dancing away, evidently as aware of the flames as she was.

Giving up on rousing him, she grabbed his arm and tugged. "Oh Jesus! You weigh a ton." Frantic, she bent down, lifted one of his shoulders and shoved, trying to turn him over. His upper body twisted at an awkward angle. She pushed harder. She doubted that a back spasm would be nearly as painful as being barbecued.

When she had managed to flip him, he moaned in protest but at least he was on his back.

"Come on." She shook his legs as sweat popped out on her forehead. "You've got to help me. Move! Do you hear me?" Nothing.

She grabbed one ankle in each hand and began hauling him feet first toward the door. It was only twelve feet away. But that distance seemed like twelve miles. Thankfully, her Doc Martins helped her keep traction. Another day she might have been in stilettoes.

Two hundred and forty seconds. How many of those seconds were left?

The room around her began to roar, as if a wind had

suddenly sprung up. But it wasn't wind, it was heat. Flames crawled up the wall on the far side. Others snaked across the bare concrete floor in a weird pattern she couldn't stop to think about because it was coming toward the man. Scratch that. Toward her.

She tugged harder, cursing his bulk and her recent absence from the gym. Not that she could bench press two hundred pounds of man at any point. For a derelict, he was amazingly well fed and muscular.

Sweat streamed into her eyes. Something unseen but suffocating snaked further down her throat with every breath. Every impulse told her to abandon her burden and run. Save herself. But her hands wouldn't let go of the body. Only her thoughts were free to run on.

I'm not a Good Samaritan. I'm so not! Please get me out of this, Sweet Baby Jesus, and I promise I'll never do a bad deed again. Ever!

Where were the police? The EMTs? The help she'd called for what seemed like an hour ago hadn't materialized. Why had no one come in answer to her call?

And then the dog was there beside her. He grabbed a mouthful of his owner's pants leg and began tugging, too. The shepherd was strong, stronger than she was. His owner's body began to slide a bit more easily across the floor.

Carly was too scared to be grateful. Too winded to even utter a word of encouragement. It was the door or die.

Fumes stung her throat and eyes but she didn't pause to wipe away the tears blurring her vision. It was as if the flames were chasing them as she and the dog pulled the man along behind them in a mad dash for the door. It was only six feet now. Five feet. Four . . .

Carly tripped as she back-stepped over the threshold. It was metal, to keep refuse and water from the alley from easily entering the store. But it was enough of a speed bump to stop their progress.

Abandoning his legs, she reached forward with both hands to grab fistfuls of his jacket to try to haul him into a sitting position.

No good. He might as well have been a sack of wet cement.

She knelt down and straddled him at the chest. "Damn you! Wake up!" She struck him in the face, desperate to get a rise out of him.

She screamed as heavy hands fell on her shoulders. For a second she thought someone had come up behind her. Then she realized the man had reached up for her.

"Get off! Get off me!" Frightened, she struggled against his grip. But his fingers were like vises, making it impossible for her to get away.

The shepherd, realizing his owner was coming round, barked brightly and stuck his head in under Carly's arm to lick the man's face.

He was cursing under his breath and gripping her so hard she moaned. Then he lifted his head and spoke. "I don't want to die."

His rough husk of a voice went over her like lightning striking much too close.

The plea was a bare whisper but the look in his eyes— he'd opened his eyes!—said all that she'd been thinking. They were in absolute mortal danger.

She didn't want to die either. Every instinct said that trying to save this stranger would only get them both killed.

As if he'd heard her thoughts, he released her with a hard push. "Go. Now!" He was giving her permission to abandon him.

Move, Carly. Move or die!

She stumbled back against his dog, who was pushed in protectively behind her knees. Even as she did, the man collapsed onto his back, his eyes falling shut.

Hopeless. You're hopeless.

A dozen other responses zoomed through her thoughts but she didn't have breath for any of them. Instead, she grabbed two handfuls of his jacket and pulled him upright again. "Wake up! Now!"

He moaned, his lids fluttering. Finally he seemed to realize that she was still trying to help him out of the doorway. He gripped her forearms, this time using her to leverage himself in an effort to move. His legs weren't co-operating much, making scuffling sounds against the floor, but it made all the difference. They were moving over the barrier of the door sill.

Once in the alley, their movements activated the security lights, spotlighting them like a soundstage. For the first time she saw him clearly. He still held her shoulders, his face revealed by the alley light. He had light hair and blue eyes. A strong clean-shaven jaw, and a nice mouth even though it was twisted in pain. He was no derelict. Even in agony, he was gorgeous.

For one second all she could think was that she had probably saved the life of this very good-looking man. Even as she thought it, Carly scolded herself. The fact that he was good-looking was about as useful as noticing the color of a balloon attached to an eighteen-wheeler that had just run her down.

The heat from the doorway suddenly pushed against them like the belched breath of a dragon.

Carly was up on her feet in an instant.

Close the door. It was the only thought in her head. As if by doing so she could contain every bit of the super-heated inferno inside.

He grabbed her ankle and sent her sprawling into the concrete walkway. Even as she fell, the man who minutes before had been unconscious flopped over her, covering her body with his. A second after that, something exploded inside the store, spewing heat and flame through the exit.

Too stunned to cry out, it took her three tries to draw a breath. Even then, all she could do was lie there and sob.

"It's okay. It's okay." Still lying over her, he was whispering into her ear and awkwardly patting her cheek. "You did—good."

Carly closed her eyes and just tried to breathe.

"We've got all we need tonight. I'll let the EMTs finish checking you out."

Carly didn't even smile at the man who identified himself as an arson investigator. Before him, a police officer had interviewed her. Both had asked questions until she no longer had breath or answers for them.

Breathing in oxygen through the mask the EMT had given her, she sat on the bumper of an ambulance parked well away from the fire. Other than hugging the dog who had miraculously ducked in under her arms while the EMTs looked her over, she had no energy left for anything. The dog, poor baby, looked as miserable as she felt. Probably that was because his owner had been scooped up and carted away.

She had watched the ambulance containing the man pull away from the curb, sirens blaring, and felt nothing but relief.

He wasn't her problem anymore. That man was not part of her world. Not her responsibility. Even so, she glanced up at the EMT hovering over her.

"Is he going to be okay?"

The EMT shrugged, avoiding eye contact. "I heard them say he was breathing. You a friend?"

Carly shook her head. "Never saw him before in my life."

The EMT's gaze shifted to her face. "They said you pulled him out of the fire. That took a lot of courage."

Carly's turn to shrug. "I was just trying to save a dog." Instantly, she was ashamed. Yet accepting the burden of admitting she was trying to save another human being seemed like boasting on her part. But to say less would be a lie. "That's how I found him. I couldn't not help."

"You have professional training as a first responder?"

Carly shook her head.

"Most civilians would have waited for first responders." The EMT grinned at her. "Still, I respect what you did. Can I do anything more for you before we load you up for the ride to the hospital?"

Carly shook her head. "No hospital." She just needed to lie down somewhere quiet for a very long time. But no! She had a ton of things left to do before the opening of Flawless.

It wasn't until that moment that she thought to turn her head back down the street toward her shop.

The front door was open and a huge fire hose penetrated it. Which meant . . .

"Oh no!"

CHAPTER TWO

He was in class. Again. First day. Subject: primary search.

The thing about primary searches is this. You'll be going in for live victims, often before the first hose is full. It's not like in the movies. Flames don't dance around behind and in front of you, backlighting your fellow firefighters like goblins in a Halloween cartoon. The flames don't show you stairs or furnishings, or holes in the flooring. There's only smoke. You can't see shit.

But you can feel things. Like heat. Lots of it pressing in everywhere.

And you'll hear things. Some sounds can help you. Some you won't ever want to hear again. And some will make you wish you'd never heard them in the first place.

The whole time the smart part of you will be telling you to get the hell out of there. My job is to teach you to manage, not ignore, that very good advice.

Safety is not part of the job. It's how we do the job.

Coughs erupting from his throat woke Noah Glover. The short-breath hacking shot pain through his lungs and abdomen, cutting off the air supply coming through the mask attached to his face. Without bothering to open his eyes, he snatched it off. He felt like shit. Dizzy, nauseated. Throat burning from smoke inhalation. Throbbing in his head. The hiss of oxygen and the slow annoying beep of machines told him where he was. Hospital. He must have messed up. Whenever he'd made a mistake as a firefighter, he went back to school, if only in his dreams.

He was trained in how to extricate himself from dangerous situations. Yet his breath tasted like ash on his tongue. He must have lost his head gear.

You never get used to the smothering blindness of the smoke. And he'd gotten two lungs full.

Was that why he felt like he was dying? His thoughts kept sliding away from him. Couldn't remember a thing about the fire. Wait. He had bigger problems. Just staying alive for instance. Instinct was telling him that if he didn't concentrate on his breathing it would stop.

Old panic spiked adrenaline through his system. *Been there. Done that.* Every firefighter had had a moment, sometimes several, when he knew everything was on the line, his life versus his will to live.

He tried to lever himself into a sitting position. All that got him was a quick ride on a drunken Tilt-A-Whirl. His stomach heaved as he grabbed for the bed rail.

"Morning, Sleeping Beauty."

Noah blinked the room into focus. Across the narrow length of the curtained private room, Merle Durvan, the informal head of the arson investigation unit had made himself at home in a straight-back chair. His legs were crossed at the ankle, showing the well-used soles of his steel-toed boots. His fingers were laced across his abdomen, admirably flat for a man of forty-nine. Behind his thick but well-groomed mustache, his face wore no expression. Only his squint revealed the intensity of his gaze.

"How are you doing, Glover?"

Noah grunted, trying to catch a thought. Durvan was the most experienced arson investigator and bomb technician in Fort Worth. He also headed the training program for arson investigators. If anyone in the unit had a problem, question, dilemma, Durvan was the man they looked to. His presence meant Noah had messed up big time.

Noah tried to clear his throat only to choke. He reached for the cup of water on the bedside tray and drank. Tap water felt like gasoline going down.

When he could draw breath again, he locked eyes with his boss. "I feel like I died."

"Funny you should mention that." Durvan reached for a computer tablet he'd stashed under his arm. "Dying a particular wish of yours these days?"

"Not funny."

"I don't think so either." Durvan uncrossed his legs to lean his hairy forearms against his knees, the tablet held in both hands. "Tell me about last night."

Noah opened his mouth and snapped it shut. Last night. *What had happened last night?* He didn't have a clue. Couldn't remember the call. The fire. Why he'd been called in. Who he'd gone out with to investigate a possible arson. Nada.

A chill ran over Noah's skin. The sensation of trouble he couldn't quite place told him to choose his words carefully. It wasn't smart to be answering questions about events he couldn't recall.

His gaze ran quickly over Durvan. He was in the uniform of an on-duty firefighter, gray polo shirt with insignia over the heart, navy pants, and radio. He also carried his duty weapon. An arson investigator—part police officer part detective—got involved often during a suspicious fire, to determine the cause of the blaze and if criminal activity was involved. By the time the fire was out, valuable evidence could be lost to the firefighters' efforts to put out the blaze. The title Arson Investigator was a prestigious position. One Noah earned two years ago. But right now he had a more pressing concern. Durvan was watching him with the calm evaluating gaze of a professional. This was not a friendly visit.

Noah sipped more water, his larynx seeming to scrape against his throat as he swallowed. "What the hell is going on, Durvan?"

"That's what I'd like to know." Durvan sat up, as if he'd completed some sort of assessment. "Just wanted to hear your take on last night while it's fresh. If you're up to answering some questions."

"Sure." To hesitate would only make Merle suspicious. He was just going to have to play along until he could tease out a clue about what Durvan wanted.

The head investigator looked at his computer tablet. "Why did you start the fire?"

"Start the—? You think I started a fire?"

Durvan looked up with a bland expression. "You already admitted as much."

"The fuck I did!" The spike in his voice made Noah's throat burn.

"We have your admission." Durvan's tone remained flat.

Noah glowered at his friend. "No way."

Durvan tapped a few things on his tablet then stood up and walked to the bed so Noah could read the text message that he'd pulled up.

The screen was blurry due to his burning eyes, but Noah saw enough to read it.

I'm tired. Failure no longer an option. Fuck it. The end.

Noah winced. *Fuck it. The end.*

That was an expression his best friend and firefighter buddy Bailey Jefferson often used when he was tired of arguing about a topic, usually the chances of how his ball team would do that season. It was also the last thing he had said just before he died after a wall collapsed on him in a fire last year.

Noah could feel his temper rising. "Where'd you get that?"

"It was sent at eleven last night. The entire fire investigation unit received the same message. From your cell phone."

"Not from me."

Durvan shrugged and resumed his seat. "I know it's been hell of a year for you, Glover."

Noah held his gaze. "I've handled it."

"Maybe handling it became too much."

Noah stared at a man he thought of as a friend. Durvan couldn't really think he—what? "You think I tried to off myself?"

"You tell me."

Noah let surprise wash over him. Something had happened. Something bad. It was there at the back of this man's flint-gray stare. The last time he'd encountered it, Durvan had come to tell him Bailey was dead.

That thought cleared Noah's head. He fought the urge to curl his hands into fists. He was in serious jeopardy. From now on, every word he spoke would be to step up out of it, or toss another shovelful on his professional grave.

"I was in a fire. I don't remember why—or where." He swallowed against the dry mouth grating his voice. "Obviously, something went wrong. I'm in a hospital. That's all I got."

Durvan put his tablet down. "How did you end up in that store? Did you choose it beforehand? Does it have a special meaning for you?"

Noah glanced at the wall clock. It was 7:19 in the morning. Durvan hadn't wasted any time in starting this investigation. "Maybe you should stop trying to humor me like I'm a goddamn head case. The truth is, I don't remember a thing about last night. Nothing. But I do know I didn't try to off myself."

Durvan leaned back in his seat and crossed an ankle over a knee. "I'm here to get your side of things. What do you remember?"

"There was a woman." His own answer surprised Noah. *Woman?* He didn't know he remembered a woman until the words were out.

Durvan smirked. "I met her. Where did you pick her up?"

Noah frowned, as if he could squeeze another memory out of his smoke-blurred brain. Something emerged. "She just appeared in the fire. Is she okay?"

He nodded. "She says she saved your ass. What do you remember about her?"

"Tall, slim, pretty. Lots of curls. Quite a looker." Noah had no idea where the description came from. But he was trained to remember details. Unfortunately, the major facts of the night before still refused to take shape. "That's her, right?"

"From your description it sounds like she had your full attention. Did she go to the building with you?"

"Never saw her before." That felt like the truth.

"Sure you didn't hook up earlier? In a bar maybe?"

Noah just stared at him.

"Okay. Anything else you remember about last night?"

"He doesn't have to answer that."

Both men turned to see a woman standing in the doorway. She was tall, dressed in skin-tight slim jeans, hand-tooled boots, and a white embroidered Mexican blouse covered by enough turquoise jewelry to pull down a lesser woman.

Durvan was on his feet in quick Texas gentleman fashion. "Good morning, Sandra."

"We'll see about that." Sandra Glover stalked over to her brother's bedside. "You can't talk to a man who's being unduly influenced by medication." She pointed to the bag on an IV pole to which Noah was attached.

"It's only saline, Sandra." Noah eyed his sister suspiciously. "What are you doing here?"

"Looking after your best interests. I got a call before dawn. So I hopped in the truck and drove over from Abilene." She eyed Durvan accusingly. "Seems some people don't remember they're friends."

Durvan jumped as though stung. "I would've called when I had the facts."

"Merle, you don't want to tangle with me this morning."

Noah hid his smile. Even after two years in the unit he'd never called this man anything but Durvan. Of course, he wasn't a curvaceous blonde with as much brass as Merle had balls. Though neither would admit it, he suspected they shared a past, however brief.

He reached out and touched his sister's arm. "I have nothing to hide."

She looked down at him, her wide gap-tooth smile as engaging as a toddler's. But the squint around her hazel eyes said "tough west Texas wildcat." She had two ex-husbands to prove it. "That's what I'm worried about, Noah. You look like three miles of bad road, by the way. Let Merle take a statement now and he'll twist your words into so many pretzel shapes even you won't recognize them."

"That's not fair, Ms. Glover." It seemed even Durvan knew when to back off. Luckily, he remembered she'd retained her maiden name. "I just need to hear from Noah what he remembers of last night's events. Then I'll get out and let you two have a proper visit."

"It's okay, sis." Noah offered her the best smile he could

muster despite the killer demon operating a pile driver through his skull.

Sandra frowned. "You should have a lawyer present." She turned to Merle. "Since I am one, I'm staying." She walked over and took his chair.

The experienced investigator blew out a breath. Unflappable before a serial arsonist, he'd almost lost his cool with the best-looking woman he knew. "Fine. Only don't interrupt."

Sandra sat and crossed her arms, one boot toe tapping impatiently.

Durvan turned back to Noah, a look of exasperation on his face. "You were telling me what happened."

"Went out for a drink with some of the firefighters from station house number two."

"You drink a lot?"

"I'm on duty today. Ordered Dr Pepper. You can check."

Durvan's gaze flicked to his tablet and back. "Various witnesses say you were unsteady on your feet by the time you left the bar."

"I remember feeling a bit out of it. Thought maybe I was coming down with something. Flu's going round. But then . . ."

"Yeah?"

Noah locked gazes with him. "I got nothing until the woman pulling me out of the fire."

"Had you two been out drinking?"

Noah's mouth tightened at the repeated question. "Ask her. She'll tell you she never met me before the fire."

Sandra's chair squeaked. "What caught on fire, Merle?"

Durvan's gaze remained on Noah. "Why don't you tell your sister what happened before I have to? It'll be easier that way."

Sandra was up out of her chair. "You can stop the bull, Merle. Noah's told you what he remembers. You need to tell my brother what you know."

"If you'll take a seat, ma'am." This time Texas-flint-met-wild-cat-feistiness. After a moment, the wild cat flicked her blonde mane and resumed her chair.

Durvan turned again to Noah. "I'm giving it to you straight, Glover. We've got evidence that ties you to a fire that was deliberately set."

He held up a hand to stop Sandra's interruption. "Hear me out. Two gasoline-soaked mattresses were propped against a wall. The fire was set to burn quickly. The only reason you're alive is because the woman pulled you out. We've confirmed she's the same person who'd made a call to 911 about an unconscious man. She claims the fire was triggered after her call. Sure you didn't ask her to do you one last favor?"

Noah was too angry to be cautious. "Right. I'd ask a total stranger to set me on fire? Makes no fucking sense."

Durvan gave up the slightest smile, an indication he'd gotten to Noah. "I'm trying to understand, Glover. But it's suspicious as hell that you can't remember anything."

Noah rubbed a hand down his face. "It's just gone. Like those hours never happened."

"You trying to tell me you were drugged?"

Sandra was on her feet again. "Wait. What?"

Durvan's expression sobered. "Maybe someone put something in your drink. Is that it, Glover?"

Noah stared at him. "You've got proof of something."

Durvan shrugged. "They had to pump your stomach last night, in case you'd taken pills. You'd downed enough booze to impress a frat house. You tested positive for drugs, too."

Noah slung his head left and right, each move sending

a wrecking ball against his skull. "Hell. Maybe I was roofied by the bastard who left me to fry."

Durvan leaned in close over the bed rail, as if in a friendly gesture. The expression on his face was anything but. "I've done what I could to keep you off the psych ward. Suicide usually earns a person a trip to La La Land. But if you start some paranoid sh—bull"—he glanced at Sandra—"about being drugged by persons unknown, you're going to have a problem with more than me."

Noah stared right back, ignoring itchy eyes that streamed. "You said they pumped drugs out of me. Can't they do a blood test or something for roofies from what they took from me last night?"

"Maybe. But even if it turns out positive, it could put you in a worse position."

"How's that possible?" Sandra's voice intervened.

Durvan didn't even acknowledge her. His full attention was on Noah. "You know as well as I do, suicide by fire is nearly impossible. Once the higher functioning goes, even the most determined crazy can't take the heat. You ever seen a burning corpse crawl out of a house on fire? I have. We got called to a blaze a few years back, started after a suicide hung himself. Fire burned through the hanging rope. He tried to escape. Made it halfway over the threshold on fire before he expired. Passed out on roofies would only show you had a well-planned-out suicide attempt."

Noah shuddered internally at the images Durvan conjured, but he held his interrogator's gaze. "I'm innocent."

"Then that only leaves one question, Noah. Who wants you dead?"

Noah's face went blank. "I don't know."

Durvan nodded once then reared back. "Just so we're straight, I look after my arson people. So far, nothing's been leaked to the media about your circumstances. The official line is there's an investigation underway of a fire in which one of our people received minor injuries. But, as the saying goes, I'm not your biggest problem. If you become a liability or public relations problem the department heads won't hesitate to throw you to the wolves.

Durvan stood up. "Lucky for you, I've got a dog in this fight. You. I'll protect you as long as I can. But if it turns out you fucked up and pulled a lame-ass stunt last night, I'm going to arrest your sorry ass personally in front of as many cameras as I can gather. No one shits on my unit."

When Durvan had closed the door behind him, Sandra came forward and patted Noah on the shoulder. "It's okay, sweetie. He believes you."

"No, he doesn't. I wouldn't believe another man in the same circumstances." He smiled at her. "You better call the folks before this gets out. Tell them I'm fine but not to talk to anybody until they hear from me personally."

"I'll do that. I just wanted to make certain first that you were okay." She patted his cheek affectionately. "Now, what's this about someone trying to burn you up?"

Noah wished his sister hadn't heard that part. "I have no idea that's even true. Maybe I was out and came across something suspicious. When I stopped to investigate, the perp got the drop on me."

"Bull turkey." Sandra had perched a fist on each hip. "Someone's tried to off my little brother. I need to know all the details."

"Look. I've got nothing more to say and won't until I can get out of here and do some investigating on my own."

She stared at him, Glover to Glover, and knew that the blood that ran through both their veins made him just as stubborn as her. She wouldn't get anything more out of him now.

She dropped her fists and crossed her arms. "You'll

need my help if you really think Durvan doesn't believe you."

"If you want to help, tell me who called you about me."

"He didn't give his name. Just that there'd been a fire and you were in the hospital." Sandra frowned. "I was too rattled to ask who it was."

The answer was unsettling, but he didn't want to rile his sister any more than she already was. "Like I said, I need to investigate. Would you check at the desk and see when I can get out of here? Hospitals make me sick."

She smiled. "Sure thing. Sit tight."

Noah watched her go in relief. They had a good relationship, even if ten years separated their ages. His sister had never been especially touchy-feely, yet she'd been there for him when he needed it during his very messy divorce. But this wasn't her fight.

Noah closed his eyes, willing his brain to remember something. Anything.

A pair of dark eyes, widened by fear and worry, came into focus. Who was she? Durvan hadn't given him her name, but he had ways of finding out. She would have given a statement at the scene. He knew who to ask to get it.

He reached automatically into his breast pocket for his cell phone. It wasn't there, or on the bedside table, or in the drawer. That's when he remembered Durvan showing him a text message he'd supposedly sent. Had Durvan confiscated his phone? He knew Durvan well enough to know he'd been holding back on what information he did have.

Or was his phone still in the hands of the man who'd tried to burn him alive?

Anger surged through him, setting his heart to pumping heavy strokes. Someone had gotten the drop on him and almost succeeded in killing him. Who hated him that much?

Burning was one of the more terrible ways to die. He had scars from burns gotten during his years fighting fires. The pain was memorable. This was personal. Someone wanted him to suffer. And then die.

He shoved the creeping sense of vulnerability away. Wouldn't help. He was alive. A major plus. What else?

He opened his eyes and, without really seeing, focused on the chart on the wall that named his nurse and doctor. He was a detective. His memory wasn't a total wipe. What did he know for certain?

He hadn't been drinking.

Yet Durvan said emergency had pumped a stomach full of alcohol and other stuff out of him.

Therefore, he'd been drugged and force-fed alcohol. Perhaps together. Then he'd been left to die with his dog

Harley!

CHAPTER THREE

It wasn't in the papers. Or on the local news channels. He'd bought the paper, which he rarely did, and recorded all the local channels at the same time to make certain he didn't miss it. The fire hadn't made the paper at all. It had gotten fourth lead, after the weather report, on only two channels. No mention of a body. No mention of anything of importance but the loss, due to water damage, of a women's boutique scheduled to open soon. That couldn't be right.

Unless he'd fucked up.

No, he'd seen the fire catch from a block away before self-preservation told him to leave the vicinity. That fire should have taken all but the evidence he'd deliberately left behind. He knew how to cover his tracks. He was an expert at what arson investigators looked for. He'd also had lots of practice. He'd left a trail pointing to the victim as perpetrator that a blind man could follow. Something had gone wrong.

No way to ask. Not yet, anyway. For the rest of Fort Worth, it was just another ordinary day.

Someone would have to pay for that.

CHAPTER FOUR

"What's the matter, fella?"

Carly looked from the dish full of dog food into the shining dark amber eyes of the shepherd standing nearby. As she did so, his ears pricked forward and his long thick tail began to swish. "You're a handsome devil. Why won't you eat? Did you get too much smoke?"

As if he understood her he barked twice, the light happy sounds of a healthy animal. He was a beauty with tall ears that were velvet soft inside, and a strong nonslanting back with a small black saddle on his otherwise golden body. A black streak down his tail finished off the details. That, and a tendency to smile with his tongue lolling out of one side of his mouth.

She'd gotten up with the sun to make phone calls cancelling the activities planned for Flawless's grand opening scheduled for next week. Then she'd done a dog food run, grabbing several kinds from the shelves because she wasn't certain what her canine guest would eat. Surely she would hit on a favorite. But, not so much.

"I wish I could understand you. You don't seem to like dry or wet food." She'd heaped a serving of each kind into the bowl. He'd drained the water bowl twice, but the food remained untouched.

Her canine guest sniffed politely at each kind but then looked up at her, his head canted to one side, as if expecting something more.

"Have you tried making him work for it?"

Carly looked up to find her cousin Jarius Wiley standing in her aunt's kitchen doorway. He was still in his police uniform of navy blue shirt and pants with black tactical boots. His black felt cowboy hat sat low over his eyes, a position at once jaunty and intimidating. That hat also drew attention to his green eyes set in a medium brown face. But that wasn't the only reason why women looked at Jarius Wiley with open-mouth admiration. Jarius was gorgeous, from his close-cropped hair and chiseled features to the ripped physique he kept toned by a daily workout at the gym—which was a necessity, since this thirty-three-year-old man ate like a teenager with a tapeworm. No food was safe around him.

"Hey, Jarius. What are you doing here?"

"I'm just off duty. Moms likes to feed me when I've worked the night shift." He came into the kitchen, shedding his tactical equipment, which he piled safely on top of the refrigerator. "What are you doing here?"

"Borrowing Aunt Fredda's yard. My loft doesn't allow pets. I need a place to keep this dog while I go check out my store. I'm expecting an insurance adjuster later this morning."

Jarius frowned. "Yeah. I heard about the fire. Condolences, cousin." He gave her a big hug that squashed her against his shirtfront. "I would have come by last night but we were working a wreck in the Mixmaster. Snarled two major interstates for hours. State troopers worked the incident. FWPD had the pleasure of rerouting traffic through miles of gridlocked neighborhoods."

"It's okay. The fire department boarded things up after I was taken to the emergency room."

Jarius's brows flew up his forehead. "Moms didn't say nothing about an emergency room. Why were you in the emergency room?"

"Because I was sort of there when the fire started." She glanced at the dog, not wanting to tell the whole truth about finding the unconscious man. "But I'm fine. The trip was only a precaution. I was released almost immediately. I didn't tell Aunt Fredda that part. Just took a taxi here."

Jarius glanced at the dog sitting politely by her side. "This the animal you saved from the fire?"

"How did you know?" Damn, he'd faked her out.

He pointed to his badge.

"Oh right."

"You know Moms. She called me the second she hung up talking to you. That should have been you, cuz. You're in trouble, you call me. I'm the *po*-lice."

Carly sighed. After she told her aunt, she'd had to caution her not to tell anyone. If she hadn't stopped her, her aunt would have immediately phoned about half of Fort Worth with news of her niece's adventure the night before.

Jarius bent down and held out the back of his hand toward the shepherd. "Hey there, big fella. How're you doing?"

The dog sniffed then licked Jarius's hand. "Yeah. That's right. We're friendly." He reached under and stroked the dog's chest. "You're a fine specimen, aren't you? Bet you got all the neighborhood bitches in heat dogging your tracks." He grinned. "Kinda like me and women."

Carly watched her cousin in fascination. Jarius seldom

wasted his considerable charm on anything that wasn't a two-legged female.

"I can't get him to eat. Think I should take him to a vet?"

"Looks okay to me." After another scritching under the dog's neck he stood up. "You should try making him work for it."

"What do you mean?"

"Certain types of dogs are trained to be fed solely on a reward system. They got to work to eat. Bet he's one of them. See how he's watching your every move? He's waiting for a command. Ask him to do something."

"You mean like a trick?"

"I don't know. I'm not the dog whisperer."

Carly picked up a handful of dry food then turned to her furry guest. "Sit."

The big shepherd immediately sat down, long heavy tail swishing back and forth.

"Good dog." Carly placed a nugget of dry food in her palm and offered it to him.

He leaned forward, sniffed a couple of times, and then delicately took it from her.

Carly grinned at Jarius. "You were right."

"Can I have that in writing? No, better a banner." He held up his hands spaced wide. "Cousin Jarius is correct, again."

"Cousin Jarius is full of himself." Carly made the hand motion for down. The dog quickly complied. She offered him another nugget. This time he just stared at her. "Oh. Good dog. Good dog."

The canine lunged forward and licked up the treat, swallowing it whole.

Carly beamed. "Poor baby. He must be starved. But one treat at a time is going to take me forever to feed him."

"Yeah." Jarius had moved to start opening cabinets. "You could take him out to fetch sticks or something.

That's a lot of dog to fill up." He reached for a box of cereal, saw that it was one of those healthy granola mixes and shoved it back on the shelf. "But you should probably give him back to his owner."

Carly sent him a startled glance. "What makes you think I know who his owner is?"

He shrugged. "You saved the man's life. Thought you'd know his name."

Her eyes narrowed at his tone. "Hold up. What do you know about last night? And don't say "nothing," because I know first responders gossip like teenage girls."

"The fire? Nothing interesting." He looked away and shrugged. "It was pretty routine."

"It wasn't routine for me." Carly shivered and reached for more dry dog food. "Heel, boy." The dog complied and got his treat. "A guy nearly died."

"Right. About that. Don't do that ever again." Jarius moved to the pantry and stuck his head inside. "Even professionals won't go into a fire without gear. There's a thin line between bravery and stupidity." His head popped out, a bag of chips in hand. "You crossed it."

"Thanks for the tip." Carly's expression soured as she made a motion with her hand for her dog to sit and feed him another morsel. "For the record, nothing was on fire when I went into the store. I heard this dog whining and went to investigate."

"Like I said, you're brave but also seven kinds of stupid."

She knew he was right, which really annoyed her. "I saved a man's life."

He opened the refrigerator. A sign, she knew from experience, that meant he was done with that subject. But she wasn't. He was police. He could answer her questions.

She made the hand signals for "down" and then "roll over," doling out treats when the dog complied. He was a champ, just like Cooper had been. "I was surprised there wasn't a mention about the guy in the news."

His answer came from the depths of the refrigerator. "Moms is definitely falling down on the job. There's not even cold cuts in here." He slammed the refrigerator door, hunger making his features sharper. "Guess I need to cruise by Mickey D's."

"Aunt Fredda's out now buying groceries. Probably buying bacon and those sweet rolls you love." She watched his eyes roll heavenward. "While you wait, you can tell me about the man whose life I saved. You have to know something about him."

He rubbed the back of his neck, as if it ached. "I wouldn't say anything to anyone about him. In fact, it'd be best if you just forgot about him."

"Why? Oh no." Her stomach took a nosedive toward her Doc Martins. "He didn't die, did he?"

"No, nothing like that. Only, well, you'll want to stay away from the inquiry. All right!" He'd spied through the entry to the dining room the fresh pound cake cooling on a rack on the sideboard.

"What inquiry? What's going on, Jarius?"

"Did I say anything was going on?" He pulled the longest knife from the wooden knife block on the counter and headed for the dining room.

Carly trailed him. "You're evading my questions and trying to put the burden on me. Just like you used to do when we were kids."

"I don't need to evade." He grinned as he positioned himself before the heavenly smelling confection that was his mother's pound cake. "I'm a grown-ass man, in case you haven't realized."

"Not so grown you didn't just give yourself away. That cocky smile doesn't fool me. What's going on? And don't lie. I'll make you pay. Just like when we were kids."

"I don't think so." He slid the blade into the cake. "You got nothing on me."

"Oh yeah? Who just cut the pound cake your mom made for the church social tomorrow?"

"*Aw damn!*" Jarius dropped the slice of cake he'd scooped up like it had bitten him. "You're still a menace, you know that?"

"And you never learned to say 'may I.' And don't think you can mend the cake by pinching the edges together like that. You're only making it crumble." She leaned in to better watch his efforts. "You'd better tell me what you know about last night so I can help you think up a reason why her cake is ruined."

Jarius hauled back from the sideboard with a big sigh and began licking cake crumbs off his fingers. "And here I thought we were tight, cuz."

"You were saying?"

He wet his lips then glanced at the cake as if it was the site of a horrific accident. "There's a reason the fire wasn't on the morning news. It's because the department refused to give out any details. Said the cause of it was undetermined."

Carly folded her arms. "Why would they do that?"

"Because of who was involved."

"Me?"

He grinned. "You may be a certain kind of famous in some places but the man you saved is the reason the authorities shushed things up like a morgue."

"Stop trying to be mysterious."

"I'm going to give it to you straight but then you forget it. He's a fire investigator named Noah Glover."

"Why would a fire investigator be passed out in a vacant building? That doesn't make any sense."

Jarius shrugged and reached down to rub the ears of the shepherd who'd come up to him. He got his fingers licked for cake crumbs in return. "So, you two didn't talk, or anything?"

"Jarius, I swear if you don't answer me!" She pointed to the cake.

He glanced at it and winced. "Apparently, he was trying to commit suicide."

"Really?" She folded her arms. "You used to tell better lies."

"I'm serious as a heart attack. Before Glover was a firefighter he was a cop. That's how I know him. A little. But don't you go telling anyone, at all, what I just told you. The department is on lockdown where this investigation is concerned. The only thing you'll get if you talk about it is deeper into a mess you don't want any part of."

Carly chewed her lip. "Why do they think it was a suicide attempt?"

"You promise to fix this mess?" He waved a hand at the cake. She nodded. "Everybody in his unit got an email from him last night. It was his suicide note."

Carly felt all the air leave her chest.

The man had been unconscious before the fire broke out, impossible to rouse. Even when she'd prodded him to consciousness, and told him of the fire, he'd seemed reluctant to help himself.

A chill stole through her as she remembered how he had pushed her away at the doorway, telling her to run, even before they reached the alley. Was that because he wanted to be left behind to die? It was too horrible to be believed.

I don't want to die.

No. He'd gripped her like his last salvation as he whispered those words to her. She'd felt them reflected in the deepest part of her soul. And she believed him. He was strong and hard and certain, a life force refusing to relinquish its hold.

And yet, when she'd hesitated, she'd felt his readiness to die. She'd looked into his eyes a second time and seen his preparedness for sacrifice. She'd thought it was on her account. What if she'd been wrong?

She began to pace. "Why would he want to commit suicide?"

"Guess he had nothing to lose."

"Nothing." Carly paused and looked at the happy shepherd wagging his tail. "He had him." She pointed. "What kind of man makes his dog part of a suicide?"

"Somebody who doesn't like loose ends?"

"No jokes, Jarius. I nearly died last night."

"I know." He came over and gave her another bear hug. "I was scared to death when I heard. By the time I was relieved of duty and could get to the site, the overhaul crew told me you were okay and had gone home."

"I came here instead. Didn't want to be alone."

"Makes sense." He held her at arm's length. "No more stupid sacrifices. Okay? You're not trained for it. It's over now. Put it out of your mind."

"Okay." She turned to pick up more dry nuggets for the dog. Yet the more she thought, the angrier she became. "Something doesn't make sense. There has to be more than I know."

He shrugged. "There's always more."

That caught her attention. "What do you know?" She walked up to him, anger making her flush. "Spill it or I swear I'll feed the cake to the dog and tell Aunt Fredda you ate it."

"Easy." Jarius spoke softly and spread his arms, like a police officer showing a frightened child that he doesn't pose a threat. "There's been some talk about Glover ever since he and a firefighter were trapped inspecting a fire last year. The roof collapsed on them. The other guy didn't make it. Glover took it hard. Everyone did. First responders are tighter than most families. But we thought he'd, you know, worked through it." He wagged his head. "I guess you never can tell. They've kept him overnight at the hospital for observation."

"Which hospital?"

"John Peter Smith. Why?"

Her heart pounding against her ribs, Carly watched as he continued to pet the shepherd. "He tried to kill his dog!"

Suddenly all the anxiety and fear—gut-watery fear she'd been stuffing down too deep for the light of morning to reach—came roaring back into the front of her mind. She stiff-armed her cousin aside and headed for the kitchen.

"Wait." Jarius followed. "Where are you going?"

Carly snatched up her purse from the kitchen table without pausing. "To meet Mr. Glover."

"You can't—" He seemed to know that was a useless argument as she pushed through the back door. Instead, he went after her, the shepherd at his heels. "What about the dog? And the cake? You said you'd fix this for me."

She spun around. "Put the dog in the yard behind the fence. Then go to the store and buy two cans of butter cream frosting. Next go to a florist and ask for a bunch of edible flowers."

"What if Moms comes back before you do?"

"She's at the beauty salon." She yanked open the door of her Mazda. "Then there's her monthly luncheon bridge game. You're safe."

"I forgot." He shook his finger at her. "You played me, cuz."

CHAPTER FIVE

Carly moved slowly down the hospital corridor, as if the sound of her footsteps were an intrusion. She'd hung around in the lobby, cooling her heels but not her temper, after being told that there was no Noah Glover listed as a patient. Then she'd spied a fireman in uniform and followed him into an elevator on a hunch. Maybe he was making a social call on Mr. Glover. Her visit would be a lot less friendly.

"Can I help you?"

Carly paused as a nurse stepped into her path. The fireman paused, too, to talk to someone at the nurse's station. "I'm looking for Mr. Glover's room."

The nurse's eyes narrowed. "We don't have anyone by that name here."

Thinking fast, she answered, "I know that's not the name he's here under. Noah called me to come over and bring his cell phone." She unpocketed and held up her own phone as a kind of proof. "He didn't say locating him would be an issue. We're family."

The nurse's expression soured. "Really?"

Carly gave her a look. "You got a problem with multi-ethnic families?"

"Of course not." Her eyes said she just didn't believe Carly.

"Okay, but how am I to get Noah his phone?" No response. The nurse was well-trained. "I suppose I can call him and see if he will tell me where he is."

"You can do that from the lobby."

"Fine. But you can tell him for me that I don't appreciate wasting my time on running errands so he can be all mysterious and paranoid." She dialed her old Manhattan apartment and waited through the message announcing that this number was no longer in service, all the while scanning the hallway for clues.

Finally, Carly made a face and hung up. "I've a million things to do beside play errand girl for Mr. Tall Dark-Hearted Attitude."

"He is good-looking, isn't he?"

Got cha! But she didn't let on, only shrugging. "You'll have to ask someone else. We're cousins. Now about seeing him. Can't I just slip him the phone? I promise not to breathe on him, or anything."

For the first time the nurse looked indecisive. "I'll have to check. You stand right here while I make a call."

It was the call that told Carly she'd get through to her quarry. The nurse was no match for Carly Harrington-Reese on a mission. As a once up-and-coming model—read that poor and unknown—she'd learned to talk her way around bouncers and through security and into the most exclusive clubs and private parties in six different world capitals. But this time she didn't feel good about lying. This wasn't a party, or a game. A man had tried to commit suicide, which was sad. But how dare he burn his dog alive in the process.

But maybe life was telling her it wasn't her place to deliver that message.

A woman dressed in jeans, boots, and a thick mane of blonde hair worn by only a certain breed of Texas woman, and the singer Adele, pushed open a patient's room door at the far end of the hall. "You know how long it takes to check out of a hospital, Noah. I'm going to your place and grab some clothes. Bet I'm back before the paperwork is signed." She let go of the door and came down the hall directly toward Carly.

She offered Carly a big smile and a "Hi there" as she passed.

On an impulse she couldn't explain, Carly blurted out, "Do you know Noah Glover?"

The woman stopped, her expression now as intimidating as the nurse's had been. "Why?"

Carly offered the woman her best smile. "I'm a friend."

The woman gave Carly an up-and-down glance, taking in every piece of clothing. "Is that so?"

It suddenly hit Carly that she might be talking to the man's wife. "Look, I don't mean to intrude, but I'm the woman who found Mr. Glover unconscious just before the fire started last night." *And I want to yell at him for almost torturing his dog.* But she probably shouldn't admit that.

The woman's expression brightened. "You saved my brother?"

Glover's sister! "Yes. I was working late in my shop next door when—"

The woman had thrown her arms around Carly and was squeezing her, hard. "Thank you. Thank you. You saved my little brother's life."

She let Carly go, backing away quickly. She wiped tears from her eyes, smearing her mascara. "I'm so sorry. I don't usually go in for big displays of emotion."

"That's all right." Carly handed her a tissue from her pocket. "He's okay, isn't he?"

"Ornery as a bear with a sore tooth. But he's fine otherwise. You go right in and introduce yourself. I've got a couple of errands to run."

"I wanted to but the nurse said—"

"You let me handle the nurse." She patted Carly on the arm and after giving her the number moved on down the hall toward the elevators, boot heels clacking.

Carly didn't even look back over her shoulder before heading toward the door. She hadn't exactly lied about why she was here. Okay, she had. But she was compelled by a moral urgency that wouldn't be denied.

She knocked softly at the door. When she didn't hear a reply, she hesitated. Maybe he had fallen asleep. Doubtful, the way his sister's voice carried. But, just in case, she pushed the door open carefully. Despite the sunny morning outside, this room was dim. A curtain was pulled halfway around the bed to shield it from the door. "Mr. Glover?"

"I told the last nurse I'm not giving any more blood. Go away." That hoarse voice sounded vaguely familiar.

Carly stepped past the curtain to look at the figure on the bed. Only he wasn't on the bed. He must have just come out of the shower because his hair gleamed with beads of water dripping from his hair. But that wasn't the most significant fact.

He was naked. Standing by the bed, his back to her, with phone in hand.

Years in the fashion industry where scads of women and men wearing nothing at all during prep backstage before a show had made her somewhat indifferent to the human body. Human coat hangers was how the models thought of themselves, to be dressed and made up and coiffed for someone else's view.

But this man in this setting arrested her attention. He wouldn't have made it as a runway model. He was too muscular. Broad back, defined arms, and a tight sexy ass.

He exuded a flagrant virility that would never fade into the background. That meant no fashion buyer would notice the clothing if it were on him. While she was ogling him, he half turned to her.

"Can I help you?"

She should have averted her gaze. That's what people did in awkward situations. But her gaze remained long enough to notice his strong calves, hard hairy thighs, and the shadow of his package. She'd seen it all on some of the most physically–blessed people on the planet. Still, it was more than a bit impressive, that flash. Not that she was interested, or looking, or even remotely curious.

"Who are you?"

Without being able to see them, Carly recalled his hard blue eyes and the force of his hands gripping her shoulders the night before. The rest of him hadn't registered. Until now. No wonder she'd had the devil's own time of it pulling him to safety. He must outweigh her by fifty pounds.

She realized she needed to answer him, but she was still having trouble making her mouth form words.

"If you're looking for the visitor's lounge, you missed it," he said.

Carly suddenly remembered why the room seemed so dark. She was wearing sunglasses. She reached up to lift them to her forehead.

"I'm looking for Noah Glover."

He turned fully toward her, expression set in challenge. "You found him."

For a moment it all registered, every gloriously naked inch of him, and sensations sent a shiver through her body.

Her physical response so surprised Carly, she gave herself a mental shake. Whoever and whatever he was, he wasn't a nice person. In fact, his attractiveness made her even angrier. How could a man who'd been blessed with so much, or at least enough advantages to turn heads while in a hospital bed, treat his dog, an innocent creature, with such cruelty?

Instead of ducking or reaching for the nearby bedding, he folded his arms and stood his ground, looking imposing and unapologetic. "You got something to say? Or did you just come by to get a good look at my junk?"

Unwilling to give in, Carly took a step toward the naked man, letting anger surge through to the intimidation she felt. "I came by to see the asshole who ruined my life."

CHAPTER SIX

Noah didn't know where to land his gaze. A most attractive woman had just appeared in his room after a knock. "Mr. Glover?"

She wore a black leather jacket, the expensive lightweight kind that clung to her lithe body. Underneath it she wore some kind of sheer black T-shirt that allowed her bra to show through. More amazing were the brown leather drawstring shorts cut high up on her thighs. Underneath she wore dark stockings that seemed to have been put in a blender before she put them on. The pairing showed off a toned body and legs so long and curvy he couldn't help staring. She should have looked ridiculous, or vulgar. What she looked was sophisticated, and scorching hot. And angry. And, unless blusher came in sepia, the flush of her bare skin was genuine.

The linking of "bare" and this woman in the same thought sent a jolt straight through him. Yeah. About that. Suddenly he remembered his package was swinging in the breeze. That, and his bare ass had had her full attention.

She didn't seem disturbed by his nudity. Of course, he

couldn't see her eyes. She wore circular black shades with thin silver frames that suited her slim face. And then she lifted them with two fingers to peek under them.

"I'm looking for Noah Glover." She repeated his name through soft lips the color of black cherries.

He turned fully toward her, expression set in challenge. "You found him." Something about her was vaguely familiar. Not that he'd have forgotten meeting her. Her hair was—well, the closest he could come to describing it was a fountain of tiny blonde curls that fizzed over her brow like a bottle of just-opened champagne. The sides were masculine short and darker. Yep, she was east coast hot. And furious with him. And he didn't have a clue why.

Then it struck him. She was probably a news reporter. TV, judging by her glamorous style. She'd somehow wormed her way in here to get an exclusive. No wonder she was looking so impressed with herself. He'd give her an exclusive, all right.

He turned fully toward her and folded his arms. "You got something to say? Or did you just come by to get a good look at my junk?"

He watched her eyes widen at his blunt question. She looked taken aback. Not at all the way he'd have expected from a conniving reporter who'd thought she was about to get an exclusive. She looked, well, like a stranger confronted with a deranged man. And then the impression vanished.

She took a step toward him, anger surging through her expression as she advanced. "I came by to see the asshole who ruined my life."

That scowl. That look was one he'd never forget.

This was his angel of mercy. Yes. Those eyes. Dark and liquid, they seemed enormous in her delicate face. But she was no Bambi. Those dark eyes stared at him as if penetrating past his professional attitude all the way into him, into places even he seldom visited. Could she see every shortcoming, regret, and dissatisfaction with himself he'd ever experienced?

It was disconcerting.

Intimidating.

Arousing.

And he was not ready to deal with even one of those feelings today. Not on any day for a long time. She wasn't going to be the one to crack a hard case like him. No one got to him like that. Certainly not a gorgeous stranger whose face was registering a lot of emotions. None of them to his credit. He needed to refocus.

So, this is the woman who'd saved his ass, and all his other parts, the night before. Oh yeah. About those parts. First things first.

"Towel."

She frowned. "What?"

He pointed to the pile of linen on the window ledge. "I'm getting a towel."

He grabbed one and wrapped it low on his hips, tucking the ends into the waist just below his navel. The terry cloth gaped open over long hairy thighs, but it seemed to be enough to set the temperature of the room back several degrees.

That was before he looked up at her. She was seething. He was angry now, too, and didn't know why. "What can I do for you?"

Now why did he give her attitude? He saw his tone register on her face and knew he might as well have insulted her outright.

"I just wanted to see for myself, the man who—"

He put up a hand. "I know who you are. You saved my life."

"Yes, I did, you selfish prick." She came toward him, eyes nearly slits, as a cascade of words tumbled out of her mouth. "Do you even realize how lucky you are? If your dog hadn't alerted me that you were there, you would have died. You owe him your life. I suppose that means nothing to you. But you should know that even after I freed him, that sweet dog still wouldn't leave you in the fire. Clearly he adores you. But you were about to repay his loyalty by burning him up with you. Shame on you. Just because you've given up doesn't give you the right to take an innocent animal with you. You could have dropped him off anywhere—a shelter, a rescue, even dumping him in the street would be humane compared to what you tried to do to. Not to mention what that fire did to my store. But I suppose a guy with your good looks is used to getting things handed to him. Some of us work hard for our dreams and you have no right to destroy them like they're nothing."

"Gown."

She blinked. "What?"

"Hand me one of those gowns. Please." Talking to her with his dick behaving in unruly ways beneath the towel was beginning to tax his concentration.

She grabbed a gown from the same stack as the towels and threw it at him. "Have you heard a word I've said?"

He backed up to the bed, sat, and unfolded the gown. "You called me good-looking."

"I called you a selfish prick, too."

Something close to a smile cracked his hard mouth. His voice dropped to a rough whisper as he thrust his arms through the sleeves. "Thank you for saving my life."

"Oh no. You don't get to say that. Not after your actions ruined my shop next door. I don't know what your problems are, and I don't care. It's not any of my business you wanted to burn up yourself. But you made a mistake when you ruined my future trying to do it."

"I didn't—"

"What? Didn't mean to burn down my life? Didn't mean to torture a defenseless animal in the cruelest way imaginable?"

"No. I didn't—"

"What? Didn't stop to think? There's a surprise."

"I didn't—" He paused.

She waited three seconds. "What?

He smiled. "Can I finish this time? Thank you. I didn't do it."

"Didn't do what? Start the fire? Try to kill yourself? What?"

He nodded, sucking in a breath. "All of the above."

"Humph." Folded her arms. "You left a note."

That popped him upright away from the bed. "How did you hear about that?"

She just stared at him.

"I've got to get out of here." He jerked the towel out from under the gown.

Carly glanced away, but not quite quick enough to miss another glimpse of his man parts. Not that it was a big deal to her. Still, it was just a bit impressive, that flash. Not that she was interested, or looking, or even remotely curious about a man who'd take his own life.

Then he turned and reached for the phone, and it was too much.

"Would you mind not mooning me?"

He looked back, frowning as he realized what had happened, and reached around to close his gown. But he took his time, not at all embarrassed. "Sorry but you need to get out of here."

"Hey." She waited until he turned his head her way. "I'll tell you what I'm going to do, Mr. Glover. I'm going to find a lawyer and sue your ass . . . and all your other parts."

Noah smirked. "Get in line, lady."

She gasped softly but in the next breath came back

harder. "No wonder people don't like you. But believe it, I'm going to sue you. You, the city for hiring you, and your mother for not rearing a nicer son."

His lips twitched. "You'd sue my mother?"

"Okay, not your mother." She began rubbing the place between her brows.

. . . .

She has impeccable brows. Now why the heck did he think that?

"I'm sure she tried her best." Oh, right, his mother. "But you, yes." She pointed a finger at him. She didn't wear nail polish. "You ruined the lives of women who were counting on me."

Noah frowned hard, drinking in the details of her slim figure again. "You saved my life? How much do you weigh?"

Those big dark eyes snapped with hostility. "Screw you."

He forced himself to take a deep breath. "Sorry. That was rude. I'm just thinking you don't look strong enough to have been able to move me."

"You're welcome."

"Look, I'm grateful you were there last night. I'm grateful you came to see me. But can we put this conversation on pause so that I can move on to other priorities? Because, believe it or not, there's something more pressing on my mind than chatting up a beautiful woman."

"No. You don't get to do that." Her hand was moving again, that slim finger waving back and forth in front of her. "You're going to stand there in that funky gown and listen until I'm finished." She took a step toward him. "And stop smiling at me. Don't you take any of this seriously?"

Noah took a breath. "I take all of this very seriously. I didn't attempt suicide. I certainly wouldn't harm my dog. And I didn't take the drugs or the alcohol willingly."

"No, the Jack Daniels and coke just snuck up behind you and did a beatdown until you gave up. You think I haven't heard that excuse before?"

His eyes widened. "Who are you?"

"You don't need to know my name. I just came to tell you that you lack the integrity of a tapeworm."

He wanted to laugh but it hurt to after having his stomach pumped. "Are you always this sweet and sensitive?"

He watched her take a deep breath before she continued. "Look, I don't mean to be insensitive about your suicide attempt. I have a great deal of sympathy for people who are in such deep emotional distress they would even consider giving up their lives to end the pain." She paused again. This time a shadow skirted her expression. "You look like you've got all the resources you need to get help. So do that. Get some help, okay? And *please* don't ever get a pet again until you've gotten the help you need."

His expression hardened. "How about you mind your own business? I'm fine."

She straightened to her full height, sympathy ebbing from her gaze. "See. That's why I didn't accept your apology. Your dog may be sleeping soundly with no idea what could have happened, but I can't look at him without—"

He perked up. "You have Harley?

Carly rolled her eyes toward the ceiling. "What?"

"My dog—do you know where he is?"

"I . . . I'd rather not say. And anybody willing to burn up his dog doesn't deserve one. I think I'll call all the local shelters and have them put you on a watch list. No more dogs for you."

Noah felt his teeth grinding. "I didn't try to burn up anything."

She cocked her head forward, tossing bright gold curls over her brow. "I know about the confession."

She'd hinted at that before. Now it dawned on him the

importance of that fact. Durvan said it had been kept out of the paper. Someone was leaking information. "Who told you about that text?"

His question was a snarl, startling her. By the look of fear that entered her gaze she must have remembered too late she was supposed to keep that information to herself. But she rallied quickly, her lids lowering over her fear.

"I just heard. Around."

He bit off a quick string of profanity meant to impress with its viciousness. She just watched, still and alert as a cat confronted by a bulldog. Fear didn't rattle her. He was impressed.

Switching tactics, he lilted his head to the side, much like his dog did when trying to figure out what he was saying. "I'd like you to tell me who gave you that intel."

She shrugged. "Confidential source. But you can trust him."

Him. "Right."

She hung onto the door latch a few seconds longer. "There's more to this, isn't there?" Her voice was quieter, curious.

He held her gaze. "I had no intention of committing suicide last night, or any night. I'd like to tell you more, but it'll just draw you deeper to this mess. I don't think I can ask that of you."

She seemed to consider this, then folded her arms. "I'm already involved." She stood patiently.

He raised a skeptical eyebrow. "Remember. You asked. Someone tried to kill me last night."

He watched half a dozen emotions chase one another across her expression as the fingers of her right hand played with the zipper on her jacket.

"Someone tried to burn you up?"

He nodded. "The confession is a lie. The fire was a trap."

"That somebody must really not like you. Deciding to burn up a person is hate on a very personal level."

"Let's say I agree. Now about my dog."

She shook her head. "He's in my custody now, where I know he'll be safe."

"Seriously? You'd take an injured man's dog from him?"

"I saved his life. He belongs to me now."

He smirked. "You saved my life, too. You know what that means?"

Her lids lowered again. "I have an underdeveloped sense of self-preservation."

He smiled finally, letting it come despite his attempt to hold it back. "I like you. You're brave. You're smart. You're a good—"

"Don't say it."

"—person. No, a Good Samaritan."

"Damn." She jackknifed away from the door. "I promised God last night that if He got us out of that inferno, I'd go to church every Sunday for the rest of my days."

"I wouldn't recommend what you did, but I'm grateful. Truly grateful."

She stared at him. "You would have died. And you didn't mean to. Do you have family? A wife? Kids?"

"Yes. No. A son."

"Where is he?"

"With my folks. He's four. My wife walked out on us shortly after he was born. My job is too crazy to allow me to rear him alone."

"So you let your parents do that job?" Again, disapproval of his conduct in her tone.

He hesitated. He seldom talked to anyone about his home life. But maybe he owed her this pound of flesh as proof of his desire to stay alive. "I'm home with him as often as I can be."

"How often is that?"

"Most nights."

"So, you live with your parents?" A smile teased her mouth.

"They live with me. Moved in after my wife left. That's all the speed-dating questions I have time for now. Show yourself out." He picked up the bedside phone again. "I have some things to take care of."

"I see. Well, good luck with that." She opened the door.

"His name's Harley."

She looked back and lifted a brow as if she didn't know who he was talking about. "Who? Your son?"

"My arson dog. Harley Davidson Brown."

"Why Brown?"

"Seemed like a good idea at the time."

"You're a strange man. Does your son like HD Brown?

"Harley? Adores him."

"He would."

His smile turned very persuasive. "So you'll give Harley back?"

She rolled a slim shoulder. "I don't know any Harley."

"Look. I need to know. Is my dog okay? If he needs to go to the vet, please take him. I'll pay."

He thought he saw her gaze soften, but her frown didn't clear. "Wherever this Harley is? He's fine. Safe and fed. Promise."

"But how did you—?" Before he could finish the sentence she slipped out.

Noah stood staring at the door after she was gone. He wasn't certain what had just happened, but he knew he'd lost the match. And he wanted to go another round with her. Badly.

CHAPTER SEVEN

Carly adjusted her hard hat as she stood in the midst of Flawless. Nothing was burned. Nothing was even singed. But everything, everywhere she looked, was ruined. The sprinkler system had done its job, soaking every surface to prevent the fire from spreading. And then the firefighters had come in to make certain the sprinklers had delivered enough water to keep any embers from reigniting. And the smell of smoke permeated everything, even with the door flung open. The space had been pronounced as safe to navigate, but her eyes were reddened by the fumes still lingering in the air.

She picked up one of the handmade silk cushions that had bled their vegetable colors into one another. The painted concrete floor had disappeared beneath the debris of collateral damage. Racks of accessories that looked as if they had been pushed aside by busy hands, lay trampled. Other items drowned in the funky water that smelled of smoke sloshing at her booted feet. Water might not have ruined everything, but then the ceiling had fallen in, heavy plaster smashing counters, tables, chairs, whatever broke its fall.

"It's not too bad. You have the integrity of the walls holding and there's no visible fire damage to the rafters." The insurance claims adjuster who accompanied her to survey the damage sounded almost cheerful as she pointed upward.

Carly stared up at the jagged hole in her ceiling. She vaguely remembered the fire chief explaining to her the night before, as he helped her secure her store to keep away looters, that old buildings have cocklofts, a word that sounded medieval. It was a narrow crawl space above the ceiling, what she would have called an attic. Fire went up, he'd explained. Heat, smoke, and embers from a fire in a room below naturally spread up into the cockloft. Fire-fighters had gotten on the roof and pumped water into the cockloft above the burning shop. Old buildings like this one often didn't have a firewall between each shop cockloft. Flawless shared cockloft space with the shop next door, so the water had flowed along the rafters above her shop as well. Water equals weight equals ceiling collapse. Total disaster for her shop, and her immediate dreams.

Carly did not cry as her gaze lowered to the mangled space she rented. But she sucked on her lower lip. Hard.

"Your landlord will need to get a structural engineer in here to verify that the integrity of the shop remains sound. That's his responsibility to his tenants. But I see no reason your insurance won't cover this damage." The arson investigator had signed off on the paperwork stating that "nothing in your store was the cause of the fire."

"I know the cause of the fire. I was here." Carly grabbed her lower lip again with her teeth. Not. Going. To. Cry.

The woman blinked. "That was you? The woman who called in the blaze? You're a witness then."

"I guess so." No one had said anything about her being a witness. Not yet, anyway. More involvement was the last thing she needed.

"What happened?"

The agent's suddenly avid expression warned Carly to be careful. She'd already tangled with the supposed victim this morning. She'd been relieved to find her name wasn't attached to the scant news reporting of the blaze the night before. But raising the suspicious hackles of her claims adjustor by telling her side of the story didn't seem like a good idea. "I don't think I'm allowed to talk about it until the authorities say."

The agent frowned. "In any case, I'll have to check with the fire chief. To make certain—well, to cross the t's and dot the i's."

Carly moved to pick up the soggy remains of an organic cruelty-free chicken-feather headband. She'd hoped that confronting Noah Glover would make her feel better. It hadn't. Her shop was in even worse condition than she remembered from the night before. But by the time she'd locked up with the fire extinguished, she was past feeling much of anything but relief that she was alive. Now every sense was being bombarded with the full impact of what she'd lost.

She held up the headband by its leather thong. "What do you need me to do? I have no idea where to begin."

"Collect and make a detailed list of your damaged merchandise, along with their individual value. Photos and receipts will greatly help us. Since you're a brand-new business, you shouldn't have trouble categorizing what was in the store."

"Then what? Most of my inventory is ruined beyond repair."

"You may be surprised." The agent offered her a gentle smile of reassurance. "We have a list of remediation companies that do a remarkable cleanup after fires. Of course, you can choose your own, providing the company meets our standards. I'm really sorry for your loss." She glanced around. "I'll be one of your first customers when you reopen. So many lovely things."

Carly wasn't at all certain that she would be a reopening. "Most of the items I have—had for sale were handmade crafts. Not replaceable by simple reorder from a warehouse. I'll reimburse my suppliers for their loss from the insurance. But replacing things could take months."

"You might be able to save this." The agent fingered the dripping feather headband Carly held. "Chicken feathers, right? My sister had a bohemian-themed wedding last August and the bridesmaids wore head wreaths decorated with chicken feathers. One of the gals accidently dropped hers in the outdoor fountain at Sundance Square while participating in the official wedding party photo shoot. My sister rinsed it thoroughly then popped it in a pillowcase and tossed it in the dryer. She'd read about the technique online. Turned out great. The bridesmaid got to wear it for the ceremony."

Carly inspected the headband anew. "I had no idea."

"Check with your vendors. They will know their products better than anyone else. And how, if possible, to salvage them."

"I will." Just as soon as she got up the courage to tell them what had happened to their dreams and her hopes. Lots more calls lay ahead of her today.

The agent paused, staring at Carly longer than she had at any time earlier. "I'm sorry. I know it's not professional, but I can't help staring at you because you look so familiar. I know we'd never met. But you have such a distinctive look. So polished yet edgy. Should I know who you are?"

Carly never knew how to answer that particular question. Should a person recognize her? As if it was her responsibility to make an identification for the questioner. "I did some fashion work years ago."

"Magazine?"

"And other things."

For instance, *Vogue. W.* A stint as a Victoria Secret's model. But not going there. She knew the woman would go home and Google her. And then she'd know.

The insurance agent smiled. "Let me see what else I can find out for you. In my business I meet all kinds of restoration specialists. Of course, insurance might not pay for all of it."

"Not my biggest problem at the moment."

"That must be nice not to have money issues." Again, the agent sent her a probing speculative glance Carly rebuffed with a shrug.

"So, thanks for the information about cleanup services. With tomorrow being Sunday, I suppose I'll have to wait until Monday to get someone out."

"No. Professional water-damage restoration experts are available twenty-four hours a day, seven days a week."

"But what about my things? I need to make certain things don't get trampled before I let people in." She glanced around vaguely, her eyes unable to focus on anything in particular because of the sheer number of possibilities. "There're pieces of jewelry scattered everywhere, for instance."

"I hadn't thought of that. You should probably hire a security person until you've had a chance to retrieve those items. But don't wait past tomorrow morning to call the remedial people in. You might be held responsible for creating a sidewalk hazard."

Carly glanced out the front window, half obscured by the plywood boards the fire department had put up to discourage looters. Beyond those windows, water still drained from under her door into the street.

After the agent was gone, she waded through the shop, picking up a necklace here, a bracelet there. She laid them out on a dry area she found under a tarp. Within half an hour she had collected one of a pair of amethyst earrings, several silver bracelets, leather purses that had been protected by the tarps, and a half a dozen necklaces. But working alone and moving carefully made it a very slow process. After an hour it was clear that it would take more than her solitary efforts to salvage the dozens of items hidden beneath the dirty slush. She needed help. But who?

Not her aunt Fredda. With her asthma, she shouldn't be in this environment. Jarius would help, but it seemed to need a woman's delicate touch.

That's when it hit her that she hadn't renewed a single friendship in the three months since she'd been home. She'd come with a dream and put all her energies into bringing it to fruition. The fact that she had no friends suited her. Less distractions. Less need to make explanations. Less . . . everything.

Disheartened and growing worried, she scraped a chunk of ceiling off a table and hitched a hip on it to rest. Closing her eyes, she let herself imagine back twenty-four hours to the bright bazaar quality this space had been. Swirls of color and textures and shapes and scents filled her memory. She loved the scent of pear, clean and spare and bright and ripe. Her stomach crimped at the thought. Pear. She hadn't eaten yet.

She glanced at her phone. 11:03. She'd work until lunchtime.

The knock on the front door surprised her. Prepared to tell another curious person that, no, they weren't open. And, yes, there had been a fire. Duh!

Through the glass in the door she could see a young man in a white jumpsuit and reversed blue baseball cap waving at her. She went to the door but didn't open it.

He didn't seem at all worried about that, yelling through the door, "Hi there, ma'am. I'm with CowTown Fire and Water Disaster. We've been hired to clean up next door. Mind if I talk with you?" He pulled a card from his pocket and pressed it to the glass.

Carly's gaze went from wording on the business card, past his shoulder, to the van parked next door where the words COWTOWN DISASTER: FIRE, WATER, AND HAZARD-OUS MATERIAL RESTORATION stenciled on the side.

She unlocked the door.

The man came in. "How are you, ma'am? Are you the owner?"

Carly nodded.

He did, too, and held out his hand. "I'm Cody. I'm sorry about what you're going through here." He glanced around. "Looks like you had a really nice place."

"*Had* being the operative word." She glanced at the left pocket of his jumpsuit where the name *Cody* was embroidered.

He nodded sympathetically. "I know. I know how it looks. You can't imagine things could ever be the same. But I'm here to tell you you'll be surprised by how fast you can bounce back. That's where we come in. CowTown Fire and Water can be the first step in getting your shop back in order. After you've had your insurance people in, of course."

"I've already done that."

"Good. As long as we're doing that job—he glanced at the shop next door—I thought I'd check to see if you'd hired anybody."

"Not yet."

He grinned, a kind of nervous energy driving his speech. "Now I don't want to be pushy, but it might be simpler for you to hire us, too. Seeing as we're already on-site."

Carly fingered the card. "I need to think about it, okay?"

"Absolutely. We'll be here a while. Mind if I look around, since the damage next door is connected to what's happened in here?"

Carly nodded. "Please step carefully. There are pieces of jewelry in the water."

"Will do." Even so, his thick rubber boots made waves as he waded a few feet in. Carly watched him closely, alert for any hint of a crunch. But he moved slowly, shuffling along so as not to step hard on anything.

He wasn't as young as she first thought. He had the loose-limbed body of a teenager. His suit didn't fit him anywhere except in the shoulders, which were broad. But she decided he was older, more than thirty, maybe even thirty-five. Plain-featured, he had skin permanently roughened by a bad case of acne.

When his visual inspection was done, he turned back to her. "I can see you are busy, so I won't take up more of your time." He came back toward her. "Whoever you get in here, do it soon. You don't want to wait. Terrible things happen in standing water. Mold begins and then you got to worry about more damage than having holes drilled in the wall boards to drain them."

"Do you own the company?"

"No, ma'am. That'd be the Dodd family. Been doing this for a while and let me just say you're lucky. What if the fire had started during the day and you'd been here and all?"

Carly shivered involuntarily. "I was here."

His eyes bucked. "You were? Gosh, that's terrible. You must have been scared to death, what with a fire breaking." He came toward her, eagerness making him smile too hard. "Did you call the fire department?"

He was asking too many questions, like the claims adjuster. "I'm not supposed to talk about it, the police said."

"I see. Yes, I can see that. Guess there'll be a lawsuit. Happens often enough when there's a fire. You might even bring a case, since the fire wasn't your fault, starting next door and all."

Carly looked away. "I need to finish so let me show you out, Mr.—"

"Cody. Just Cody, ma'am. You have a good day now."

CHAPTER EIGHT

Noah turned into the parking lot behind the Fort Worth Fire Investigation building located at Texas and Macon at a little after ten a.m. It was the home to the Fort Worth Arson/Bomb Unit. The two-story buff-and-cream brick Art Deco–styled structure sat next to its architectural building mate, Fire Station #2, the oldest station house in the city. The elaborate multibayed fire house with red-tile roof still boosted a brass firepole. That pole was the viewing delight of every visiting school class, and the curse of rookie firefighters required to polish it regularly to keep it gleaming.

Usually the sight of the building representing firefighting tradition gave him an uptick in pride. Today the place might have been razed and rebuilt with Legos for all the attention he gave it.

He'd had to borrow his father's truck because he had no idea where his own was. And he needed to find Harley. The woman who'd come to his hospital room all but admitted she had his dog. He didn't know who she was, or how to find her. But before he went in search of Harley, he needed to see the lay of the land at work.

Usually, he came in the back way, using his pass. But with his ID in his truck, at least that's where he'd left it, he needed to get buzzed in at the front door like a guest.

The older building was utilitarian-white inside, the broad hallway bisected by a large desk where all visitors were stopped. Crissie, the administrative assistant who controlled access through the front, gasped softly when she saw him. "You're okay?"

"Just peachy, Crissie." Noah moved past her without breaking stride. Had she received a text of his so-called suicide message, too? If not, she'd certainly been told about it. Everyone in the unit knew, according to Durvan. He just wasn't up to dealing with questions now. Probably not ever. The suicide text was a sham. No explanation necessary. Once he found the person who tried to do him in, he'd simply let the truth speak for him. Until then, he'd be silent as Buddha.

That's what he'd counseled his father when he called home from the hospital. His dad, a retired fireman, didn't need the advice.

After an earlier call from Sandra, his father had refused all calls from anyone and made the decision to keep Andy home from preschool today. "No need to explain anything to me. We know you didn't do whatever they're saying. Like I told your mother, you being okay is enough for us. Andy doesn't need to even know that was an issue."

Noah never stopped being surprised by the content of gossip on the playground. Andy had come home asking about everything from Miley Cyrus's latest video to whose parents were divorcing. Kids heard *everything*. That lesson had prompted him to suggest to his dad that now might be a good time to head south to Padre Island for a few days, where his parents had a beachside timeshare. They seldom went in March, during college spring break season. But his father only said, "Already packing, son. Figured you'd do better with us safely tucked out of the way."

Noah had been the focus of media attention before, usually after solving an arson crime. This time, it was going to get ugly. Andy didn't need to be confronted by things his dad was just beginning to wrestle with. But Andy's old man needed information. Lots of it. Which is why he was here, at work.

Now that his head was clearing of the alcohol and drugs, the analytical parts of his brain were kicking in. The only reasonable way to treat what had happened was to push it to arm's length, approach it as though the crime was about someone else.

Someone had set a man up to die without the victim being able to defend himself. At the same time, by making it appear a suicide, the perpetrator may have wanted to disgrace his victim. Having the victim die in a self-started conflagration would virtually guarantee the destruction of his career reputation. *Arson investigator dies in fire set by his own hand.* Catchy headline.

A ripple of bad feeling washed through him. He'd been chosen, special. The perpetrator hated him in ways he could not yet understand. He'd even hated him enough to include Harley in his scheme.

It took a beat for the heat of his anger to subside. An innocent animal. He was dealing with a depraved soul.

Yet, he learned while still a patrolman with the police force, that there was always some kind of logic in the minds of even the craziest perpetrators. Crazy logic, maybe, but reasons for what they'd done. He'd sent arsonists to prison, some for a long time. One to death row. That was the place he would start digging for suspects. Men who had a reason to hate him.

Not wanting to talk to anyone until he had gotten to his

computer and gathered some facts, Noah merely nodded to the two other arson investigators on duty as he passed their doorway. To his annoyance, one of them, Mike Wayne, got up from his desk and followed him to his office.

Mike was a year older than Noah, but they'd come into arson investigation together. Mike had always been a fire-fighter. Built solid with arms and thighs like tree trunks, he was usually the most fit in a room of very fit peers. Noah had the edge of his years as a police officer. Mike had the advantage of fighting more fires. They'd traded their knowledge on the job to learn their new jobs ASAP. Mike was more than a colleague. They were like brothers, loyal but competitive.

Mike paused in Noah's doorway and leaned a shoulder against the jamb. "Heard some crazy shit went down last night."

Noah reached down out of habit to pat Harley, usually under his desk when he worked. Annoyed to find his dog missing, he turned to his computer screen. "Thanks for the news flash."

"Don't be more of a hard-ass than usual. I'm just asking. You okay?"

Noah glanced up. "Durvan came by first thing. Guess he's taking the case. Thought you'd all be filled in by now."

Mike snorted. "Whatever Durvan knows he reported only to the captain. All I know is what the fire department grapevine says. You were involved with a suspected arson fire and had to be taken to the hospital."

Noah frowned as he scanned his computer screen. "Thought the news would be full of the details by now. What happened to media coverage?"

"You got lucky. Thirty minutes before the call came in about your fire, an eighteen-wheeler struck the guardrail at the top of curve of the I-30 East exit ramp onto I-35W North. Shut down all arms of the Mixmaster. Seemed like every news crew in the Metroplex with a van or copter tried to capture it. Backed up traffic headed in all directions for hours."

"Lucky me."

Mike waited a beat. "Captain wants to see you. Said to let him know when you came in."

"You can tell him I'm here."

Durvan appeared behind Mike. "Didn't expect you today, Glover."

Noah glared. "A little smoke can't keep me off the job."

Durvan tapped Mike on the shoulder so he could get past him. He looked almost angry as he came to stand before Noah's desk. "You should know the captain just gave me the job of getting a warrant to pull your cell phone records."

Noah finally looked up. "Why?"

Durvan's gaze bored into him. "Something to do with your phone being used to remotely start an electronic device last night."

"Do tell." Noah didn't let the news rattle him.

"Yeah, I do. You used a WeMo." The company made customizable products that allowed a person to control plugged-in electronics from anywhere using one's computer or phone.

"Nice try. I don't have an account."

Duran shook his head. "You're going to have to do better than that." He held up a cell phone in an evidence bag. It was burned and warped. "Found it in the fire. Want to bet a WeMo app is right here among your phone apps?"

They had his phone. Then they probably had his truck as well. But he needed to stay focused.

Noah leaned back in his chair. "Then it'll be a new account, as of yesterday."

Durvan frowned. "Doesn't change anything. You could've decided yesterday to use the device to end your life."

Noah shrugged. "Sounds sloppy. Not like me. I'd never stake my life—or loss of it—on something I hadn't used before. It might not have worked."

"Of course, it would work. Arson fires are often started remotely by professionals. Didn't you have some cases last year using a WeMo?"

Noah ignored the jibe. "You ever set up a new Wi-Fi device? Did it work for you the first time?"

Mike snickered.

Durvan grunted. "Fine. But you should know I'm close to probable cause on arson." He glanced at Mike. "Need you to get a warrant for Glover's cell phone records. And one for WeMo to see if our boy's among their clients, and when he last used his account."

Mike glanced quickly at Noah. "How soon you need it? I'm working two cases at the moment. Another coming up for trial next week."

"Put it in your mix. As senior investigator, I'm delegating the responsibility for the warrant to you. Homeland Security is coming in first thing next week to test our explosives unit's readiness. Got to drill over the weekend. I'll message you the wording to take to the judge." He turned and wagged the bag with the cell phone at Noah. "Tick tock, Glover."

Ignoring both men's speculative looks, Noah turned his attention back to his computer screen.

When Glover was gone, Mike came forward, his voice on low volume. "Man, tell me you didn't—" He paused and suddenly backed up, both hands held up in surrender. "No, I don't need to hear nothing. Better that way."

"Your call."

Noah first checked his bank account and his credit cards, in case he'd been induced to give the guy money. But no withdrawals had been made last night. This wasn't about robbery. Or theft. It wasn't even just about killing him. It was about ruining his reputation in death. So then, who would want him that kind of dead? Someone with a grudge. A felon.

Noah studied his screen for a moment before looking up to find Mike studying him from his desk across the room. "You remember that fire bug we put away three years ago? Somebody Wheatley? I see he just got out."

Mike shrugged. "Don't remember him."

"You know any of our convicted arsonists who've gotten out of prison recently?"

"No. Only felon I know is my former neighbor Chet Haggard. I kinda feel for the old boy. Lost his wife. His house. All on account of breaking up a TV."

"He did the crime."

"Yeah. But there're times when I have wonder about some of our laws. Here's a good old boy, fed up with his wife watching HBO. So, he takes a baseball bat to the TV. The wife calls the police and has him arrested for destroying her property. Turns out he didn't have the right to destroy property in his own house because this is a community property state. She owned half the TV. The poor bastard should have taken his bat to something beside their brand new 60-inch 3D smart TV. Cost more than three thousand dollars, which made destroying it a felony. Doesn't seem quite fair."

"Poor impulse control." Noah twisted away from his screen. The arson investigation squad often discussed motivation and legalities of a crime. It kept them sharp and up to date. "Could be the wife was worried that next time he got worked up, he'd take that bat to her, or one of their kids. Probably why she left him."

Mike stroked his chin. "Hadn't thought about it that way." He glanced speculatively over Noah's shoulder. "You're pulling up everyone you ever incarcerated?"

Noah pegged him with a look. "Someone wants me

dead. Seems like a good place to start looking for suspects."

"What about old girlfriends? Some bitches be crazy."

As the last word echoed through the room, a man in the
uniform of an officer appeared in the doorway.

"Glover. In my office. Now."

The position of arson investigation captain was mostly
bureaucratic. Often the arson investigation captain hadn't
been on an engine truck in years. A few had never fought
a fire. Administrative all the way. Such was the case with
Captain Jillian. He'd come to them from the Fire Preven-
tion Bureau, where he'd been a commercial sprinkler and
underground pipes inspector. His background made him
good at dealing with city hall and city commissioners,
pressing the flesh and negotiating the budget for the department. But that meant he didn't know anything about
what it took to do the job of the men and women he super-
vised. The best captains, from morale point of view, con-
sulted with the experienced men and women who went
out on the job on a daily basis. The arson investigators
preferred it what way, too. But Captain Jillian wasn't one
of those. He wanted to be in charge of every case that
had any potential for recognition. Not too surprisingly, he
and Glover had bumped heads a few times since he'd joined
the department sixteen months ago.

Captain Jillian was big man, tall with wide shoulders
and military bearing. But at age fifty-three his middle had
spread, and he'd grayed so that his thick mustache had a
steel-wool quality to it. Right now he was staring at Glover
with undisguised dislike.

"Where have you been all morning?"

"Working a case." Noah met his superior's gaze
squarely. He wasn't going to let the man get to him. He

could afford a little scrutiny. Because he'd solved a lot of cases since becoming an arson investigator, he'd had a lot of autonomy about where he was at any given time. But he could see in the man's expression that his superior was about to give him some cheap grief.

"I don't much like you, Glover. But you clear cases, so I haven't said anything."

Noah kept his mouth shut. The captain had said plenty over the past six months since they tangled about a case that the captain had insisted on running, over Noah's objections. The fact that it didn't turn out well had sealed their relationship as one of mutual bad feeling. It just hadn't affected much, so far.

"But now I have a problem with you in front of me I can't and won't ignore. I received an odd text from you at one o'clock this morning. Now I'm told you started a fire last night with the intent of killing yourself."

"No, sir. Someone tried to murder me last night."

Jillian looked more surprised than he should have. "That's quite an accusation."

"Less wild, sir, than an arson investigator unaccountably deciding to take his life by fire instead of using the weapon he carries daily."

Jillian blinked. "Yes, well, men with disordered minds aren't usually thinking in such terms."

Noah felt himself getting pissed off. "And yet, I am."

"You have a point. According to investigator Durvan, the circumstantial evidence is compelling but not yet probable. Until then, we will continue to behave as though nothing has occurred. But I wanted you to hear it from me. If and when Durvan gets probable cause, I won't jeopardize the reputation of the unit to shield your ungrateful ass."

"Ungrateful." That was the key word. If he wanted to grovel . . . Yeah. Sure. If it would speed this up.

Noah looked down, staring at his boot tips as if he'd never seen them before. "I appreciate all you do for the arson unit, Captain. And for me. Any help you can give, under the circumstances, will be greatly appreciated."

"It's damn little. The media, so far, haven't caught a whiff of this. But I expect that to change swiftly. As of now, you are not to have any part in this case. I would put you on inactive duty, but I need every man working. Besides, it won't look good for the fire department and the administration if . . ." *If it turns out we are in error.* Jillian let the thought die. But they both knew this was now as much about managing damage as it was about the truth. As Durvan had already warned him, the administration would do whatever necessary to shift the blame onto his shoulders, if it came to that.

Jillian reached out to move a pen on his desk that had been lying there minding its own business. "But if I get whiff of you interfering in any way with this investigation, I'll put you on leave without pay." He looked up to make certain Noah was listening. "Are we clear?"

"Yes, sir."

Noah made it into the hall without cussing. But when he looked up he whispered, "Fuck." His father and his son were talking with Crissie at the front door.

"Hey, son." His father lifted a hand, face eased into smile lines and crow's feet around identical blue eyes. Father and son were amazingly alike, same height and coloring, though Shiloh Glover's wavy hair was heavily salted with gray. And his waist wasn't as trim.

"We're all packed for a few days of surf, sand, and redfish." He ruffled Andy's blond curls with a big hard hand. "Isn't that right?"

Andy nodded then flew down the hall and grabbed his dad by the knees. "Come on, Dad!"

Noah bent and picked up his son, anchoring him with

an arm against his chest. "How're you two going to catch redfish?"

"Brown shrimp!" Andy held up his hand for his father to give him a high five.

"Don't go teaching the boy the wrong way around." Shiloh Glover grinned as his son walked toward him. "This time of year, redfish go after plugs. Shrimp are summer bait."

"Whatever Grampa says. He's bigger than us, so we have to listen." Noah poked his son gently in the belly. That never failed to make Andy collapse in infectious giggles.

After a few more pokes, Andy struggled to be set down. Usually, his father complied. But this time Noah held onto him a little tighter. Twisting his head around right and left, Andy asked, "Where's Harley?"

"Visiting a friend." Noah kept his voice conversational.

"Like a sleepover?" Andy had just had his first sleepover with a cousin.

"Yeah, definitely a sleepover. But he's coming home today." Needing to change the subject, Noah made eye contact with his father. "Where's Mom?"

"In the car, using her phone. She's arranging to get some groceries delivered so we won't have to stop and shop tonight when we get down to Padre. They got this new phone app where a grocery store will deliver to your door whatever's on the list you send them." He met his son's gaze with a question he did not want to ask aloud.

Noah turned to Crissie. "Would you mind showing Andy where to find the Men's?"

"I don't need to go, Dad."

His father grinned at him. "Padre Island is a nine-hour drive. Think you can hold it until then?

Andy gave him a disbelieving look. "We're going to stop at Buc-ee's for lunch. GiGi says they have the cleanest restrooms."

"Then I'll buy you an orange juice to drink on the way down so you'll be prepared. Now scoot."

When father and son had stepped into Noah's office and shut the door, Shiloh spoke. "Didn't want to tell you over the phone. A warrant was served as we were packing up to search the house."

"Did they wreck the place?"

"With your mother watching? Not likely. They were fairly respectful. But they did take a few things. Your personal laptop, all your work files, a few tools from the garage, and the gas can for the lawn mower." They both knew what that was about. Most likely the fire had been started using gasoline. It was ubiquitous, cheap, and effective.

"Sorry to put you through that, Dad."

Shiloh nodded. "You put me through worse growing up." He reached out and grabbed Noah by the back of the neck and pulled him close, whispering in his ear. "You clear your name, son. Your mother and I got Andy in hand."

Andy came sprinting back just as they opened the door.

Noah grabbed him about the waist and swung him high off the floor. It was a game they played. "Give me a hug, Andy. Grampa's ready to go."

Andy looked from his grandfather to his dad, his eyes suddenly shining like crystal blue lakes. "You aren't coming?"

Noah smiled. "You see these people in here? If I leave, some of them will have to work extra hours. We've talked about how being a man means pulling your own weight, right? I need to pull mine now."

Andy's lower lip began to tremble. "Can you and Harley come after work?"

"Maybe in a few days, if my work's done. Meanwhile,

you and Grampa fill the freezer with fish so I can grill up a batch when you get home. And watch out for jellyfish."

Andy turned back for help. "We can wait, can't we, Grampa?"

Shiloh smiled. "Maybe. But the fish can't."

Noah gave his son a hard hug, feeling the fragile bones of his ribs through his jacket. Something powerful and protective and dangerous all in one moved through his chest when he considered his child. *To his last breath.* That was only way he knew how to describe the feeling.

When they were gone, Noah turned to find Durvan leaning out of his doorway, staring.

"You saw my kid." He pointed back to the closed door. "Andy lost a mother. You really think I'd do anything that would take his father away from him?"

He didn't wait for an answer but turned and walked back into his office.

Half an hour later, Noah strode out of the Arson Investigations offices. He was loaded now with more information and a place to start. That place was the woman who had saved his life the night before.

At least now he had a name. Carly Harrington-Reese. After that, Google had inundated him with enough information to make interrogating her an even more interesting prospect.

Picked up by an agency at seventeen, she'd become one of those supermodels, accustomed to the best of everything. She came from the eastside. Probably grew up in hard times. Then her looks turn out to be her ticket out. She's instantly famous because of the body God gave her. Hard times nothing but a bad dream. She's certain the good times will go on forever. But something happened. Five years ago, she dropped out at the top. Lots of speculation but no explanation in the tabloids.

Noah didn't need much imagination to fill in possibilities. Money made in that world comes and goes fast. The high life is expensive.

Maybe the key word was "high." She could have snorted her fortune away. Other supermodels had been known to do the same.

Now Carly Reese was home, out of the blue, and sinking money into Flawless. Everything she had left? No way to know. But he did know some things. Arson was often about money.

He let his mind wander down possibilities, however remote. She might have had second thoughts before the boutique opened. Had she hired a professional to get her money back via insurance? Then changed her mind when she found a man and his dog—?

He rubbed a hand down his face. None of that explained why he was there unconscious in that blaze. Not likely a boutique owner was involved in that. Someone wanted him, Noah Glover specifically, dead.

The thought carved out a space in his middle. He knew fear. Every firefighter did. The professional learned to control that fear, use it as a tool to fight the fire, and protect himself and his fellow firefighters.

So, no, Carly Harrington-Reese wasn't his arsonist. But he couldn't wait to question her.

It had nothing to do with the images that had flooded his screen when he went in search of images of her. Not pornographic, or pervert paparazzi sneak shots, these professionally done images showed the stunning model in all her glory. Most were less provocative than his nude stance in his hospital room.

A flush edged up the back of his neck at the recall of his behavior. It had to have been the residual of the drugs still at work. He'd done some stuff in his life, streaking on a dare through a women's dorm at the University of

Texas, for instance. But flaunting himself as an adult before a stranger? Definitely the drugs.

Now that he was thinking straight, he wanted two things from Ms. Harrington-Reese. One: answers about the events of last night. Two: Harley.

CHAPTER NINE

"I know who you are. You're the lingerie model Carly Harrington-Reese."

Carly turned to find Noah Glover filling her rear entrance doorway. He'd yelled her name because of the noise from the giant fans set up next door to dry out the space.

He walked right in like he owned the place. "I read all about you."

Carly rolled her eyes and kept folding one of the crocheted ribbon sweaters she'd discovered untouched under a tarp. "Good for you. I hope it was an edifying experience."

He paused as his gaze slid over her in that way men have when they want a woman to know they are looking and liking what they see. "I don't know about edifying. But it was informative. And entertaining."

He'd seen the photos! French *Vogue*. But if he thought that knowledge was going to ruffle her, he truly *didn't* know who she was.

She put every bit of skepticism and scorn she could muster into her voice. "You speak French?"

He smirked. "Let's just say the photo spread didn't require translation."

She shrugged and continued to fold. "So we're even. Not that I care." Which wasn't really true. She remembered thinking when she saw the layout that she'd never felt more naked in her life. European magazines preferred their models to look more realistic, dimpled flesh and all. Not that she'd had that problem at nineteen.

She glanced sideways at him, prepared to verbally abuse him right out that door. But to her surprise his mouth had lost its humor.

He backed up a step though he wasn't actually too close. "About this morning. I apologize." The strain of shouting raked through his voice "What I did was insulting. That's not my style. All I can say in my defense is that I was still feeling the effects of the concoction that knocked me out last night."

An apology was the last thing she'd expected. Concoction? No. She didn't need to know. She absolutely didn't want to deal with anyone else—especially not this man—today.

"Apology accepted. Go away."

Instead, he moved closer so that the shouting, at least, would end. "You wanted to talk so badly this morning you came to see me."

"Yes. And we talked."

"No. You yelled and I listened."

She shrugged. "I'm yelling now. Go away."

"Not gonna happen." He stood his ground, looking around casually at the disaster as she piled a few more items in the two handmade wicker baskets she'd uncovered under another tarp. The firefighters had done a better job of shielding her wares than she'd first given them credit for.

"You need remediation in here, pronto."

She looked up, about to spend a bit more of her frustration on him. But the sight of him stopped her. He looked, well, he looked like hell. She was pretty sure she'd missed that in the hospital. And it wasn't her anger. She remembered him as impressive, vital, and sexy.

Or, perhaps, she'd been paying more attention to his pelvis than she'd given herself credit for. How else had she missed his utter exhaustion?

The whites of his blue eyes were still an angry red, and she could've packed for a week in the bags underneath. The reddish blond sketch of a day's worth of stubble stood stark against his washed-out complexion. Whatever had happened to him last night, he was the worse for wear for it.

Instinctively, she offered him the thermos she'd been drinking from. "Drink some of this."

He took and upended it. Just as quickly he grimaced and lowered it, sputtering, "What the hell is that? I was expecting coffee."

"Kale and green tea smoothie. It's loaded with polyphenols that function as powerful antioxidants. Your body's stressed out. That depletes your immune system. You could end up ill after last night."

He tried to hand it back. "No thanks. I got plenty of antioxidants at the hospital."

"Sure you did." She waved off the thermos. "Green tea's got caffeine, too. You like coffee, right? Drink it for the caffeine lift. You look like you need to lie down."

He grinned then, a slow, heat-you-up-from-the-inside grin.

Carly crossed her arms. "Drink it, Investigator Glover. It's the only good thing being offered here today."

He took another sip, this time swallowing it all. Then he glanced at his watch. "I haven't eaten yet. There's a place across the street where we can talk and eat. Like you said. I need to keep my strength up."

Carly waited a beat as her stomach reminded her that it was an hour past her usual lunchtime. "I didn't hear a please."

She watched his jaw work and decided his dentist must spend a lot of time worried about the investigator's enamel. "Please. Across the street. Now."

"Attitude, much?"

He frowned. "How old are you? Twenty?"

"Thirty. In December. You know all about me. Remember?"

He opened his mouth, couldn't think of a thing that wouldn't sound cheesy, patronizing, or close to an insult, and closed it.

She picked up her purse and keys and began locking up. When she was done, she piled one wicker basket on top of the other and headed toward the rear entrance without so much as glancing at him.

It took him a couple of seconds to catch up. "Where are you going?"

"I have a dog to feed." She put her baskets down to lock the back door.

He smiled. "Harley."

She shrugged. "You can come with, or follow me."

"Come with." He grabbed up her baskets.

As he slid into the passenger side of the Mazda he didn't know why he hadn't just agreed to follow her. He never "came with." He drove everywhere and anywhere he needed to go. He wasn't a chauvinist. He just didn't like the way most men *or* women behaved behind the wheel. He'd seen too many accidents, pried too many injured people—and a few dead ones—out of wrecked vehicles.

But he didn't put it past Carly to simply drive away and lose him in the traffic. Plus, riding with her gave him an excuse to be in her presence a little longer.

It had been a long time since he simply wanted to be in a woman's company. He had needs and found women willing to accommodate them. But the rules were clear up front. Not looking for anything but a good time. Some relationships lasted a night. A few others, a few months. Nothing he couldn't walk away from. He had a child to protect. There'd be no parade of women in and out of his son's life, giving him hope and then snatching it away.

Why the hell was he thinking of that now? He wasn't sure he wanted the answer to that question. But something about her drew his interest. It wasn't only her beauty.

He glanced at Carly's profile. She had a delicate narrow face with a soft full mouth and a stubborn chin. In the fashion pictures, she'd looked remote, regal, very much like a sculpture of Nefertiti he'd first seen in a book in high school. It was cheekbones and skin tone, he supposed. In every way, Carly was better in the flesh than in her pictures. Her skin was a warm shade of brown. Her hair a celebration of her African American heritage. The fashion photographs resembled art house stills. As much about her body being a sculpture in the space of light and shadow and color. Hers was a gorgeous, slim body with just enough curves to make a very touchable sculpture of female perfection. But it wasn't real.

The real woman was sitting next to him now. He could see her pulse beating in the hollow of her throat. Could watch in real time the unedited expressions crossing her face as she maneuvered through traffic. There was a tiny mole on her left collarbone just above the neckline of her oversized sweater. Tiny curls bounced happily against her forehead each time she moved her head. The hair said *Don't Worry, Be Happy.* Her expression said *Woman at Work.* The dichotomy stirred his investigative juices.

He didn't think it was only the store that drew the two lines between her brows. From what he'd read, she'd lived a lot of her early life in the fast lane. And what about that gap in her life story? What thirty-year-old has three years unaccounted for? What had happened to pull her off her pedestal?

He glanced again at her, mind-warping images of her body artfully posed in ways that showed off her nakedness running through his mind. Suddenly he was thinking about how long it had been since he'd spent a night with a woman.

So maybe the second reason he was sitting in the passenger seat wasn't the only other reason. She said she pulled him out of the fire by herself. Tall and still slim, she'd lost the coltishness of her youth—another thing he liked better about the real Carly. But what did she weigh, a hundred twenty, a hundred twenty-five? She didn't seem capable of dragging his one hundred and ninety pounds out of a building alone. What if there was someone else?

He didn't want to think about what that might mean. But it was his skin in the game, and he was going to find out.

He half turned to her in his seat. "We need to get one thing straight. I came to see you, not just to get Harley back. I need you to tell me everything, in great detail, that you remember about last night."

She didn't say anything. She just kept driving. Finally, she sighed and looked at him. "I don't want to be any more involved. You get Harley back. We're done."

When Noah glanced out the window, they were climbing a terraced hill with flowing shrubbery lining the drive. "Where are we?"

"Off Riverside, eastside."

They crested a curve to find a large traditional two-story white brick house coming into view. Beyond it the grounds fell away in all directions. It was a mini-estate of several acres in the middle of a neighborhood.

"Who lives here?"

"My aunt Fredda. Why do you sound so suspicious? You were expecting the hood?" She laughed. God, she knew how to get to him.

Talking with her was like drinking whisky, neat. It packed a kick but then went down with fiery smoothness, leaving him with a warm stimulating craving for more.

He rubbed his eyes with his fingers. They still stung from the smoke. "Actually, I know this place. Mrs. Fredda Wiley lives here. Worked for years as president of Eastside Citizens on Patrol." He grinned as she turned to him, brows lifted. "This is my town. I get around."

They pulled up into a broad paved space large enough to park half a dozen cars easily. At present the only car there was a late-model Mercedes.

Carly sighed when she saw it. No sneaking in and out of Aunt Fredda's house without having to answer questions.

Carly exited her car and hurried across the lawn instead of heading toward the house. Noah followed and grinned when he realized why. She reached a long fenced-in area behind. And there was Harley, tail wagging. Then he saw Noah. He stepped back a few feet and then jumped and cleared the five-foot-high chain-link fence with ease.

Noah heard Carly call out in surprise just before he was hit by ninety pounds of happy K9. Barking and leaping and wagging his tail so hard it seemed like his rear end might break off, Harley did happy all over his handler.

"I know. I know. Hi, Harley. Missed you, too." Noah went down on a knee to accept the slobbering licks of his

K9 buddy. "Sorry to leave you alone so long. But you're lucky to have a nice lady take care of you."

Carly watched them wrestle with a bemused expression. When the mutual love fest slowed down, she offered, "He's probably starving. He wouldn't take much from me. Bring him in the house. You can feed him."

They followed her in through a side door that led directly to the kitchen. Before she could say a word, an attractive fiftysomething woman dressed in silver skinny jeans tucked into high-heel boots and a black velour sweater with a rhinestone zipper confronted them, a hand on each hip. "Who's this young man?"

"He's the man I—we met last night at the fire." Carly began fluffing the curls atop her head. No need to start more rumors than necessary.

"Are you the owner of this animal?" Aunt Fredda pointed to Harley, who was still doing a happy dance all over his master.

"Yes ma'am." Noah pushed Harley away, a game they played. The dog skidded a few feet across the spotless tile floor. Almost instantly he got traction and galloped back to throw his full weight into his handler. Noah *oofed* softly but did not go down behind the knee block.

Aunt Fredda's lips pursed as she watched. "I want you to know that dog is a menace. He ate my pound cake."

Carly gaped at her aunt. "Why would you think that?"

Her aunt pointed to a piece of paper lying on the breakfast nook table. "That's what the note Jarius left me says. Now what am I supposed to do about the church social tomorrow? I always bring my pound cake. Folks expect it."

"I'm sorry, ma'am." Frowning at his K-9, Noah gave Harley the "down" sign. The dog instantly complied. "Harley has a history of food boundary issues. I'd be happy to replace your missing cake. How about one from Blue Bonnet Bakery?"

Aunt Fredda worked her mouth, trying not to smile. "They do make some decent cakes. But I have my reputation to maintain. Everybody is expecting my pound cake."

"I'm sure that's true." He looked again at his dog. "Bad dog, Harley."

The German Shepherd gazed up at his master, head kicked over to the side with ears on high alert.

Noah smiled. "He says he didn't do it."

Aunt Fredda glanced down at the animal. "You'd take that shaggy bag of bones' word over mine?"

"Harley didn't eat the cake." Both parties looked over at Carly.

"Are you sure?" Noah looked at her doubtfully. "To be honest, Harley does have a history for unreliability around unsupervised food. That's why he's not a seeing-eye dog."

Aunt Fredda tucked her arms together. "I'd like to hear about that."

Noah smiled. "He was kicked out of the guide-dogs-for-the-blind program after he ate a burger off the plate of a blind man during his probation period."

Carly burst into laughter before she could clap a hand over her mouth. "Are you serious?"

He grinned back. "Yep." He reached down to pet his partner. "But Harley's been retrained to eat only from my hand. And, honestly, he doesn't like sweets. So you might be right, Carly. There might be another culprit."

"Harley hadn't come up against my prize-winning pound cake before." Aunt Fredda looked almost pleased to have tempted the dog beyond his training. "You keep him away from my cakes, he'll be fine."

"Yes, ma'am."

Carly glanced again at the note. She didn't want to throw poor Harley under the bus, but she hated to rat out her cousin to his mom.

"You two had lunch?"

"Yes—No." Carly and Noah glanced at each other as they had both answered at the same time.

Aunt Fredda chuckled. "Men don't lie about hunger. I got some chicken salad from Costco this morning. And some grapes. You go sit while I pull some lunch together."

"That'd be much appreciated, Mrs. Wiley."

Aunt Fredda turned to Noah. "You know my name. I know you, too, don't I?"

"Yes, ma'am. I'm Noah Glover." He held out his hand. "You were kind enough to invite a member of the fire department arson investigation unit to speak at your Neighborhood Watch group last year. That was me."

She nodded and shook his hand. "That's why you look so familiar. I don't usually forget a handsome face." Then, as if a light bulb went off, her friendly expression hardened into her courtroom face. "But that's not the first time we met, is it?"

"No, ma'am." Carly was astonished to see Noah blush. "I came up before you once in juvie court. I was hoping you wouldn't remember that. Not my finest moment."

Aunt Fredda frowned as she shifted through her memory. "Ah, yes. Noah Glover. Joy-riding without a license in a stolen vehicle. Your uncle turned you in, said he did it to teach you a lesson."

"Yes, ma'am. That was me. I'm amazed you remember that."

"I didn't often see young men before me who looked so repentant. You admitted your guilt. That's why I didn't sentence you to juvenile detention. I figured a year of community service working with other kids headed down the wrong way might wake you up."

"It did." He turned to Carly. "I tutored juvies for a year. Best education on what not to do in the world." He looked back at Aunt Fredda. "I wasn't a bad kid, but your verdict made me choose a career in law enforcement. Thank you."

Aunt Fredda's expression turned friendly again. "*You* did that. I only pointed out the path." She patted his hand before glancing at Carly. "I take it your being together has something to do with that fire last night."

Presented like that, Carly couldn't lie. "Yes. And we need to talk."

"I see. Then you might want to take that discussion into the dining room. For privacy."

Carly headed in that direction, not at all certain they wouldn't be eavesdropped upon anyway. Aunt Fredda was worried. She could see that in her aunt's eyes.

Carly indicated that Noah take a seat as she rounded the table to sit opposite him. Harley came in quietly, as if he understood Fredda Wiley's beautifully appointed dining room was no place for misbehaving. Carly smiled at the dog when he sat next to Noah and set his big head on his thigh with a sigh. "Was Harley really a seeing eye dog?"

"He was mostly a see-food, eat-food dog." Noah stroked his dog calmly. "When he's on duty, he's alert and all business. But when he's off duty, he's pretty much a total slob. He's either looking for trouble, eating, or sleeping."

"What kind of work? I thought he failed as a service dog."

"Ever try a sport and been terrible at it? Then you try a different one and excel? Harley's like that. He's now an explosives specialist. It's not unusual for a canine who fails one service-dog program to be handed off to another professional K-9 program. They've already been screened for intelligence, diligence, hardiness, and trainability. After the seeing-eye gig didn't work out, Harley went to the Bureau of Alcohol, Tobacco, Firearms and Explosives to be trained as an explosives K-9. He's got a great nose. And he's thorough. A year ago he was offered to our arson investigation unit as part of Homeland Security cross-training. He's trained to detect a variety of components used in bombs, as well as the explosives and accelerants themselves. I've always had dogs, so I got him."

Noah reached into his back pocket and pulled out a notepad. "Now that the polite talk is over, I want you to tell me everything that happened last night. No detail is too small."

"I don't think that's appropriate."

He glanced up at her, the friendly wrinkles around his eyes going squint hard. "Why not?"

Carly lifted her chin. "You're a suspect in a crime. I'm a witness. Discussing what happened could—what's the word?—taint my testimony."

"What makes you think you'll need to testify?"

She simply stared at him.

He rubbed his forehead. "Let's get this straight once and for all. I was the target. Someone tried to murder me last night."

The words hung in the air as Fredda Wiley entered with a tray containing plates with generous scoops of chicken salad on lettuce cups, piles of green and red grapes, some kind of cheese, and two long sections of fresh baguette. She said nothing directly, but the look she gave her niece crawled right up Carly's nape.

"I've got coffee brewing. I'll be in the kitchen."

They waited until she was gone, then Carly met Noah's gaze, gorgeous chocolate-drop eyes boring into his. "I sympathize with you, truly I do. But I've already given my statement to the officers handling the investigation."

The truth struck him in the chest. Before, at the hospital, he'd thought she was a bit hysterical, and rightly so. She'd had a bad scare. But now he didn't see fear in her eyes so much as opaque disinterest. "You don't believe me."

Silence. Then, "I don't know what to believe. And I

want to do the right thing here. For the moment that seems to be not taking sides."

He folded his notepad. "I get it. I respect that. If you're scared, I can—"

"I'm not scared." Carly popped a grape in her mouth and chewed. "I've been fifteen rounds with Death once before. And lost. I don't like losing, okay?"

He looked deep into her eyes and believed her. "Someone you cared deeply about? Right?"

"Don't push me. I bite."

He believed her. It would hurt like hell, too. But he suspected he wouldn't mind. "Fine. Then tell me how I can win your trust."

To his utter surprise she seemed to consider his question. She wanted something from him.

She reached over a cut a wedge of cheese and nibbled one end before speaking. "I'm worried about my shop being vandalized before I can get my things out of there. I'm still looking for pieces of jewelry. Some are quite valuable. The insurance adjuster suggested I hire security until I can collect them all."

He nodded. "Done."

"I wasn't asking for help. I was going to ask for a trustworthy recommendation."

"I know. I know someone reliable, diligent, and trustworthy."

"He sounds expensive." She reached for another grape but only stared at it like it was crystal ball. "Like I have much of a choice. Can he do it on short notice?"

Noah nodded. "I guarantee he's available."

She smiled at him. The effect of it went all the way to his groin. Harley, nose practically in Noah's crotch, made a whiny noise. Just what he needed, a dick odometer.

He picked up his fork, salivating at the food before him. "We'll talk later."

She didn't smile again, just cut another wedge of cheese.

While Noah and his dog went out so that Harley could do his thing before they headed back downtown, Carly stacked their plates and went in search of her aunt.

She found her peeling potatoes at the sink.

"Thanks for lunch. And I'm sorry about your cake, Aunt Fredda. I'll find a way to make it up to you."

"No need." Fredda looked over at her. "That dog didn't eat my cake."

"How do you know?"

"I'm not saying I'd put it past a dog to eat cake. But then wash the platter?" She pointed her potato peeler at her best cake plate resting in the dish rack. "You ever known Jarius to wash a dish he didn't use?"

Carly almost felt sorry her cousin. Caught out by his mom. And Aunt Fredda was not one to be crossed.

CHAPTER TEN

Hemmed in by scrub brush and barbed wire, the driver sped along Shelby Road, a rural lane south of town, at sundown. As the turnoff for Village Creek Motocross passed his window, he scowled. He'd planned on making an appearance at the 4th Dealer Series competition next weekend, followed by an evening celebrating at Bikini's in Arlington. But now all his plans were shot to shit.

He rubbed his gloved hands over the steering wheel. He needed this fix very badly, to work off some stress before he made another mistake. He needed to relax. Clear his head.

Only one solution for that.

After a few minutes a black-humped shape appeared in an empty field off on the right, backlit by the embers of the sunset. That's what he was looking for.

He checked his rearview mirror. No car on the road. Piece of luck there.

He shut off his headlights and braked hard, fishtailing off the blacktop and onto a gravel road where the truck bounced over the metal cattle grate into the field.

The bouncing continued, jarring his teeth, until the truck jolted to a halt as a tire slammed into a deep unseen rut.

He gunned the engine twice, hoping the tire would grab traction and spin out of the hole. But the only things ejected from the rut were clods of dirt.

Swearing viciously, he slammed the truck door shut and walked back to inspect the tire. At least it hadn't blown.

He swung his head left and right, the plastic shower cap he wore under his baseball cap crackling. A car was in the distance, but he doubted they would notice a truck in a field with its lights off. If they did, it was too dark to make out much. Even so, he didn't like being out of his truck before nightfall. He might be spotted and later described. For that reason, he'd stopped to take off the truck's license plate when he hit open country. It was a risk worth taking if he was stopped.

Lost my tags, officer? Didn't even know it. That's the last thing I need about now.

Then he'd have casually mentioned he worked for Cow-Town Fire and Water Disaster, then revealed his volunteer fire department credentials as he went for his license. Funny how that always worked up a conversation. Didn't matter if he or she was a trooper, deputy, or patrol. Law enforcement seemed to get a hard-on when talking with firefighters. Most times he got away with a friendly warning. What did they call it? Oh yeah. Professional courtesy. That's what he was. A professional firefighter. Even if he worked for an all-volunteer fire department. Why didn't the shit-for-brains candidate review board of the Fort Worth Fire Department get that?

He went to the back of his truck, shifted free a section of planking, and shoved it under the stuck tire. It didn't matter that he got mud on his clothing. The disposable biohazard coveralls he wore from work didn't shed, leaving no fibers for forensics. It and his booties would go into a Dumpster in Mansfield.

Once back in the cab, he reversed his engine and stepped on the gas. This time the truck moved, tire gripping wood to move up and out. Problem solved.

He was good at thinking on his feet. Problem solving. This last time, he'd scored well enough on his third attempt to make the cut from thirty-two hundred applicants to seventy real contenders.

He exited the vehicle and tossed the board back onto the truck bed. Never leave even casual evidence. Details. The devil and difference between success and failure was in taking care of the details.

That's why he'd liberated this truck from a dealer of junk cars over in Kemp. Everyone suspected that not all the vehicles were legally obtained. If a truck disappeared from where he kept his merchandise in his front yard, who was he going to call? Ghostbusters?

He snickered at his own joke. First time he'd cracked a smile all day. He put the truck into drive and continued toward his destination.

His failure three weeks ago to make the final cut from seventy to the final thirty selected to become firefighters came at a high price. It caused him to make a mistake. A big one. The result was lodged in his brain, humming like a hornets' nest night and day.

FIRE KILLS HOMELESS MAN: ARSON SUSPECTED.

Every day since, the headline played through his every thought like the crawl at the bottom of a newscast.

He jerked the wheel to avoid a water spigot in the field.

He wasn't a killer. He scouted his sites regularly, never knowing when he'd need one. No evidence of squatters, or even the occasional homeless seeking shelter that night. He'd walked the perimeter himself.

Should have checked the second floor.

He would have if he hadn't been sobbing so hard he couldn't hardly function. He was always careful.

No, he wasn't a killer. He'd been made a killer.

By Noah Glover.

He'd nearly gotten his revenge too.

But then his most detailed and cunning plan was wrecked. By a woman.

He pulled up in front of the abandoned mobile home. Gloves on, he grabbed a can from the rear and moved toward the trailer, anticipation a boiling rage in his gut.

Finally, he drew out the lighter, the only thing his father ever gave him.

Bright flames of light soon licked at the structure.

He stood well back and watched as dozens of glowing cinders flashed through the rising column of smoke like fireflies on a summer night. The anxious gnawing in his stomach soon turned to butterflies.

Finally, cleansing release.

And a new plan began to emerge.

Of course. Why hadn't he thought it before?

Better than death. Prison. Glover would be alive to suffer, a long time.

He grinned, wishing he could stay longer. But that would be careless.

He didn't turn on a light until he reached the road again. He could see cars coming. The fire must be seen for miles now.

He pulled onto the highway, watching to see if anyone noticed. But the first vehicle slowed and then turned into the field that he'd just left. Maybe he hadn't been seen. His gaze flickered back and forth from rearview mirror to unlit road. When the second vehicle paused at the same turn in, he knew he'd gotten away.

He drove into Mansfield and left the truck with a friend who let him park it on his property. He checked the truck carefully, grabbing up the floor mats his feet had rested on. Then he carefully folded up the plastic drop cloth he'd sat on while he drove. Finally, he walked over to his fire truck, emblazoned with the Edgecliff Village Fire Rescue decal and dumped his evidence inside, along with the gloves and shower cap.

His mind was clear.

All of his problems began and ended with Glover. No Glover. No problems.

CHAPTER ELEVEN

She couldn't breathe. Blistering heat pressed in on her from all sides. Smoke invaded her nostrils, forcing its way into her throat, blocking her scream.

She couldn't move. Merciless darkness held her down.

Her chest heaved. Spasms of fear quaked through her.

In the distance a dog howled, long and mournful.

She was dying. She didn't want to die. Not yet.

Carly sat up in bed, cold sweat trickling down her back. Even with eyes open, she couldn't shake the sense of terror. Darkness blanketed what should have been familiar. Where was she?

Possibilities skittered through her thoughts as she strained for clues.

Was this Brooklyn? The track of an elevated train ran at eye level outside the tiny efficiency apartment that she'd shared with two other hopeful models. But no, no sounds of that urban lifestyle filtered back to her.

Was she in the Parisian Left Bank studio she'd later shared with several rotating flight attendants? They'd seldom slept there, only dropped off bags and changed clothes between parties and flights.

She held her breath, waiting to hear the ancient wrought-iron elevator that clanked up and down the building like an elderly relative.

Nothing.

Piombino, Italy? No, the suffocating sense that still held her in its grip was the opposite of the fresh, sea salt–tinged air of the Italian port city where she and Arnaud—

Where was Arnaud?

She felt in the darkness beside her. The bed was empty. Then she remembered.

Dead. Arnaud was dead.

Shivering, she reached to turn on the bedside lamp that revealed the small bedroom of her latest home, a loft apartment on Vickery in Fort Worth, Texas. She lived alone. She was alone. As she had been for the past four years.

"Get up, Carly. Get up and move!" The command, spoken out loud, gave her motivation.

She picked up her robe, opened the door, and stepped out onto the third-floor balcony that ran the length of her apartment. Downtown Fort Worth shimmered in the near distance like a movie set backlit by a haze reflected from the canopy of clouds. Wind whipped past her body with a chill factor unexpected. March in Texas was like that. Eighty-five during the day. Thirty-five by dusk. Tornado weather.

But tonight there was only the cold breeze that felt good against her skin after her dream of unbearable heat. Yet the restless feeling supplanting it wasn't better. It stung like the winter-tinged air.

Restlessness was dangerous. It was the call of the nomadic life she'd left.

She'd come home, after a decade away, to put down roots. To make a stand, on her own terms. But the fire the night before had destroyed more than merchandise. It had put an abrupt end to her hopes that the transition would be simple, and easy.

Once more she was a tangled mess of loose ends. With nothing to show for her efforts. So then, who was she?

Carly Harrington-Reese was no longer a simple eastside girl. Nor was she a world traveler, with too many high-profile acquaintances but few real friends. She'd jettisoned both former selves for Arnaud. And lost everything. Now here she was again, with nothing to show for putting everything she had into a project.

"Not now," she whispered to herself. Tonight the dead should stay buried.

Once pushed aside, the anxiety of her dream descended again.

Carly pulled her robe closer, eyes darting right and left. Why did she feel spied upon? As if it was possible for someone to search her out on her third-floor private balcony. No reason to fear anything.

Yet, at the moment, she felt very unsafe. Unsheltered. She could have died the night before. She hadn't let herself really think about that until now. It was too scary. But that explained the dream. Her unconscious dealing with what she refused to. It didn't explain why she was suddenly thinking of Noah Glover and Harley.

She knew next to nothing about Noah Glover. She did know he commanded the loyalty of a dog willing to risk his life to save his handler. Harley had brought his owner to her attention. If not for the big bear of a shepherd, they might both have died in the fire. A fire deliberately set.

Carly shivered and wrapped her arms tight about her waist. Who in her life would be willing to risk death to save her? Cousin Jarius? Yes. But he was a police officer. Protecting the public was part of his job description. Not that she needed saving, exactly. She needed comfort. The nudge of her body down low confirmed what she hadn't been thinking, waking her libido.

"Fat lot of good that'll do you, Carly." There was no one to call.

Suddenly she remembered how Noah had looked in the nude, his jaw set in defiance while his body arrogantly ignored all proprieties. No defensive gesture on his part to cover anything. He didn't need it. Everything on display was worth staring at.

He was hard, everywhere. Muscles strapped his shoulders, rippled down his arms and impressive thighs. Yeah, about those thighs. Firemen spent a lot of time climbing and carrying heavy equipment as they did so. Noah must still work out with them to stay ready, if needed.

A suddenly warmth spread across her skin. She'd seen tons of perfectly toned bodies before. Slept with a few. But gazing at Noah had been a distinct departure. This was a real man, built for real life, not the runway or a perfectly staged photo opportunity. They weren't movie muscles. His body was built for work.

It was a novelty to look at a man who hadn't been man-scaped within an inch of his life. Noah was all raw male with just enough red-blond hair covering his chest to make examining him interesting. For instance, whorls of hair encircled each of his flat male nipples, erect in the chill of the room. That light furring tapered down his chest to flank his navel before arrowing down to the payoff.

And it was worth it.

Even half aroused in a nest of red-gold curls, there was no mistaking the potential of his johnson, yet to be fulfilled.

Carly slapped a hand against her cheek, shocked that she'd remembered so much of him in such detail. "You don't even like blonds."

Not exactly true. She had just never been drawn to light-haired men. But she wasn't thinking about "men."

She was remembering in pulse-accelerating detail one man. And to think she thought she hadn't paid that much attention.

She suspected most women only had to look at Noah Glover to want to crawl into bed with him. Despite his ordeal, he'd looked like an ancient gladiator standing in that hospital room—solid, hard, willing, and able to have whatever he chose.

Stirrings of sexual warmth surged through her, bypassing attraction, longing, and desire. The punch it packed was one hundred percent lust spreading into her breasts and clenching low down in her pelvis.

She was lusting after Noah Glover. That thought astonished and embarrassed her.

Carly shook her head, harder this time. "Waste of time, building fairy tales about a man I'll probably never see again." He was most likely even now tucked up against his girlfriend somewhere, sated and safe.

It had been a long time since she'd thought about being sated and safe.

"Not a good time for this, Carly." Lusting over an unobtainable alpha male was giving in to passion without reality. She needed a dose of reality, badly. Frank, irreverent girlfriend talk. That's what she needed.

She turned back from the balcony and went to pick up her cell phone. 1:27 a.m. Too early to call Gillian in New York. Though, knowing her, she might still be out on a Saturday night. Sunday morning in Paris. Allete would not soon forgive her for interrupting her beauty rest. So, no one to call. She pocketed the phone.

She took a step and froze as something gave a shrill squeak.

She looked to see what she'd stepped on. It was a fuzzy duck with a squeaker in its bill. She'd bought the doggy chew toy along with dog food for Harley.

She picked it up and held it against her chest. She hadn't realized until Harley spent what was left of last night with her, how much she missed having a pet of her own.

"Now see? You need a dog." Once said aloud, she felt better.

Maybe she'd name it Cooper II. No, that wouldn't be fair to a new pet who'd come with her or his own personality. But a dog suddenly sounded like a very good idea.

Dogs were always there, ready to cuddle and happy to see you, with none of the entanglements that had ruined the relationships in her life. A dog would watch TV with you, share your popcorn, and not comment on how inane chick flicks were. And hadn't she already watched *Bridesmaids* twelve times?

Yep, dog not guy. Much safer. If not nearly as satisfying in one major area.

Not that there had been that many guys. Arnaud had come along when she was barely nineteen, and taken charge of the scared ingénue's career. As one of the hottest fashion photographers in the business, he knew the culture inside and out. He'd made her a star while she'd fallen for him so hard, the foundation of her life shook, and then cracked.

"Stop, Carly. No going there." But the sensation of feeling trapped rose up around her for a second time. She needed to do something. Never one to sit and stew, she needed to be active to work through her demons. That meant getting out of here. Fast.

Without thinking about the reasonableness of what she was doing, she slipped into a pair of skinny jeans and pulled a heavy sweater over her head without bothering with undergarments. It was a habit from years of having to strip for lightning-quick changes at shows. Bras and undies slowed down the process and left marks on the skin.

Besides, she wasn't going far, or meeting anyone. She just needed to get out.

Instinct drove her into the night.

Noah sipped his thermos of coffee. At his feet was a plastic bag containing a can of dry-roasted peanuts, a couple of protein bars, a pack of gum, and a sack of doggy treats. He and Harley were set for stakeout.

Harley suddenly sat up and woofed quietly from the backseat. It was followed by a soft *poot*.

"Geez. You're killing me here." Noah waved a hand before his face as he rolled down the driver's side window. Harley barked again, this time a little brighter. "Yeah. I know. Time to take a doggy dump."

Harley was off schedule. Having not eaten until late in the afternoon, he'd demanded both morning and evening portions together. Or maybe it was the pieces of bratwurst his owner had slipped him at dinner. Either way, Harley was manufacturing farts foul enough to run off the baddest bad guy.

Noah exited his truck, parked in a lot diagonally across the street from Flawless so that he could simultaneously watch the front and rear exits of the building complex. While he couldn't see the rear door, he could see if a vehicle turned into the parking lot behind the strip of stores.

He stood perfectly still, ignoring the buffeting north wind that had turned a warming spring back into a wintery shiver. Only his eyes moved as he scanned the area from A to B to C. Nothing moved in the shadows on either side of the street. Two cars passed as he stood watching. One blasted a beat that registered in his chest from a block away. Nothing to hide there. The other was moving fast, late for something. Or moving quickly away from something. But not interested in him, either way.

He really wasn't expecting his arsonist to return to the scene of the crime this long after the event. The man after him was smart. He'd gotten the drop on Noah because Noah hadn't suspected anything until it was too late.

He shook his head. He was thirty-four and jaded as hell by a life in law enforcement. He should've seen trouble coming. He should have bruises or cuts, something to prove he'd put up some sort of struggle. But he didn't.

What women said after being roofied was true. He didn't know what he'd said and done, agreed to or argued about. The lost hours were a complete blank, as smoothly opaque as polished black marble.

He scrubbed a hand up and down the back of his neck. He felt stupid. He felt violated. He felt he'd somehow let himself down. He didn't like any of those feelings. Or the fact that the men and women he worked with in mutual respect were now eying him with suspicious gazes. As if he were no longer one of them, maybe even a traitor.

Damage control. He needed to do it, and fast. He wasn't here just because he'd promised Carly he'd make certain her store was secure. He wanted to watch the place. Maybe something would jog loose in his memory of the night before if he sat here in the dark.

Finally, satisfied that the night was empty of threat, he reached for the leash he wore like a second belt around his waist.

Harley, breathing excitedly with the opportunity for fresh air, waited patiently for the leash to be attached to his collar.

Once out of the car, he sniffed around carefully on the ground but never lost eye contact with Noah for more than a few seconds at a time. He was in his harness. That meant they were working. Harley didn't know whether this was the real thing or a test, with a whiff of accelerant or bomb-making component hidden anywhere, even in the wheel rim of their car. His handler was like that, hiding test strips in a drawer or waste basket right in the Fire Investigation offices. It really didn't matter that Harley couldn't make the distinction between a test and a real search for explosives. But Noah suspected that Harley detected the pheromone change of excitement in his handler's scent and so knew when he'd done something important. Those were the moments the K-9 lived for.

Bright eyes shining in the darkness, Harley kept a close eye on Noah's hands, waiting for a command to "Seek." Instead, Noah said, "Free," which was permission to take care of his doggy business.

Snuffling in the night the way his handler had drunk the details through his human eyes, Harley processed the scents of the grassy patch at the edge of the parking lot. The area was perfumed with cigarette butts, chewed gum, gas exhaust from the hundreds of cars that had passed, raccoon scat, and the faint scent of cheeseburger from a wrapper that had landed briefly before being blown away in the chill breeze. But overwhelming everything was the strong urine of other dogs. Male and female, young and old. One with a gastric infection that made Harley back up a step. Another fresh pile so rich in the remnants of prime rib and pork chops, he was tempted to sample.

He swerved his gaze toward Noah, who would be sure to stop him if he tried. He sneezed, blowing the temptation out of his nostrils. And moved on to find a place to squat.

As Harley finished, a flashlight winked in the darkness across the street. Noah's pulse jumped and his body went rigid. Yes, there it was again, inside Flawless.

"Damn." He spoke softly but it was enough to stop Harley from investigating whatever new odor had taken his doggy fancy. He came quickly to stand before Noah, ears forward and head straining up toward his handler.

Noah reached back to touch his pancake holster, nestled

behind his right kidney at his back. Inside was his Sig
P239. As an arson investigator, invested with arrest pow-
ers, he was allowed to carry at all times. It would be just
too good if the arsonist had come back. More likely it was
a B&E trying to pick up some easy loot to fence.

He gave Harley the command for "silence," then crossed
the street quickly on the opposite side, glad for the boarded-
up plate-glass windows. While they prevented Noah from
seeing inside, they also protected him from being spotted
easily from the inside. He scanned the shadows before and
behind him as he proceeded down the side street across
from the shop, looking for any signs of a lookout.

After a moment of dawdling, while Harley marked a
fireplug, Noah determined that his B&E was probably
alone. And just as probably he was a novice at robbery, or
desperate enough not to care that his flashlight was dancing all over the interior.

Noah gained the nearside sidewalk quickly and made
the decision to go in at the rear, the way the culprit had
most likely entered. Sure enough the door was standing
ajar. He glanced back at the rear parking lot, one last time,
and noticed a familiar Mazda in the only occupied space.
Well, hell. Carly Harrington-Reese was inside.

He gathered up Harley's leash and pulled out his own
flashlight. Just in case she was of the kind of woman who
carried, he knocked hard on the doorframe before entering and called out, "Police. Show yourself."

"Okay. I'm Carly Reese, the owner." She often omitted
Harrington when she didn't want to call attention to her
former occupation.

He recognized her voice and switched on his flashlight,
sending the high beam straight at her as he stepped through
the backdoor of the store.

Her dark eyes were wide as a nocturnal creature's. Her
hair was equally wild, streamers of curls exploding in

every direction about her head. *Happy hair,* he thought fleetingly, but pinched off his smile. Because the last thing he expected tonight was to find her stumbling about in the dark. Anything—and he had been a cop who knew first-hand the results of those possibilities—could happen to a woman alone in an empty building.

Fear for her safety expanded in his chest as anger. He and Harley moved inside and closed the door before releasing a bit of it. "What the hell are you doing?"

"Noah?" She swerved her light his way for confirmation, then shoved a hand through her crazy hair, setting off little curl quakes. "I forgot to look for something earlier."

He bit back an expletive. "You'd think last night would've discouraged you from taking risks. Even a child knows, once burned, twice shy."

That pricked her. A chin lift and frowny stare came into play. If she hadn't looked so pissed off, he might have smiled at her. He was learning her temperament.

"My place. I have a key." She stuck her flashlight into something so that it stood upright, flooding the ceiling with light. "Why are *you* here?"

"Protecting your property. And now your beautiful butt."

She cocked her head to one side. "You took the job? Why?"

He hated giving her a clue to his thoughts, but what the hell? "Because I figured I owed you."

"So you put yourself in—hah." She pointed a finger at him. "You're hoping the arsonist will return."

His mouth straightened from downward grim to flat annoyed. "This isn't about me." He came toward her, Harley at his side. "We're discussing you. Were you born without the self-protection gene? Or, do you have some kind of martyr complex?"

She didn't back away from him. In fact, she stepped into his path. "Why are you so angry?"

"Because." Because she was a little too close for his comfort. It was a hell of a time for his libido to wake up. Just being close to Carly, his body suddenly remembered what it was like to get an erection, and ache for release.

"What if I'd come in with my gun drawn, thinking you were a thief, and shot you?"

She folded her arms and cocked a softly rounded hip to one side. "I'd have sued your ass for reckless endangerment."

Damn. She had an answer for everything. Why did that please him so much? Most women found him intimidating. She wasn't easily impressed. Even if her greatest defense was her mouth.

With that thought his gaze latched onto her mouth. Those full soft lips knew how to take him to task and put him in his place. He wondered what they tasted like. Would they be as sweet as they looked, or as tart as her tongue?

She seemed to realize the exact second he stopped thinking of her as a crazy lady and began viewing her as a most desirable woman. He expected her to back up, self-preservation, an instinct in the female/male world of lust. She only stood there.

Harley, also brought on line by the testosterone spilling off his owner, began a nervous dance. It was called "emotion down the leash."

Noah almost smirked. With the hard-on he was getting, poor Harley should be howling at the moon.

Not professional. The phrase flashed across his mind. He was on the job, informally or not. This wasn't the time or place to indulge his ego, and other parts.

He took a step backward but she went with him, her face lifted with a question in her gaze.

"You don't—" His voice gave out. He didn't want to talk. He didn't want to follow protocol. He didn't want to do anything but kiss her.

CHAPTER TWELVE

He'd been out prowling.

The high from the fire on Shelby Road hadn't lasted. Maybe it was the static charge in the air. About midnight the wind had changed directions, stirring up the atmosphere with electrical energy and reigniting his urge.

Two beers in, he'd left a dive in White Settlement without bothering to inform the crew he regularly drank with. Another beer, and he might have said things he'd regret. The only way to prevent that was to stay sober, and be alone.

With the native paranoia of a creature with many predators, he never slept long when the urge was on him. Or in the same place two nights in a row. Sometimes, like tonight, he roamed.

But a man had to be somewhere. Driving around aimlessly might draw attention. The last thing he needed to deal with tonight was cops. "The Boss's" song *State Trooper* hummed through his head. *Please don't stop me.*

He knew to stay away from Glover until he was ready. But that turned his thoughts to the woman who'd ruined his perfect crime.

Curiosity had sent him to her apartment complex. Finding her was as simple as looking her up on the internet, courtesy of the Flawless card he'd pocketed.

Carly *fuckin'* Harrington-Reese! A real honest-to-god nasty girl. He'd seen the pictures to prove it. Sure, they said it was fashion. But, fuck that! She was naked. That was nothing but high-class porn.

Sitting in his truck in her parking lot, he hadn't expected she would appear on one of the top-floor balconies. Picking up the binoculars he kept for fire watching, he'd watched her while he chafed with an itch he hadn't scratched in weeks.

That was because Darlene hadn't let him back in after he'd slapped her around for burning the pizza she was reheating.

He would have forgiven her tonight. If she'd opened her door. Instead, she'd threatened to call the police. So, he'd driven on. And ended up at the Reese woman's location. When she went back inside, he'd almost finished jacking off to the fantasy she'd evoked. Deprived of the sight of her, he'd slowed down and made the pleasure last.

Then she'd suddenly appeared in the parking lot. He thought he'd been made. Panic made him fumble his glasses as he ducked behind the steering wheel. And, fuck, wouldn't you know it? One lens had struck his gearshift and cracked. By the time he'd looked up, she was getting in her car. He followed her.

Here—to Flawless.

Christ! It was like she knew he was there, waiting for a chance to get her alone. His hands were slick on the steering wheel. The bulge in his jeans harder than before the handjob.

Good thing he'd had the presence of mind to circle the block and park a ways beyond. She'd barely entered through the back door when Glover appeared.

Watching the store now, knowing they were inside together, he had half a mind to finish what he'd started. They were probably in there fucking, while he hid in the bushes like a pussy.

The searing unfairness of it all made his heart pound and his eyes burn. The urge to do something made his hand shake as he reached for one of the incendiary devices he'd pocketed before leaving his truck.

It wouldn't be neat, or solve all his problems. It would, however, ease the tension coursing through his veins like corrosive acid.

But instead, he swerved his hand at the last second to his Ka-Bar at his ankle. He withdrew and pulled it across his palm. He stared at the blood pooling, letting the sting of the wound remind him that he had made mistakes lately. He couldn't afford for rage to control his actions.

Whatever was going on inside, he would wait and use it to his advantage. When he was calm and ready.

CHAPTER THIRTEEN

Carly blinked when Noah shut his flashlight off. Then he reached out and did the same with hers. She could no longer see him. But every one of her other senses intensified to make her aware of his presence.

They weren't quite touching. Even so, she could feel the heat from his body, judge the expanse of his body from it. A moment before he touched her, she sensed the raising of his hands. She met him halfway, her arms lifting to rest on his chest as his hands found her shoulders and pulled her close.

When his lips found hers in the darkness, she sighed in relief.

It was the moment they had been building toward all day, perhaps even since the night before. It didn't make sense. Desire never really does. That hunger for another person doesn't consider anything but its own needs. And right now, her desire was running the show.

She felt his hands sliding over her, one moving up to cup the back of her head while the other moved down low on her hips. Without breaking the kiss, he pressed into her, bone and muscle, molding her perfectly to his harder frame. Somehow her hands found their way inside his jacket and then around to his back until she was clutching his shoulders from behind. He was hard and sinewy beneath the soft cotton of his shirt. He tasted of peanuts and coffee, and some subtle indefinable essence that was his alone. She even liked the drag of his whisker-roughened jaw along hers. In every way, this tough guy seemed to have the answer to a question she wasn't sure she'd asked.

She heard him moan low a moment before he released the kiss. Shaken to her core by a simple kiss, she was no longer certain of anything.

When he dropped his hands from her body, she knew she should do the same. They weren't a couple, or anything close. Not even friends. Clinging was definitely not part of the scenario, whatever the hell the scenario was.

Her hands came away slowly, sliding down the firm contours of his back before falling free from beneath his jacket. And then she retreated, back into the shell she had developed years before, when too many men thought "model" equaled "sex object" and were more interested in what she was than who she was.

She even knew how to let him off easy. "Mistake, huh?"

She felt him staring at her even though she couldn't see him. Staring and wanting her, without a doubt. It was in his voice, deep and a little harsh with flecks of surprise, when he finally spoke. "I've been wanting to do that ever since I opened my eyes last night and saw you bending over me like a guardian angel."

The confession startled her. She'd expected his interest was more recent, fanned by the pictures of her he'd seen. It took a few seconds to form a flip reply. "You're just saying that because I saved you."

She couldn't see his smile. But she knew she felt it.

"Is that what you were doing just now, saving me?"

Saving him? Her heart had started to pound. She had no idea, no idea at all, what she was doing. She only knew she didn't want to stop now.

She ran her hands up his chest and clenched her fingers over his pecs. "Shut up and kiss me again."

This time there was no pretense at moderation or control. His mouth engulfed hers, hot and demanding, his tongue stroking hers in urgent persuasion. She'd never felt weak-kneed before, as if her passion demanded instant surrender, on the floor, right now. But suddenly she was all wobbly and clutching him for balance.

He seemed to sense her problem, because he back-walked her until she came up against a thigh-high counter covered in a tarp. He didn't stop there. He lifted her up onto it and then pushed her knees apart until they framed his hips. Then he cupped her butt and pulled her in tight against him so that she could feel the strength of his arousal.

All the while raw need poured from his mouth into hers. He kissed with his whole body, every muscle straining in aching need. The tough man driven by desperation.

A little desperate herself, she ran her hands up and down his back, seeking without asking for him to touch her more intimately.

Finally his hands slid upward, under her sweater. She heard his soft intake of breath when he realized she wasn't wearing a bra. Before she could register how that affected his already impressive arousal, his hands were sliding around to the front. Then his fingers were framing her breasts in a slow massage that pebbled her nipples in the center of his palms.

She was reaching for his belt buckle when he lifted his head, gasping for breath as if the oxygen had left the room. Smiling to herself, she slid the tail of his belt back through the loop and pulled it loose.

But his hands were there before she was done, warm hard palms embracing the backs of her hands. "Wait."

Carly froze. What did he say? *Wait?!* "No. No waiting."

Noah gripped harder as she went back to work on his buckle. Though, damn it all to hell, there was nothing he wanted more than to watch her lower his zipper, slip his jeans over his hips and—

"Jesus." His voice sounded as ragged as his grip on reality. To save himself, he reached over and switched on her flashlight. It the sudden arc of light he saw one very puzzled, or very pissed off, expression on her pretty face. He must've looked like an idiot to her.

His body was vibrating with images of doing things with her he'd done without for so long, he'd been half-convinced his sexual nature would need a hit of Viagra to kick start it. Turns out, all he needed was a woman with Happy Hair. Even though she was no longer touching him in any way, his senses still drank her in. Every sensation registered as bright hot sexual attraction.

But he was nothing if not practical. He had to be, a single father with job responsibilities that had no neat boundaries. And that was before last night. She needed to understand how little he had to offer her.

He reached up, resting a hand on each of her shoulders. She tensed but didn't shrug off his touch. Instead she regarded him with a wide dark gaze that still shimmered with desire. He'd done that. It made him proud, and ashamed. He had no right.

"Carly, I'm battered goods. I'm also hemmed in by choices I'm happy to deal with, but which make any kind of relationship nearly impossible. You're young, no entanglements. You could have any man. Do anything. Do whatever you want."

She held his gaze steadily. "What I want to do at the moment is you."

Noah thought he was beyond surprise after the events of last night. Christ. He wasn't close. *She wanted him.*

He didn't have to answer. His dick was there. He could see in her eyes her understanding of his predicament. And she smiled and leaned in to kiss him again.

He didn't have the strength to deny her. Oh, but she tasted good. If happiness had a flavor, she was it. She had the kind of smile that made a man glad he was male. And when she'd looked at him with that directness that was her own, he could only answer, if only in his head,

He sighed in gratefulness when she backed away, sensing, perhaps the dialogue going on in his head. So he went vocal. "I'm not a good bet for a relationship. I'm likely to be arrested any minute. If I'm found guilty of arson, I could go to prison."

She framed his face in tender fingers. "Sounds like we don't have a lot of time to waste."

She was killing him. "I'm not—"

She slipped her thumb over his lips and pressed. "You can't talk me out of wanting you. Is that what you really want to do?"

What he wanted was to take her now, on a tarp, on the filthy floor, against a wall, wherever and however he could find the best and fastest way into her. But she deserved better. She deserved a lot better than him. Yet he wasn't strong enough to walk away. "My parents took Andy to Padre Island for a few days. We could go to my place."

She shook her head. "Someone wants you dead. That person may be looking for you."

Damn. She had enough presence of mind to think of that a beat ahead of him. Of course, his brain was in his pants at this point.

She kissed him softly. "My place is just a few blocks away, over on Vickery."

"What about your property?" He glanced around in the dark. "I won't be here to guard it."

She touched his shirtfront, making him aware that she could feel the too-rapid rise and fall of his chest. "I came tonight not knowing what I was looking for. Now I want what I'm holding onto."

He grinned. "That would be me."

After a quick stop at a nearby pharmacy, both knew there'd be no preliminaries, just a rush to get through the door before they began undressing each other.

They'd taken turns playing "touch me here" as they drove over. Mostly, he kept one eye on the scant traffic while discovering with one hand that she wasn't wearing panties when he'd slid a hand down the front of her jeans and into the wet slick center of her. She was so ready for him her lids dropped closed as he softly stroked her. By the time they reached her apartment building, she had tightened her thighs to hold his hand in place.

He stole a glimpse of her face, tight in concentration, and grinned. "Getting a little needy?"

Her eyes popped open, her gaze throwing shade for days. "Just so you know, payback's a B." She smiled. Even when seen by the scant light of the dashboard, the lustful look she gave him had him ready to cream his shorts.

Meanwhile, Harley made a few comments from the backseat, most of them whiney sounds of confusion. And one of his signature farts that had them rolling down the windows.

Once parked, Noah set Harley up with partially rolled-down windows and locked him in. "I'll be back for you in, *hm*, an hour."

Harley licked his hand and curled back into a ball to sleep. Noah wasn't worried about his dog, who often spent hours in the truck when they were on a call. Certainly no one ever stole anything out of his truck—something flirted across his mind and then disappeared when Carly slid in beside him to pet his dog.

"Be good," she whispered. "I'll take really good care of your handler. Promise."

She turned around so that she was facing Noah. "Ready?"

More than she could ever understand.

They ran like a pair of teenagers, arms tight around each other as they crossed the parking lot. They stopped in the shelter of a stairway to kiss and giggle.

Noah shook his head as she grabbed him by the wrist and pulled him along toward her loft. What was it about her that made him feel lighthearted and free? He should be miserable. But all he could think about was getting her indoors where he could undress her like a Christmas package and then bring her all the pleasure she could handle. And then he'd help himself.

Access to her place was controlled by a fob on her key ring, and then he was being led through an interior that was dark except for the light from the Fort Worth skyline streaming in though her open shades.

She kicked off her shoes, pulled her sweater over her head, and shucked off her jeans. Then she paused and simply stood there for his benefit.

Noah's breath caught. She was a vision, all smooth satiny skin with small but perfectly shaped breasts with dark nipples he wanted to lick until she sighed.

He took a step toward her, looking into her warm and welcoming gaze. "You're—just the most beautiful . . ." That's all he got out before she moved in on him.

She reached for his shirt and pulled it over his head.

She ran her hands through the light hair on his chest, then twirled the curling hair over each nipple around her forefingers. "I've been wanting to do this since this morning at the hospital." She leaned forward and licked each one. The action made his belly jump with desire.

Lord. Had it only been this morning that they butted heads? This morning was a thousand hours ago. And, if she kept licking him like that, he was going to come in his pants.

He reached out and skimmed the sides of her breasts with his fingers, bushing his thumbs back and forth until they stood at full attention. Then he leaned in and licked her, as she had done him.

He heard her little catch of breath each time his tongue passed over those pebbled buds. She reached up and tightened her hands into fists in his hair, holding him to her chest so that he could lick his fill.

He smiled as he nuzzled a breast. He was just getting started.

Just as quickly, his dick did a hard jerk, reminding him that it might have been too long for everything he was thinking.

One of her hands was at his belt while the other stroked hard along the length of his erection behind his jeans. As glorious as it felt, he made a grab to still her hand.

"Whoa, Carly." He sucked in a breath, struggling for control. "It's been a while. There's a limit to what I can handle at the moment."

She smiled at him, a womanly knowing in her expression as she again took his wrist. "In that case, we better get you some relief, so you can enjoy the rest of the evening."

An evening in her company. If she had offered him anything in the world, at the moment it would have been that. An evening in her bed, in her.

She unfinished unbuckling his belt, unzipped him, and pushed his jeans off his hips. Then she plunged both hands into his shorts.

"Oh," she whispered in flattering tones. And then her cool fingers were wrapping around him, tightening even as they began to slide back in forth in a rhythm that nearly brought him to climax within seconds.

He grabbed her wrist, a single word scraping out of his throat. "Please."

Laughing in sympathy, she pulled him past the sofa and pushed him gently into a nearby chair. And then she straddled him.

Hands braced on his shoulders, she rocked her hips forward into him, pressed her warm wet core onto his erection. The sensation of her sex ready and weeping for him rocked his world to the foundation. And then she was kissing him again, slow deep kisses that melted into each other, until she felt him fiddling with his jeans.

She lifted her head, a question in her eyes.

"No glove. No love." He jerked free a condom. As she slid back on his thighs, he quickly slipped it on.

When their eyes met, she was gazing at him with her head rocked to one side. "Ready to ride, cowboy?"

He grinned at her. "I'm just a city boy, ma'am, but I surely aim to please." He took her by the waist and lifted her.

Understanding what he wanted, she reached down between them and grabbed his erection, aiming it so that when she settled again onto his lap he slid into her.

She gasped at the feeling of being filled. In fact, it took her a couple of breaths to adjust. Holding still for her was the hardest thing he'd ever done. And then she began to move. Using her feet she lifted up against him, her breasts pressing into his chest a moment before she dropped down on him, forcing him deeper and deeper with each stroke.

He let her manage the rhythm until he knew he was as deep as possible, and then his hands came up to clamp her waist, and he took over.

It was a hard fast ride. But she was with him all the way, stroke for stroke, rising up on tiptoe and allowing him to plunge her body down hard on his. The sensations were overwhelming, the rhythmic sound of their thighs slapping together, the liquid heat of her sex dampening his legs. She felt so right. More right than he had any right to expect. He was going to have to think about that. Later. Right now topping every other urge was the glorious sensation of pleasuring the woman in his arms.

"Oh baby. Carly. Damn. So good."

He knew when she reached the peak. Her body went stiff as she called his name. She was gasping, bucking against him, her head thrown back. And then she erupted in little sweet cries as he felt her rippling orgasm clasp him tight.

He came quickly after her, a thick hot eruption so violent his balls ached.

For long moments there was only her harsh breathing and the endless roll of her second orgasm. And his voice thick and low saying her name over and over as he gathered her close.

He held her for a long time in the silence as she lay collapsed over him. He even rocked her a little as he brushed curls away from her face. Her eyes were shut, her mouth a little open, as if she had lost connection with the world.

He smiled to himself and kissed her nose. He'd been with plenty of women, but never one who came so easily, so effortlessly, and with such abandon.

Carly Harrington-Reese was something special. But then he'd known that from the moment he'd opened his eyes and saw her bending over him. His guardian angel. He just didn't know what he was going to do about it.

CHAPTER FOURTEEN

Noah walked Harley through the double-gated entry in the hurricane fence that surrounded Fort Woof. The park, located on Beach Street just north of I-30, was built especially for Fort Worth dogs and their owners. There were two fenced-in areas, one for larger dogs and one for small dogs under forty pounds. Small dogs could run in the large-dog area, but not vice versa. Each area had picnic tables—though food was forbidden—benches for humans, watering stations for humans and dogs, as well as poop disposal stations with plastic bags. The park opened at 5 a.m. and was usually busy. But early on this Sunday morning, only a few eager beavers were out on the large expanse of grass.

Noah pulled the collar of his jacket up around his neck to block the chilly breeze. It would be in the mid-70s by noon, but just now winter was making a mild protest at being pushed aside.

The 40-ish degree breeze didn't bother Harley, who danced on the end of his leash in anticipation. The park was a familiar place where he could free play.

They had an hour before reporting for a side job at the North Texas Speedway. It was obvious from Harley's highly antsy attitude that the big shepherd needed to work off some edginess before they arrived to work the crowds. Make that *both* of them needed to blow off steam. Noah was feeling pretty torqued himself. With three hours of sleep under his belt, he should have been okay. But his mind was revving like a street racer before the beginning of a competition.

He'd had to pick up most of the mess left by the police searching his home before he'd turned in. Maybe that's what was wrong. He felt like he was living on borrowed time. Having sex with Carly was either the best or worst decision he'd made in years. His opinion on the subject changed each time it floated to mind. It had done so with every other thought before he fell asleep. He tried an old trick of tying a mental weight to the memory, in the hopes it wouldn't float to the surface again until he had time for it.

Noah looked around before unleashing Harley. The only other dog he saw in the main yard was a Yorkie tentatively climbing a brightly painted A-frame. The park had built an agility course for more-ambitious owners and their canines. Unfortunately, the Yorkie seemed anything but eager. The frightened pup paused before reaching the top of the A-frame and turned to yip at its owner.

A tall man in a puff vest and knee-length shorts that were exactly the color of his untanned legs waved a hand at the dog. "Go on, Larchmont. I promised Mommy you'd get the hang of it today." The man sounded as forlorn as the dog had.

Larchmont glanced at the peak that was his goal, then turned back to his owner, his lower body shimmying in fright. Three yelps, and he was headed back down the way he had come.

Noah turned away with a small smile. Clearly, "Mommy" was in for a disappointment. The little fellow wasn't Dog Agility material.

Harley, on the other hand, was born to run. As soon as he was off the leash, he barked repeatedly as he jumped back and forth before Noah, waiting for the right word.

"Release!" Noah's voice was high with encouragement.

That's all the shepherd needed to hear. He turned and shot straight across the field, as if a big juicy bone lay unclaimed on the far side of the park green.

Noah grinned as he watched his partner speed away like a shaggy arrow. Whoever had thought he'd make a good service dog had miscalculated Harley's drive. He was a natural born seeker, with a nose so sensitive he'd scored in the ninety-fifth percentile on his final test for certification as an explosives K9. No small feat for a repurposed canine. Luckily, Harley had been sent by ATF for reschooling at the prestigious Harmonie Kennels. The kennel, located in the Shenandoah Valley of Virginia, was the top privately owned school for law enforcement, as well as for specialty government and military K9 training. When ATF decided to place Harley with the Fort Worth Fire Department, Noah had volunteered as a handler.

He had been as intimidated as any police academy rookie when he'd been told he was being sent to Harmonie for three weeks to learn how to use an explosives detection dog. Harley was trained. It was all on him to prove that he had what it took to be the handler of such a gifted canine.

He could still remember his first impression of the owner, Yardley Summers. Tall, flame-haired, and gorgeous, but as intimidating as a drill sergeant, she'd looked him up and down and then turned away, leaving him feeling inadequate. That feeling quickly turned into determination to prove her wrong in her assessment. He'd worked

EXPLOSIVE FORCES 127

twice as hard, drilled after classes, kept Harley by his side
24-7 until it felt like they were joined at the hip. Harley
liked him. And he liked the goofball German Shepherd
who never saw a scrap of food he didn't like. Of course,
he'd been trained not to eat anything that didn't come from
his handler. But that snatched burger wouldn't be the last
of Harley's indiscretions where food was concerned. It
didn't matter if it was kibble, French fries, or a bit of birth-
day cake. Harley was a see-food, eat-food dog.

Noah smiled as he watched Harley sneak up on a flock
of mourning doves arrayed on the lawn and then charge,
scattering them into flight with panicky wingbeats. Harley
never caught one. Noah suspected it was because he had
no idea what to do with one if he did. Harley didn't see
the birds as food. That was a good thing.

Noah smiled as a gray bird fluttered to the ground near
him. "Good morning, dove." That's what his son Andy
called the birds: Good Morning Doves. He never corrected
the boy.

The thought of Andy pinched off his smile. He didn't
like one bit having to send his son and parents out of town
because of trouble he had brought, however involuntarily,
on the family.

He'd talked with his father on the drive over to the dog
park. They'd arrived at Padre Island the night before and
settled in. In fact, his father was up preparing for the first
day of fishing, while Andy slept in. His father told him to
stop worrying. Andy was safe. He needed to handle his
business and find the bastard who wanted him dead.

That was his dad, a man who knew how to motivate
with soft words.

Noah felt a sensation like his heart being squeezed. He
loved his parents, and Andy was his world.

He felt guilty each time he had to ask his folks to per-
form duties that were really his responsibility as a parent.

But his job required him to be places and do things, sometimes with five minutes' notice. He was a single parent, no matter how much he tried to spread himself out to cover that gap in his son's life. But he wouldn't change things if he could.

Out of all the regrets in his life, and there were a few, he had one solid victory on his side. He hadn't tried to hold on when his ex-wife, Jillian, walked out on them the day before Andy turned three months old.

Andy didn't remember his mother. Noah hadn't tried to preserve her memory for his son. His parents weren't happy with that decision, in the beginning. But what could he say to his child? *Love and revere your mother's memory though she made me buy custody of you and then never bothered to contact us again?*

He wouldn't put that burden on a young child.

When Andy was older, and asked, he would tell his son as much of the truth as he understood it. Phrases like "borderline personality disorder with abandonment issues" had no place in a preschooler's vocabulary.

He wasn't certain this was the right way to handle things. Maybe his own leftover anger and disappointment and sense of failure affected his decision. But there was one thing he did believe with conviction. His first and most important job as a father was to protect and nurture his child. To his final breath.

As Harley came sprinting back his way, Noah gave the hand sign for "stop." Harley braked so hard, momentum sent his rear end swinging around to meet his front. But the dog dug in his claws and quickly righted himself and sat.

Noah fed Harley a treat, then sent him off with "Release!" Harley shot away, this time toward the abandoned Agility section.

As he followed his dog, the phone he'd borrowed from

his sister rang. He'd given the number to the arson department, in case he was needed.

"You left incriminating evidence," Merle Durvan began without preamble. "We've matched a set of your left-hand fingerprints to those lifted from the wall above the electrical socket where we found the WeMo. You braced yourself on the wall to plug it in."

Noah frowned. "If I were committing arson, I wouldn't leave prints any rookie investigator would look for."

"Looking at it as a suicide attempt, I'm prepared to accept that you weren't concerned about leaving evidence."

Noah tamped down a spurt of anger. "You've decided I did this."

"I'm not paid to have an opinion. Just collect evidence and put it together into a probable cause to press charges."

"You coming to arrest me?"

"I've been handed the means to arrest you." Durvan paused. "I just can't shake the suspicion that someone is leading me down the garden path."

Noah let out the breath he'd been holding. Durvan still had doubts. "Stay suspicious. The man who set me up can't have executed the perfect crime. He screwed up somewhere. He just didn't expect me to live to tell you the truth. He's got to be sweating bullets over the fact you might uncover something."

"You know something, Glover? Anything that points in another direction?"

"No. But I got some questions I need to put to a few people."

"The hell you will. Stay away from anyone you were with that night. Tampering with witnesses will definitely land your ass in jail. I have one piece of news, for what it's worth. There was GHB in your blood. Doesn't change my focus. So, until I finish my investigation, don't set a toe outside the city limits or I'll have you arrested for attempted flight from prosecution."

Noah didn't need to hang up. Duran was gone.

Tampering with witnesses.

Noah wiped a hand over his mouth. He'd done a lot more than tamper with Carly last night. He'd probably compromised the key witness. Which was why he'd left her bed in a rush.

Not his finest hour.

It had taken him all of a minute of afterglow, the second time, to realize just how big a mistake he'd made in going with her to her apartment.

She, who had been gently caressing his chest, had caught up with his thinking about ten seconds later.

She'd raised her head up off his shoulder and her hands stilled, forefingers no longer circling his nipples. Then with a graceful swing of her leg she dismounted from him. He'd never felt more naked.

Not bothering to cover herself, she'd folded her arms and stood before him. "If that's regret creeping up on you, forget it. I got what I asked for. I won't be trying to jack up your life. I have enough problems. Nothing's flawless, right?"

For a moment he'd kept his mouth shut. What he could see of her in the light reflected from the city looked damned perfect.

But she was right. He couldn't afford to get distracted any more than he'd already been tonight. But that was the damnable thing. Carly didn't feel like a distraction. She was a whole other superhighway of possibility into territory he couldn't begin to explore until his life looked some kind of sane again.

He'd raked a hand through his hair, groping for the right words. "I'm not sure how to say this. You saved my life.

The least I could have done to repay you was to stay out of your life, certainly out of . . ."

"Me?"

He'd felt the back of his neck burn. "Okay. Yeah."

She'd watched him, her eyes shining in the dim light. "I invited you here. I didn't force you."

"No. I came damn willing. I just should have listened to my better instincts."

"Why didn't you?" Yep, talking with Carly was like drinking whiskey straight from the bottle.

What could he say? *All my honorable intentions went up in flame when you kissed me?* That sounded like a loser line.

He'd cracked a smile. "I wanted you. Have since the moment we met. Hell. Every time I look at you I get a hard-on. I know that sounds lame. But that kind of thing doesn't happen to me."

"No. I get it." She brushed a handful of springy curls back from her brow and then reached for her sweater. "I've felt the same way since Friday night." She pulled it over her head on one fluid motion. "Damned if I know why."

He could have told her. They'd shared a traumatic experience together and survived. Nothing like a near-death experience to make a person want to reassert the most fundamental life-affirming survival instincts. That would include sex.

But it didn't explain what he was feeling now, hours later, standing in a dog park with the sun in his eyes. Being with and in Carly had set off a five-alarm fire in his belly that lay banked there even after climax. He hadn't only succumbed to the moment, he'd let down his guard with her. That was something he hadn't done with any woman since his divorce.

Noah shoved that thought away. Then and now. He

knew the difference. He needed to be practical. Think practical. To do that, he needed to keep out of range of Carly's emotional gravitational field.

She hadn't tried to stop him leaving. She hadn't said a word that made him feel worse than he already did. She'd simply watched him as though his every move was important.

He'd finished dressing before he turned to her that final time. "You will probably be called as a witness against me, if the case goes to trial. If the authorities learn about us, this, it could jeopardize your testimony."

Her lips twisted. "You're good, but I wasn't going to take out an ad."

Ouch. Guess that put him in his place. "All I'm saying is, tonight was just about us. It doesn't change things. Tell the truth as you see it."

"I always do. I don't think you started that fire."

"That's not what you said when you came to my hospital room this morning."

She stared at him, her big dark eyes holding emotions he couldn't tease out. "A man doesn't make love the way you just did if he's given up on life."

Noah laughed at the remembrance, the bright bark of laughter so at odds with the near silence of the Sunday morning that Harley paused at the apex of the A-frame to glance back at him.

His final words to Carly had been, "When I beat this, I'll look you up."

She'd smiled, finally. "You do that."

Now, here he was in a dog park, no closer than he was twenty-four hours ago to finding out who wanted him dead. Andy and his parents, and maybe even Carly, were depending on him to extricate himself from this mess. He needed to stop thinking like a victim and start thinking like the investigator he was.

Every crime needed opportunity and motive. For now, motive was the simple desire to murder Noah Glover. More, it was the desire to make that murder look like suicide. To ruin his reputation in the manner in which he was to die. That's what the suicide note had been about. To make his failure public. As if he was at the end of his rope, or felt trapped, or ashamed. But there was nothing in his life so terrible that friends and family would understand his suicide. Or, was there something he was missing?

He frowned as he processed that idea. The desire to make his death look like a suicide limited the number of ways the murder could take place. Choosing arson as the method of death was an unnecessary complication with far more risks than simple murder. He could have been killed in a hit and run. Shot. Poisoned. Instead, he'd been roofied. Then picked up sometime later when his adversary knew he could control him, and their environment.

"Son of a B!" That meant the man knew him well enough to get close to him to deliver the drug. That had to have been at the bar.

The person was known to him. Was familiar enough with Noah's habits to quickly get inside his natural caution as a law enforcement officer when approached. Not a stranger, nor even a man he'd previously arrested. The perpetrator must be a friend, or at least a regular acquaintance.

He pulled out a note pad and began making notes. Once a cop, always a cop. It was a mindset. It ruled the way an officer entered a building, approached a store, chose a seat in a restaurant, and orientated him or herself in the world.

And his nemesis had even gotten past Harley.

He glanced at his dog, who had come running back and now eyed him with bright eyes and a lolling tongue.

He smiled and reached for a treat. "I wish you could talk."

Harley barked on cue and received his reward.

He grinned. "On the other hand, all you'd probably say is 'Time to eat? Time to eat? Squirrel! Uh, time to eat?'"

He leaned down to scratch both sides of Harley's head behind the ears. His furry companion might be a taste bud surrounded by fur, but Harley was also, like all dogs, a believer in pack. Noah was his pack leader. Noah's son was pack. So, to a lesser degree, were Noah's parents. But the pack ended there. Harley would defend Noah against an aggressor, even if the person was well known to him. He and his dad had learned that early on during a particularly heated basketball game of twenty-one. While tussling for the ball, his dad had thrown an elbow that caught Noah in the ribs and sent him to the driveway pavement. Harley had almost taken a hefty bite of out his father before Noah realized what the dog was about to do, and called him off. After that, they played basketball only after Harley was put safely inside.

No, no hostile person could have gotten close to him with Harley there. That confirmed that he had greeted the man in a way that Harley had accepted his presence without question.

Noah looked at Harley, hard. "Who did we pick up that night?"

Harley licked his hand.

"Yeah, a better question would be, will you recognize our enemy when you see him again?" Saying that aloud gave Noah an idea. He should retrace his steps that night, as far as he could remember them.

He wished he had his truck back. But it had been impounded for evidence gathering. That was a reminder, much like Durvan's curt call, that the clock was ticking on his freedom. Once forensics came back with that evidence against him, Durvan had all but said he would be arrested. Bail would depend on whether or not the judge could be persuaded that he wasn't a flight risk. No, he had to act before his freedom depended on the outcome between some assistant district attorney and some cheap-o defender—because he could not afford better.

Another thought struck him. He must have been in his truck when his attacker approached. If he'd been accosted before he reached his truck, Harley wouldn't have been at the fire. The attacker wanted his truck. Had he wanted Harley, too?

The idea of Harley dying because of some perceived hate against his handler made heat pulse behind Noah's eyes. Harley was trained to find explosives, as dangerous a job as any a K9 did. Because Harley, like any dog, wasn't aware of the danger inherent in his job. It was up to his handler to make certain his K9 did that job with as many security controls in place as the handler could manage. There were even situations where a handler could refuse to subject his K9 to danger if the conditions looked dicey.

Secrecy wasn't all that easy in the real world. Someone must have seen something. Perhaps they just didn't realize the importance of it. Moreover, there should be footage from the security cameras that nearly all businesses had.

Of course, he'd have to be careful about trying to obtain a look at such footage. As Durvan warned him, talking to people he'd been with the night of the fire would be seen an as attempt to tamper with witnesses. He'd have to come at it another way. What that way was, he had no idea. Right now, he and Harley had a job to do.

Carly. What was he going to do about her? Nothing, yet.

He whistled for Harley, who shot toward the exit like a furry cannon ball.

For four and a half years, he'd had no life other than his son, his job, and Harley. That had seemed enough. Until last night.

CHAPTER FIFTEEN

"We're almost done here. Just a few more questions."

Carly made a production of glancing at the clock above the fireplace before looking back at her unexpected guest. Investigator Durvan had made that statement the first time ten minutes earlier. "I hope so, Mr. Durvan. I'm meeting my aunt at church in twenty minutes."

"Yes. You mentioned that before." Durvan looked down at the computer tablet on which he'd been making notes and scrolled up and down, as though needing to reread every word.

After years of enduring couture fittings, Carly was a pro at not fidgeting when she was bored. But she was losing her patience with the man who'd interrupted her Sunday morning. They'd already discussed why she'd been at her store after hours. How she'd gone to investigate strange noises next door and found an unconscious man and a dog. That she'd called 911 immediately, before the fire began. Now she'd repeated it all. Why was he was still sitting on her sofa as if she had all the time in the world to entertain him?

"You're certain you never met Noah Glover before the

night of the fire? Casually. Perhaps at a social function? Maybe, at a night spot?"

"I'm not much for going out. My life is pretty busy since I've returned home. To be perfectly honest, Inspector Durvan, we didn't even meet on the night of the fire." She saw his eyes widen ever so slightly and smiled. "We met the morning after the fire, in his hospital room."

"Really? Why would you go there?"

Carly thought about telling the truth, but remembered in time her promise to Jarius not to reveal how she'd learned about the suspected suicide attempt. "I had his dog."

"I see." Though his expression didn't change, this was new knowledge to him. She'd bet on it because he made a note. "Why didn't you turn the animal over to a police officer at the scene?"

"It didn't occur to me. Things were pretty intense. Mr. Glover was rushed to the hospital before I realized I was left holding his dog. Maybe it doesn't make real sense thinking about it today. But, after I'd saved both their lives, I felt responsible for the dog until he could be returned to his owner."

"How did you know where to find Mr. Glover?"

"I overheard one of the EMTs say where they were taking him."

Those shrewd gray eyes held hers. "How did you know Mr. Glover's name?"

"I didn't." Carly looked him straight in the eye.

"I met Mr. Glover's sister in the hallway."

He looked surprised, again. "You know her?"

"No. She was coming out of a patient's room and I heard her say something about a fire. So, I approached her and I explained that I might have been in the same fire, if it was the one on Magnolia. Turns out she already knew about a woman saving her brother. She threw her arms around me and thanked me for saving him."

"I see." Durvan typed another note, using his thumbs. "Did you leave the dog with her?"

"No, she told me to go on in and introduce myself. That's when I met Mr. Glover." Better not to add *in all his glory.*

"Did he remember you?"

"No." Carly held on to her temper. She didn't like being questioned like a suspect.

"When did Mr. Glover recover his dog?"

"He came by my aunt's home after he checked out of the hospital."

"Your aunt's home?" The eyebrow twitch was the tell of his surprise this time. "Why there?"

"She has a fenced yard." She glanced around her flat for emphasis. "My apartment doesn't allow pets."

"Is there anyone who can verify Mr. Glover's visit to your aunt?"

Carly took a deep breath. "My aunt. You might know of her. Judge Fredda Wiley. She sits on the juvenile court bench."

Durvan's eyes crinkled in the corners. "I do know her."

"Then you know she's going to have something to say about me being late for church." Carly stood up. "I'm sorry but I really must go."

Durvan stood up but didn't move toward the door. "I appreciate the time you've given me, Ms. Reese. You're lucky your insurance will cover all the damage your premises sustained." He glanced around her apartment. "Of course, as successful as you've been, money shouldn't be an issue for you."

Carly held on to her smile until she thought her lips would crack. "No, I don't need to set any place on fire for the insurance."

He didn't smile, but a grudging respect entered his gaze. "Thank you for your time."

He moved toward the door, but Carly anticipated the sudden "Colombo" hesitation and turn even before he executed the move.

"Just one more thing. I understand your husband died a few years ago under mysterious circumstances." His cool gray gaze held hers. "There were rumors of suicide."

Carly felt as if he'd kicked her in the stomach. He'd delved deep into her past. Deeper, perhaps, than Noah had. But she'd had years of practice dealing with haters. Nothing showed in her expression as she stared back at him.

"There was no mystery to it. Arnaud was a brilliant fashion photographer but also a drug addict. He'd been clean for nearly two years. He backslid, and it killed him. No fires were involved. Not that it's any of your business."

Durvan nodded but didn't back down. "I had to ask. It's possible someone helped Mr. Glover execute his hoped-for demise."

Just in time, Carly bit off the words of defense on Noah's behalf. "I wouldn't know anything about that."

"If you should remember anything else, anything at all about the fire or Mr. Glover, I'd appreciate a call."

"Or, I could call the media." That got his attention.

"Have you been approached by the media?"

"No. I prefer to keep my private life private." But the implied threat had been made. Carly Harrington-Reese could be pushed only so far before she pushed back.

"I'd appreciate it if you'd keep it that way, Ms. Reese. My job is the find out the truth. Once the media gets wind of an event like this, none of us will be able to control it. Sensational headlines could hurt everyone involved, especially the innocent."

Like Noah. Carly's heart jumped. This man couldn't possible know anything about her and Noah. But he suspected a connection.

For the first time, Durvan's mustache twitched up into what might have been a smile. "Thank you for your time, Ms. Reese. I must caution you to avoid Mr. Glover should he try to reach out to you. You may be called to give testimony if the case goes to court."

"You really think he started that fire?"

Durvan didn't answer.

Once she shut the door, Carly leaned against it, waiting for her heartbeat to slow.

"Underhanded! Vicious! Creep!" She murmured each word so that Durvan wouldn't hear if he was standing just outside. But talking to herself always helped clarify her thoughts. "He thinks I'm part of the crime of arson."

The second the words were out of her mouth she knew they were true. Inspector Durvan didn't believe Noah. He didn't entirely believe her either. If this was an indication of how the line of inquiry into the arson case was progressing, no wonder Noah had bolted the night before.

A chill worked its way down Carly's spine as she walked over to pick up her purse and keys. Best not to get involved any further. That had been Jarius's advice. She wished now she'd taken it from the first. Although . . .

It had not occurred to her that the authorities might entertain the idea that she was part of Noah's suicide—No . . . arson? Uh . . . murder attempt? What exactly did the arson investigator think? He'd scattered a lot of innuendo but few facts.

She'd told Noah from the first that she didn't want to be involved in whatever mess he was in. She had been right to worry about his presence complicating her life.

"That's why you're going to mind your own business from this second forward, Carly."

As soon as she made one call.

She opened her purse and pulled out her cell phone, ready to dial the number Noah had left with her the night before. Right up to the second she began considering the possible repercussions of that call.

What if she was called as a witness, or suspect, and her phone records were subpoenaed? A call to Noah right after a visit from the arson investigator would look suspicious. And it should.

One thought toppled onto others. What if someone had seen them together the night before? Either coming out of Flawless. Or worse, entering her apartment building. What if Investigator Durvan already knew they'd come up to her apartment, and that Noah had stayed until the wee hours. One plus one would make a man like Durvan think of sex every time. Not that Noah had actually been in her bed. They'd never made it that far.

There it was again, the jolt of desire that made her body flush and her toes curl inside her sky-high heels every time her mind wandered to the early hours of the morning.

She glanced begrudgingly at the chair on which they'd had sex—made love? The novelty of her feelings surprised her. She'd wanted Noah Glover with an urgency she hadn't felt since Arnaud. And maybe not then. She'd been almost a virgin with Arnaud. Now she was a grown woman who knew pleasure—how to give it and receive it.

Last night she'd done both, with a man who knew how to give as well as receive too.

She blew out a long almost desperate breath.

She'd thought she knew what she was doing. It was just sex, after all. Nothing earth shattering, or with a future. She had heard out all his objections, all the sane reasons why they should take their hands off each other, turn their backs, and step quickly away in opposite directions. But they hadn't.

Even after the first time, they hadn't wanted to get far enough apart to make it possible to move to the softer more comfortable bed in the next room.

He'd simply held her as she lay in boneless contentment against him until it was clear that his body was rallying. His touch turned more gentle the second time. His fingers no longer held on desperately but leisurely quested out the contours of her body. He whispered into her ear. Telling her what he was going to do to her, and how it was going to be better than the first time.

The wonder of it was, he'd kept that promise. With her still astride him, he'd found a way to take control, hands holding, molding, forcing her up and down his shaft until she was gasping softly as his mouth tugged first one nipple and then the other. He was waiting, still whispering now and then in a deep voice that seemed to come from someplace deeper than his chest. And still he waited, bringing her to climax twice before he groaned and stiffened and emptied into her.

Carly smiled as she ran a finger along the back of the chair she'd never before liked all that much. She hadn't expected the power of the feelings that stirred in her lower belly even now. It wasn't the beginning of anything. It couldn't be.

And yet, the erotic images that her memory was suddenly offering up fed those hot and satisfying sensations.

Carly turned away from the chair. She'd matched his composure after they'd come back to reality, still locked in a sweaty embrace. Leaning toward him, her eyes shut, she remembered how she inhaled the scent of his skin just beneath his chin one last time. A memory to preserve until another night.

Smiling, she opened her eyes. That's when reality landed like Dorothy's Kansas house, shattering the unformed plans stirring in her thoughts.

In the faint light she had seen his expression becoming wary even before he spoke.

They couldn't have another time. This was it.

And so she'd retreated, watched him dress silently, and then let him go.

Carly turned toward the view beyond her windows.

How did she feel about Noah Glover? She wasn't certain. She hadn't had to consider a man in in her life in—damn!—years. There'd been no conscious decision to become celibate. It had just happened, first as a protection against the pain of Arnaud's death. And then because she was busy trying to reinvent herself. The drought had lasted so long, it was no surprise she'd been overwhelmed by the sensation of good sex. Oh, Noah was good. But eyes-rolling-back-in-her-head good?

Or was that just the novelty of letting go after three years of self-imposed celibacy that had turned her into a delicious mush of satiation?

"I'd have to have something to compare it to." She spoke the words to the chair, as if it might provide the solution. The only idea that formed in her head in reply was *More, please*.

But Noah wouldn't be coming back. Not to her home, or to her bed. He'd made that clear.

The very best thing she could do was go to church and pray all during the service that she wouldn't be caught up in Noah Glover's life any more than she already was. No good could come of getting in deeper.

She walked over and scooped up her laptop, lying closed on the coffee table, and curled up on her sofa. She was just going to make a list. In case she needed it. Of what she knew, what she suspected, and how it might have gone down.

Half an hour later, she had a list of questions that impressed even her. Top of the list was: *Why kill Noah in that store?* Like any city, Fort Worth had its share of down and out neighborhoods. *Why not choose an abandoned house in a derelict neighborhood where no one would have come upon the fire until it was too late?* That question spurred lots of others until she had a long list of things to be run down.

"Noah should see this."

The thought given voice surprised her. She'd promised herself at least twice now that she wasn't going to get any more involved. She'd just made the list to prove to herself that Investigator Durvan couldn't be saying all that he knew about the fire. Or that the investigator was so busy trying to frame Noah that he hadn't bothered to look at all the facts. The list made her feel more in control, more like her old self.

At least that was as good as she was going to be feeling about things for now. She had a daunting task of obstacles involving Flawless. Beginning with her calling in the restoration company right this minute.

She dug in her purse and found the card the young man had given her the morning before, and placed the call. The answering service for the company said they would send someone out by noon. She didn't need to be there. With her permission, they would get in because the mutual wall between her store and the fire-gutted one had been damaged and needed to come down anyway.

She'd begun calling her vendors yesterday, the morning after, because she didn't want them to hear from anyone else about the fire and subsequent damage to Flawless, and its merchandise. Most had been friendly, even supportive, as she promised them that they would be paid out of the insurance money. A few had been upset at the loss of their work, feeling as she did that the intrinsic value was in the creative process itself, not in how much the resulting works were worth. How did one value a painting or even a handmade scarf or wall hanging, except in terms of how appealing they were to a potential owner? Many artists struggled with the idea of selling their one-and-only favorite creation. Several agreed to recreate versions of Carly's choices from their inventory, but kept the original pieces. She understood their feelings.

Carly reached up to finger one of the silver bells that made up the necklace she wore. She had hand-fashioned each bell into the shape of the African sesame seed flower with its long narrow bell and flared ruffle edge. Each of the three dozen bells had taken days to shape. A fresh water pearl suspended on a thin silver wire served as a clamper for each. With the largest placed at the center point, clusters of smaller and smaller bells climbed up either side of the silver chain, creating a bib necklace of bells. It was the task that helped her get through the first two months after Arnaud's death. But it wasn't a memento of him or their life. It was a pledge to herself that she could and would make a life on her own, with new talents.

Carly checked the wall clock. Services, usually praise singing, had begun fifteen minutes ago and usually lasted half an hour. Even so, she was dressed. That left no excuse not to go.

Arriving much too late at St. James A.M.E. Church to miss turning every head in the sanctuary, Carly tiptoed up the aisle to Aunt Fredda's prominent third-row pew.

Aunt Fredda waited until they were rising to sing another hymn before she whispered out of the corner of her mouth, "What kept you?"

"An unexpected visit from the arson investigator who's looking into the fire."

Aunt Fredda made her famous *humph* of disapproval.

Carly sighed. She'd felt the same about Durvan's visit. She didn't like being accused by hints and by the resurrection of an old scandal of wrongdoing. So maybe *she'd* do a little bit of investigating. On her own.

CHAPTER SIXTEEN

The Texas Motor Speedway was home to Big Hoss TV, as the world's largest high-definition LED video board was known to fans. Covering more than 20,000 square feet in area, it was filled with news about the events taking place on this the final day of the Lone Star Nationals Giant Automotive Festival. Located in far north Fort Worth and spilling over into Tarrant County, the speedway routinely hired off-duty police, firefighters, and county law enforcement personnel to augment their security for big events. Noah, always glad for extra ways to earn money, had arrived with his K9 Harley an hour before the opening.

Noah led Harley through the crowded infield where the Texas sun ricocheted off the surfaces of more than two thousand candy-colored, chrome-plated vehicles. Just as he had predicted, the day had warmed quickly. He was beginning to sweat where the neckline of his collared shirt chafed his neck. It was going to be a long-ass day.

The display was open to 1972 & older models, street rods, custom vehicles, muscle cars, trucks, and classics all lined up for display to the delight of the attendees. The event also featured more than a hundred vendor exhibits, a Giant Swap Meet & Auto Trader Classics Cars 4 Sale Corral, the ultra-intense Goodguys AutoCross timed racing competition, a model car show, a free Kids Zone, and live music entertainment! All in all, it was a logistics headache for security.

Noah and Harley's job was to make certain the fun was not interrupted by anyone setting off anything incendiary or explosive. A couple of numb nuts with fireworks could do a lot of damage. Forget the ever-present threat of terrorism.

In his work harness and on the leash, Harley moved through crowds of automotive enthusiasts pushing strollers and carrying backpacks, diaper bags, small children, Texas-sized portions of vendor food, and oversized bags of purchased merchandise. Harley sniffed it all, head from side to side as he explored every passing pants leg and purse with the purpose of finding something interesting so that he would get a reward. He'd smelled the liver treats in a utility pocket of Noah's cargo pants before they left home. Liver treats were his favorite, second only to duck and sweet potato. He wanted every liver treat in Noah's pocket. The game was on!

He paused every so often to sneeze hard, deliberately blowing out the accumulation of smells in his sensory passages that could overwhelm a less well-trained dog. The sheer numbers of human smells, mingled with the odors of gasoline, motor oil, tires, leather, dust, not to mention food odors from the many vendors, made the job an ordeal even for the most experienced professional K9.

Noah, too, felt the tension of working the large crowded environment. Boston's "More Than a Feeling" blasted from the overhead speakers and was giving him a headache. Vintage rock for vintage cars, he supposed. But, damn, they were well into the second decade of the twenty-first century. How about some Sam Hunt or Beyoncé?

Most times, he could forget about everything else but the job, and how to stay safe. But today, it was more difficult to pack everything else away and focus. What if the man who'd tried to end his life were here, watching him and knowing he wouldn't be able to identify him? The place between his shoulder blades itched just thinking about that possibility.

"Get your act together, Glover." He muttered the words under his breath as his gaze swung from scouring the way ahead to watching intently as Harley paused to assess a smell.

Festivals like this were often a place where a person's trash could be a dog's poison. Aside from the main reason they were hired, there were constant and possibly fatal hazards of working a K9 around cars. The drips and drops of sweet-tasting antifreeze, as well as other acids and alkalis spilled by careless car owners were toxic to dogs. Then there was the possibility that if Noah wasn't alert, Harley might scarf up a discarded piece of sugar-free gum or candy, both of which contained xylitol, another toxin for dogs. Added to this were the temptations of remains of vendors' offerings, many of which included mushrooms, grapes, onions, garlic, or chocolate. Harley was obedient and an excellent explosives K9, but he was still a dog. Noah's job was to keep Harley on track and out of harm's way while the K9 did his job.

After an hour on the crowded infield, Noah pulled Harley off the job and took him inside to let him explore behind the scenes in the corridors that ran beneath the arena seating. Here, at least, the floor was clear of clutter and spills. The fiercest gauntlet was the one where Noah would come face to face with a colleague.

"See you drew the easy shift."

Noah looked around to find fellow arson investigator Mike Wayne coming up behind them, half suited up in his firefighting gear. He also noted three female Motocross workers standing in the corridor giving Mike's impressive torso lustful looks.

"You caught a flame?"

Mike nodded. "In the parking lot. Some idiot's hot rod overheated." He looked down at Harley, who had nudged him in greeting, and patted his head. "Hey there, Harley. Didn't expect you two would be working today."

Noah shrugged. "I can use the extra cash, same as the next guy." He eyed Harley, who was obviously happy to see Mike. Harley had been taught not to be friendly to anyone when on the job, unless given the command by his handler. But they saw Mike at the office on a regular basis. Sometimes Mike even hid things for Harley to sniff out. "You hear anything I should know about?"

Mike slapped a fireproof glove against the palm of his hand. "You know we can't talk about anything connected to the ongoing investigation. A friend wouldn't ask."

Noah met his gaze and the accusation in it. "A friend wouldn't need to be asked."

Mike grunted. "See you around."

Noah gave Harley the command to "walk on."

As they moved along the backstage corridor, available only to personnel wearing the appropriate badges hanging from a lanyard, Noah gave those he recognized a chin-up motion in greeting. Some responded enthusiastically. Others merely nodded in return. As an arson investigator, he walked a fine line in the first responder world. He was seen as a firefighter by police. Having the authority to wear a gun and arrest people, he was seen as a cop by firefighters. It was a dual existence he shared with exactly thirteen other arson investigators in Fort Worth. Not a large pool of colleagues. Even so, they were sorely missed today as he and Harley went about their job as security forces.

Noah gave Harley water from one the bottles he always

carried. After the dog had drunk, he carefully checked
Harley's paws, especially between the toes and the pads
to make certain he hadn't picked up a small stone or sliver
of glass or burr on their rounds. Satisfied his partner was
okay, he fed him a few liver treats as Noah watched the
crowd from the edge of the infield.

The beefed-up security used by the Motocross came
from all over Fort Worth and the surrounding towns in
several counties. Noah recognized several other K9 han-
dlers, both law enforcement and private security. They
paused to trade information about the day and to show off
their K9s. Then it was back to work—this time, the
parking lot.

After another hour of inspecting cars, Noah turned Harley back toward the restricted area to rest. Parking lot
paving was harder on a dog's footpads than grass.

"Well, well. If it ain't the prof."

Noah turned toward the voice. A man in a Village Creek
Motocross T-shirt revealing full sleeves of tats was grinning as he came toward him. Beneath a gimme cap with a
beer brand emblazoned on it, dirty blond hair curved away
like wings above his ears.

Noah nodded in recognition of one of his former students. "J.W. You working today?"

"No. I'm here helping my cousin Don Lee. He's got a
seventy Mustang he's been rebuilding." J.W. reached down
to pet Harley, but the K9 growled in warning.

J.W. hopped back, hands lifted in fake horror. "Say now.
We're friends. Or have things changed? What's your boss
been saying about me behind my back?"

"Harley's on the job," Noah said in defense of his dog.
They were both feeling edgy since the fire. "He knows it's
not playtime."

"Well, pardon the hell outta me." J.W. looked back at

Noah. "You want to come by the lot and see what Don Lee's done? We're over in the muscle car section."

"Might do that. Got to rest and water Harley first." Noah realized that J.W. wasn't treating him any different than usual. And, more important, he was someone he'd seen Friday night.

"You were at Murtry's party Friday night, right?"

J.W. shrugged. "More like happened to be at the place where it was going on. Some of your buddies don't allow us volunteer guys the same respect."

Noah shrugged. It was an on-going issue among some firefighters. "Professional versus amateur" was how many full-time employed men and women felt about volunteers. Others, who'd come from the volunteer world, felt differently. J.W. had the rare honor of being respected by most of Fort Worth's firefighters.

"A fire's a fire, J.W. We put it out the same."

"Wet stuff on the red stuff." J.W. laughed and grabbed his crotch as he imitated urinating. "You right there."

A woman with a child in a stroller and holding the hand of another glared at him as she passed. "This is supposed to a child-friendly event."

"Sorry, ma'am." Noah shook his head. "That's real classy, J.W."

He snorted and then pulled up his tee's short sleeve to reveal an angry-looking four-inch-long burn on his upper right shoulder. "Got that putting out a fence fire last night. You tell me we don't fry the same."

Noah nodded, debating whether or not J.W. would be on Durvan's Don't Ask potential witness list. What the hell. "You remember anything special about me Friday night?"

J.W. looked surprised. "Special? Uh, you're sorta cute, and all. But you don't have tits, so I wasn't paying much attention."

Noah laughed. "Screw you."

"Why the question?"

"I sort of lost track of the events of the evening."

J.W. grinned. "I can see how that can happen on a Friday night. But you were drinking Dr Pepper because you were working the next morning."

Noah's senses went on alert. "You remember me saying that?"

"I remember Jeb Nelson calling you a pussy over it." J.W. reached up to scratch under his cap. "You two got a beef?"

"Jeb likes to jerk everyone's chain."

J.W. nodded. "Sorry I couldn't be more helpful. I'm pretty sure I left before you did. Had a date." He winked.

"Nice talking to you, J.W." Noah gave a second's thought before bringing up a sore subject. "If you need a recommendation on your job hunt, I'll be happy to write one for you. I hear Waco's fire department is looking for experienced guys."

J.W.'s face flushed. "I got it covered. Any day now, things will turn my way."

Noah went back to the infield just in time for the Show & Shine, K&N Filters All-American Sunday competition. The air vibrated with the throbbing full-throttle sounds of late-model American-made vehicles.

Harley barked twice, not enjoying the punishment to his ears.

Noah bent down and stroked him strongly until the K9 settled. He didn't blame his partner. In fact, he wished he had earplugs.

Shortly after three o'clock, the events shut down. Unlike the rest of security, who were sweeping the infield to make certain every single item that had been carried into the stadium was being carried out, or properly binned, by participants and guests, the explosives teams were free to leave.

Harley was panting heavily by the time Noah had installed him in the back of his father's truck. He gave him more water, but not enough to potentially cause stomach problems. "You must be exhausted, aren't you, boy? I know I am. How about a steak dinner somewhere before we crash?"

Harley barked twice and licked Noah's face, leaving it glistening with dog saliva. Harley's vocabulary was limited, but he knew "steak."

Chuckling, Noah wiped his chin with the back of his hand. "Better shower and change first. Eau de Pooch isn't popular with the ladies."

He climbed behind the wheel and then inched his way in bumper-to-bumper out of the stadium parking lot and onto I-35W South.

The pricking at the base of his neck jerked him out of the stupor of barely moving traffic. He glanced over his shoulder.

Harley sprawled on the back seat, tongue lolling as he snored like a ripsaw.

Noah glanced in his rearview mirror. The driver of the car behind him was a middle-aged woman who had her steering wheel in a death grip. She must be one of those drivers who wasn't prepared for the mammoth near-permanent rush-hour crush that was the interstate under construction from the downtown Mixmaster north to the 114 cut-off.

The prickle persisted. As he reached up to rub the back of his neck he saw it. Or something. A flash of a headlight as a vehicle three or four back was veering across the stripe as if trying to keep tabs on him.

Could be a drunk driver not quite in control of his

vehicle. Despite the strict tabs on alcohol, a few patrons had no doubt left in states of intoxication above the legal level.

"There it goes again." Noah said the words to no one in particular. Harley certainly didn't care. This time, the vehicle changed lanes.

Noah had a not-so-clear impression of a battered truck, more rust than paint, three cars behind him in the outside lane. But there was nowhere for either of them to go. The traffic had slowed to a stop.

A tail? Had Durvan sent someone to shadow his actions until he could be arrested?

The thought crawled all over him and stung like fire ants. The hell with that. He was usually the hunter, not the prey. Only one thing to do about it.

He bided his time, even turning on the radio to help him keep his cool as he plotted what to do. Sooner or later the traffic would thin enough for him to make a move.

It came as a major stream of traffic on his right began peeling off onto the exit ramp for 287 North. He changed lanes suddenly and then pressed the brake, causing the car behind him to slam on its brakes with an angry blast of the horn. He could imagine the middle finger being aimed his way as the driver swung left to fill his truck's previous spot. He didn't have time to admire it.

He jerked his wheel, sending his truck over the series of hard high bumps used to prevent drivers from exiting after they'd passed the official ramp. He was prepared for the jarring ride and kept the truck aimed at the exit. Harley, on the other hand, awoke with a start and began barking wildly as he tried to maintain his balance on the seat.

"Sorry, boy."

Noah twisted his head left as he reached the pavement of the exit ramp.

The rusty truck, once three cars back and still a lane

over, moved past before the driver realized that Noah was on the exit ramp.

He drove north a while before cutting over and driving city streets through Saginaw and then past Meacham Airport. He'd be harder to spot in town than on a major highway.

Only when he reached the stockyards did he stop checking his rearview mirror.

Maybe it was nothing. He could have been mistaken. His paranoia working overtime. But he couldn't afford to be less careful. Not when he knew for a fact someone wanted him dead.

Strange how that worked. He'd never wanted more to be alive than at this moment.

He made a call to Andy, who talked in a breathless rush about the fish he'd caught with his grandfather. And how his grandmother was making those fish for dinner, though Andy had doubts about eating living things. The cycle of life had begun to register with his four-year-old. But then grandpa had explained how it was okay to eat what you caught, as part of the cycle. It was only a sin if you wasted the gift of food. And how they were going crabbing off the pier tomorrow so they could keep that life cycle going with other kinds of seafood.

Noah's blood pressure had subsided by the time the call ended. It helped to know that out in the world there were people, like his son, who worried about doing the right thing by sea creatures. Kind hearts. He wanted his son to keep his as long as possible.

Without even trying, his thoughts turned to Carly.

Where was Carly? What had her day been like? He hoped like hell it had been better than his.

CHAPTER SEVENTEEN

"This is so not a good idea." Carly put her car in park and stared at the back door to Flawless. She didn't need to look inside another single time. Nothing would change as long as the huge fans, which she could hear from the parking lot, were drying out the interior. A week, at most, she'd been told, before the mess could be cleared. A week.

She hoped God would forgive her for sitting through Reverend Morrison's sermon while her mind played through scenarios of what her next steps should be. It had been a particularly long service, this being Palm Sunday followed by the congregation's monthly Sunday Dinner.

A reasonable person would be working her business plan, trying to find a way to recoup from the devastation. Instead, she was fixated on the who and why of that devastation. She knew she wouldn't be able to swallow a single mouthful of the food being served after service at the monthly Sunday Dinner served in the Fellowship Hall. Thankfully, Aunt Fredda had been too busy with problems of her own to notice her niece slipping out before grace was said.

Aunt Fredda's explanation that, according to Jarius, a stray dog he'd taken in had eaten the pound cake she had baked for the dinner had been met with smirks and rolled eyes by her friends in the Ladies' Auxiliary of St. James A. M. E Church.

A smile tugged at Carly's mouth. Only she knew that Jarius's punishment for stealing the cake was to mow his mother's one-acre plus yard for the next month with an old-fashioned push mower!

Judge Wiley owned and kept ready a pair of push mowers, to be used by panhandlers who occasionally came to her door asking for a handout. She offered them work. Her rules were simple.

"I pay eight dollars an hour. And I know how long it takes to mow my yard because I've done it. Fifteen-minute breaks for every hour of work. I provide lunch. You don't finish on time, you don't get paid."

Carly smiled. She admired her aunt, who knew who she was and exactly how she fit into both her working and community lives. Living in one place all one's life offered that kind of stability. Something Carly had never wanted. She'd only known movement. Her parents both worked for the State Department, her father as a Foreign Service Cultural Affairs Officer. She'd lived in Washington, D.C., Haiti, Buenos Ares, and Italy, among other places. It was at one of those European postings that she'd been approached about modeling. If she'd stayed in Fort Worth, she doubted she would ever have gotten that chance.

But things changed. While her parents, now stationed in Tokyo, never tired of the adventure, their youngest daughter was ready to stop and take stock at home.

Flawless was to have been her rootstock for beginning a new life and finding a way to belong again in her hometown. But that dream, months in preparation, went up in smoke. At the moment, she didn't know how, or if, she wanted to recover. That fact made her very sad, and very angry.

She thumped her fist lightly on the steering wheel, talking aloud to herself, as usual, to help her process her thoughts. Which, not surprisingly, resettled on the list in her pocket. She didn't have to think hard to image what everyone in her life would say about it.

"Flawless was collateral damage in a crime. The reasons why had nothing to do with you, Carly Harrington-Reese. Let it go."

Except that she couldn't. The puzzle was like a scab she couldn't stop picking. Or maybe she was just procrastinating over the final call she needed to make to one of her vendors. Indija had been her hardest sell on Flawless's box store sample sale idea. Indija, a recent graduate of the Art Institute of Fort Worth, worked with reclaimed stones. Often using chunks of crystal and other stones, she wrapped pieces in copper wire to create rings and bracelets. These items weren't for the timid or traditionalists. Her jewels demanded that the wearer be as bold and daring as her accessories. But Indija had an attitude problem. She was also stubborn, hard to work with, and deeply suspicious of everything and everyone.

Reluctantly, Carly touched the young woman's number in her phone.

Indija heard her out in silence, no sound but the occasional sucking of her teeth until Carly finished. "So, I plan to open again as soon as I can. And I very much want to continue to represent you."

"No, ma'am. I don't see that. I was never for this store idea. I do fine selling online. But you convinced me to give you a try. You sounded like you had a fire in your belly. I'm hungry, too. But now you're telling me one little problem and you're quitting."

"I'm not a quitter, Indija. I'm being realistic. It will take time to clean up my store, redecorate and restock. It could be weeks or months before I'm ready to open."

"*Uh-huh.* That's what quitters always say. It could be this time or that. Vague promises, and shit. Why am I talking to you?"

Suddenly there was only that cold silence at the end of phone. Carly felt stung by one very angry wasp. She'd been hung up on.

"Great. Now I feel better."

Only she didn't. Indija's words hurt. And that made her, more than ever, determined to get to the bottom of the fire.

It wasn't about Noah. Even if she hadn't been there and the fire broke out, she'd still be in the same position. Flawless ruined.

But then Noah, and Harley, wouldn't be here.

That thought sent a rush of fear through her so strong, she grabbed the wheel with both hands until the shuddering stopped. She was there. She'd saved a life.

To hell with what Noah said. She needed to talk to him.

As she started her engine a GMC Sierra 1500 4WD Denali pulled into the parking lot. The words *WISE DEVELOPERS: HISTORIC PRESERVATION* were emblazoned on the side. It pulled up behind the burned-out store next to Flawless. Moments later a large fiftyish man in a Sunday suit climbed out. This was her landlord, Burt Wise.

She killed her engine. Now that she thought about it, she had a few questions for him, too. Having dealt with him before, she knew just how to get what she wanted.

She slid out from behind her wheel and struck a pose in the parking lot before addressing him. "How are you, Burt?"

The landlord turned in surprise to hear her voice and got an eyeful. His graying buzz cut practically bristled as he eyed her up and down, taking in every detail of her church attire. Her black sheath dress was simply cut,

fabric covering her from a modest scoop neck to below
the knee hemline. The pizzazz came from the exacting
couture fitting that detailed every curve of her body
from breasts to waist to hip to butt.

She watched him swallow hard before he could speak.
Or maybe it was his tie tied a little too tightly that made his
oversize head appear like an inflated balloon. "Afternoon,
Ms. Reese." He had a hearty Texas drawl better suited to
selling used autos or ambulance-chaser attorney services.

"Call me Carly."

She came toward him, doing an exaggerated catwalk
strut in six-inch heels that made her tower over his shorter
five-foot seven-inch frame. He seemed to enjoy the view
as a grin spread his lips, revealing two rows of capped,
Chiclets-sized teeth.

Some men were pathetically easy, depending on what
a woman wanted from them.

She threaded an arm through his and turned him away
from the building. "You're just the man I wanted to see.
Shall we sit over here and talk?"

"I guess." He must have sensed something in her eagerness, because he was suddenly wary. "I don't have much
time."

"This won't take long." She led him to an iron bench
with wooden slats on the sidewalk and sat first, crossing
one long leg over the other. "I've been so worried since
our fire."

"You told me insurance covered your loses."

"That's true. But merchandise isn't everything." She
made her eyes wide, while stifling the urge to gag at her
own antics. "After all, I was here when the fire started. I
could have been a casualty."

The tomato-pink drained from his face at the thought.
"But you look fine."

"Thank you. But since I was almost barbecued, I think

I deserve to know who did this. The arson investigator who interviewed me wouldn't give me any information. But now here you are. What have you heard?"

He blinked, his gaze growing shrewd. "I heard I'm not liable for the break-in or the subsequent damage."

"That's not what I meant. I want to know if the authorities know who did it."

"Not that they're sharing."

Something overhead caught her attention. A big smile broke over her features. "What about the footage from your security cameras?"

She pointed to the one nearest camera, mounted on a lamppost and aimed in their direction. "What did you see on that footage, Burt?"

The big man flushed. It wasn't pretty. He was suddenly the stroke-inducing color of a tomato. "Wasn't nothing to see."

"Why not? Did the perpetrator disable all the cameras?"

"Not exactly." He frowned at the device. "They don't actually record."

Carly dropped her pose. "What actually do they do? Are they monitored at a center station? What?"

Burt frowned at her sharp tone. "Do you have any idea how expensive monitored security is? All surveillance companies do if there's a problem is call the police or fire department. Any tenant would do that much. It's a rip-off paraded as peace of mind."

He must have seen something alarming in her expression because he rushed on. "Before you get your panties in a twist you should know you signed a lease in which the coverage of our security services is stated in black and white."

"You didn't spend any time pointing that out."

He snorted. "Not my job. And this isn't my only property. No, sir. Wise Developers oversees more than two dozen other buildings in the county. And not one of those tenants wants to pay the additional cost for monitored services. Way I figure it, my paying for and installing cameras was expense enough. Got them at Costco. Saved a bundle, let me tell you. To my way of thinking, if the criminal thinks he's being recorded, he'll move on to easier pickings. That's why I put signs all over the property saying that tampering with the cameras will result in an alarm being sent directly to the police."

"But it's fake peace of mind."

"Oh really? We haven't had a single break-in anywhere since those cameras were set up."

Looking at his smug face, Carly couldn't decide whether she was more annoyed or appalled by his risk-taking. "You had a fire Friday night. One of your tenants, namely me, nearly died." No point in bringing up Noah's name now.

He shrugged it off. "Yet here you sit, safe and sound. I rest my case."

"Who put the system in for you?"

He drew in his chin. "Why're you asking so many questions? You thinking about suing me?"

Maybe. When the dust settled. "I have insurance. My agent wants to know."

"You tell them to talk to my lawyer. You signed a contract. Everything's in there." He stood up, clearly annoyed now. "I'm within my rights to secure my property as I see fit."

Carly thought fast. She was losing him. She stood up. "Thanks for the conversation. By the way, I should thank you. I got a discount on my reclamation needs because I'm using the same company as you."

"That so? I do throw a lot of business their way."

"So you've had other fires?"

"No, nothing like that. They do jobs for my historic preservation projects." He pointed at the building behind them. "Most developers don't want to take on old buildings like this one because of the costs. Nearly all need rewiring, new plumbing, and things like asbestos removal and mold remediation. That kind of stuff can increase my overhead something fierce. But I'm a city backer, proud of our heritage. So I cut a deal with CowTown for all my renovations to lower the upfront layout of cash. Saves me money. *Bam*." Wise was suddenly as animated as Emeril showing off a new recipe.

"On top of that, I get a break from city hall for reclaiming historic properties. *Bam*. Saves me more money. And then there's Historic Site Tax Exemptions for historic preservation from the Landmarks Commission and the City Council. *Bam*. I'm golden."

Carly smiled. "I'm impressed." She did wonder if he'd be so golden if the City Council knew about his security shortcuts.

He shrugged, but a smile of satisfaction won out. "I do okay."

"So then, we're agreed. I will be let out of my contract. Penalty free."

"What gave you the idea I'd do that? You signed a two-year lease!"

She pointed at her back door. "Do you see anything like business going on in there?"

"Not my problem."

"You're absolutely right—if you let me out of my lease. Otherwise, I'll see you in court. And you'll get loads of publicity because I am a celeb."

He watched her through hard eyes tight in the corners. "You think you can play hardball with me?"

She folded her arms casually and shrugged. "I made a lot of money modeling. I don't mind spending some of it to out a shady business man." He eyed her up and down. "You won't find any cracks in my facade, Mr. Wise. I'm flawless."

Wise worked his mouth as though he did all his calculations with tongue and teeth. "I keep the first and last months' rent. And you promise to leave the premises broom clean. Plus, this deal stays between us."

Carly didn't hesitate. "As long as I have our terms in writing and signed."

He grinned at her. "You got the makings of a decent business woman."

"I am a decent business woman." She smiled and turned away.

"I need to use your phone."

Jarius looked up to find his cousin standing behind him in the dessert line of the Fellowship Hall. "I thought you'd left." She simply held out her hand. After juggling two plates of desserts, he handed it over. "Here you go."

"Not this one. I need your booty-call phone.

Jarius looked quickly right and left before answering. "What are you talking about?"

"Don't even start." She tugged his arm to pull him out of line. "I know you carry a burner phone so that you can call women you don't necessarily want to have your real name and number. That's cold. But right now I've got some calls to make that I don't want traced either."

"Then get your own. They're cheap."

She held out her hand, eyes like daggers.

"Okay." He reached into another back pocket. "You scare me sometimes, how you know things, cuz."

"I may need to keep this a while. Is there anyone whose messages you want me to pass on?"

Jarius shrugged. "Not really. I'm seeing someone."

Carly's brows rose. "Is it serious?"

"Maybe. That's what I'm trying to suss out. I'm not seeing anyone else while I do."

"That's a grown-up thing to do, Jarius. About time."

"Don't you start. Moms is always on me about settling down. I tell her I'm a young man in my prime."

"You need to watch you don't turn into a burn-out situation past your prime. No real woman wants a played-out playa."

He grinned at her because they both knew he was far from being burned out. He seemed to be getting better looking all the time. "So, what kind of calls will you be making? Anything overseas?"

"I'll pay this month's bill. Okay?"

He nodded. "We're good."

Carly waited until she was back in her apartment before she looked up Noah's number and called. It was past four thirty.

"Glover. What?"

"Not the friendliest hello I received."

"Carly?" He sounded very wary.

Her chest tightened. "Was this a mistake?"

"Yes. I'm hanging up now."

"Wait! This isn't my phone, if that's what's bothering you. It's a pay as you go. Untraceable."

She could practically hear him thinking. "Has it occurred to you that if I wanted to see you again, I would've called you?"

"No." Carly held her breath. He was really angry. She hurried on before she could lose her nerve. "I've been doing some thinking. I need to see you."

"Why do I suspect you've done more than think?"

"Do you want to know what I've learned, or what?"

"If it's important tell me now."

Carly blew out a breath of frustration. "Maybe I should just listen when everybody tells me to stay the hell away from you."

"You got a visit from Durvan."

"How did you know? Does he always have a giant stick up his butt?"

"Pretty much. But he's the best in the business. Tough, thorough, relentless. If he told you to stay away from me, he meant it. If he finds out different, he won't like it."

"Nobody tells me what to do."

"Tell me about it." He sounded less aggravated. "What happened to that not-my-problem attitude of yours?"

You did. But she couldn't say that without revealing feelings she wanted to keep private. "Your arsonist messed with my life and things I care about. I've got a stake in this."

He wondered if *he* was one of those things. Then he continued, "He's a killer, Carly."

If he hoped to give her pause, his words had that effect. Carly felt a chill sweep up both her arms, raising goose bumps. But fear also made her more determined. "I made a list of questions I'd like answers to."

"You want facts? Here's a fact. You're not safe. And not just when I'm around." He didn't sound angry, just cold and distant. "Why do you think the fire department has kept the details about the fire out of the media? I suspect it's because it would tell the real arsonist that you spoiled his plan to have me die in the fire. Think he's going to be okay with knowing that?"

"Then we need to get the bastard first." Brave words for someone who was shaking in her stilettos. Thank goodness he couldn't see that.

This time the silence on the phone was Siberian.

"Are you certain you want to get more involved with me?" There .vas a dare in his voice, as seductive as it was dangerous. This man played hardball.

Carly wasn't sure they were still on the topic of the arsonist. "I don't know. But I do know this. I can't stop thinking about . . . everything." Let him make of that what he wanted. "Also, I won't get any peace arguing with myself. I need to do something. Make something happen."

His voice this time was quieter, almost strangled. "I don't want you to be hurt."

"I've been taking care of myself for a long time."

"I can't stand the idea that you're being pulled into something I might not be able to control."

"Control is an illusion that only men buy into. That's why you don't read instructions or ask for directions."

"I suppose you asked for directions today?"

"I asked a lot of things. Things you might be interested in knowing the answers to."

She could feel the tension running through him. Or maybe the tip-off was Harley's whining in the background. "I'm starved. You like steak?"

"I'm vegetarian."

"Of course you are. But no meat, ever?"

"What do you have in mind?"

The playful note in her voice sent Noah's thoughts straight to his dick. He stiffened so quickly he had to take a breath.

He jerked his thoughts out of his pants. If he said no, she'd do something else. Better she was with him than out there stumbling into trouble. Still, she had to know what she was getting into.

"I may have someone tailing me."

This time she didn't have an instant reply. "Noah?"

"Hm?"

"Lose them."

He smiled despite himself. "What businesses are open on Sunday that are within walking distance of your place?"

"CarePlus Pharmacy is nearby."

"I'll pick you up in the parking lot in twenty minutes. And, Carly, dress down."

CHAPTER EIGHTEEN

Noah watched Carly cross the pharmacy parking lot toward his truck. She wore skintight jeans that showed off miles of leg and cupped her butt like a territorial boyfriend. A metallic silver hoodie, patterned with green sequin shamrocks all over the front, stopped just short of her hips, accenting that curvaceous butt as she cat-walked her way to him in knee-high, lipstick-red stiletto boots. Every step sent vibrations of sexual energy across the parking lot. Each and every one of them brushed against his crotch as if they were her fingertips on his bare dick.

This was her idea of dressing down? Just watching her made his eyeballs sweat. She was turning him on, fully dressed. And that wasn't good. Because he wasn't the only one paying attention.

Two young men in hoodies and droopy pants had paused next to his truck to watch her too. He rolled down his window and gave them the stink eye. "Nothing for you here. Move along."

The young men looked startled, not realizing anyone

was in the truck. The first to catch his drift grinned at him. "You know her?"

"Yes." Noah gave the single syllable the force of his law enforcement personality.

The other guy punched his friend in the arm. "Yo, bro. You got to know that wasn't runnin' round free." They play-scuffled for a second and moved on.

Noah's predatory gaze followed them across the lot as if they were known felons until he realized what he was doing. Hell, he was jealous of even another man's gaze on Carly!

Which was the most stupid thing he could be. She was world famous, had been seen by millions on the runway, in magazines, and on the internet.

His mind flashed to the nude photos he'd seen of her online, and a low growl revved in his chest. Maybe he wasn't sophisticated enough to deal with a woman like Carly, after all.

He shook his head, still amazed she'd had sex with him, an ordinary guy. No, not just sex. She'd taken him a million miles from the lonely place he'd lived the last five years, where sex was just mutual physical release. She'd made it personal, and intimate, and irresistible. Now he was so horny he was nearly bent double with lust.

He'd made a mistake last night. He knew that now. He'd made a worse one agreeing to see her now. But there she was, so alluring he was thinking about things that would get them arrested if he acted them out in public.

So, he was just going to have to gut it out and get over it. No, get over her.

A moment later, Carly yanked open the passenger door and slid in, a big grin on her face. "Hi."

"Hi, yourself."

Carly's smile held its ground, though his low-pitched

voice didn't sound all that enthusiastic. Was he still annoyed that she'd called? Really?

Hoping to ease the tension between them, she scooted closer, took his face between her hands and gave him a quick kiss on each cheek, continental style. "*Bonsoir, mon cher.*"

She thought nothing of the gesture until she realized he had stiffened, his mouth becoming a flat line of disapproval as if the greeting was unwelcome. Looking into his intense blue gaze, she saw that he was reacting to the commonplace continental greeting as if she'd planted a juicy full-tongue kiss on a stranger.

"Do you greet every man that way?"

The irritated rumble surprised her. Was he pulling a jealous act? Oh no. She didn't play that.

She scooted back to her side and reached up to fluff her curly pompadour. "I do pretty much what I want. Haven't you noticed?"

"All the time." His pinched the bridge of his nose, as if he had a pain there.

Confused and frustrated by his lack of enthusiasm at seeing her again, she reached back between the front seats to greet Harley, who'd been barking and dancing in joy to see her. "*Allo, mon grand garçon.*"

"Harley doesn't speak French. *German* Shepherd. " Noah sounded pissed.

You're being a butthead probably wasn't the best response, considering his mood, Carly decided.

Instead, she gave Harley a good scratching behind both ears then raised up and planted a kiss on his doggy shiny black nose.

She flicked a glance Noah's way as she settled back in her seat. He looked untouched by her nearness. She'd had a very different emotional response to seeing him again. Touching him had sent little ripples of pleasure rushing through her fingertips. He looked like she'd offered him a slap. Legs spread and one hand resting on the steering wheel, he stared straight ahead. His handsome profile might as well have been cut from Texas granite. He was dressed casually in jeans and a blue plaid dress shirt open at the throat. It took a second for her to realize that the black nylon strap over his shoulder wasn't some designer artifice but the very utilitarian right half of a shoulder holster. That made her heart pick up a notch.

He wore a gun.

He's a police officer, she reminded herself, accustomed to the sight of Jarius carrying his service weapon. Even so, her reaction to Noah carrying wasn't staying casual. He hadn't been wearing a gun the other times they'd met. A ripple of tension rolled through her. Something had changed.

She lifted her gaze to his face, but her question died on her lips.

He looked big, solid, and very dangerous. Felons probably backed down from this man. But she wasn't afraid. Not when her body was still vulnerable to memories of the night before. Even now she could remember the feel of his warm hard hands sliding over her body, directing her up and down and all around his shaft. And the feel of his day-old stubble brushing her nipples.

Yet there he sat, lost in some male reverie, completely unaware of his effect on her. Maybe she needed to come at this from something less than her usual very direct angle.

"How do you like my outfit?"

He frowned at her. "You call that dressed down?" His voice was a little too neutral to be natural.

She touched her shamrock-spangled hoodie. "Too much?"

"Not if you want to start a riot. You're wearing goddamn fuck-me boots." He reached forward to start the engine.

She leaned in and grabbed his wrist. "Hold on. You said dress casually. I'm causal."

He turned a hard face toward her. "Well, I'm not.'

His gaze skimmed her hoodie, pausing where her breasts thrust gently behind two big shamrocks with golden-circle centers. Though he couldn't possible see them, Carly felt her nipples harden in response to his stare. When he looked up, his gaze was no longer angry, or disapproving. It was hot, his pupils blown wide by his own arousal. She suspected he must be seeing the same in her gaze. So then, maybe he wasn't so angry as horny. This she could work with.

She scooted sideways in her seat, drawing close enough so that she could lean into him. She felt him tense, as if to move away, but he didn't. Encouraged, she pushed her nose into the collar of his shirt, the better to inhale the scent of the man inside. He had showered recently. Just past the end of her nose, a bit of shaving gel still clung to his jaw. It was sexiest thing she could imagine.

"Carly." He said her name as a rasp of sound.

"*Hm?*" She heard his breath catch and then hard hands were framing her shoulders. Not to pull her close but to push her back into her seat.

His gaze was hot, avid, something she'd never thought blue eyes could be. But his expression said, *Back off.* Totally mixed signals. "What's wrong?"

Noah shoved a hand through his hair, completely devastating the neatly combed rows of tawny waves. "I can't even think about answering that question without getting us both so far off topic I might not be able to crawl back to it."

As if to prove the point, one wayward curl sprung forward forming a C-hook above his left eye. The result was impossibly boyish, and totally at odds with the stern lines of his face.

Okay, so maybe he was feeling as much at sea about his feelings as she was about hers. She didn't have to be told he didn't share easily or much of himself with others. She supposed that came with the territory of being an officer of the law. Or, something else entirely was going on. That made her really *really* look at him. And reevaluate.

He looked exhausted, and tense as newly strung barbed wire. She remembered what he'd said over the phone about being followed. Her playful mood evaporated.

"Maybe we should find a more private place, to talk."

"Damn straight." His gaze generated enough heat to perk coffee before he looked away and put the truck in gear.

As they pulled out of the parking lot, Carly hauled into her lap a large purse Noah hadn't noticed her carrying. Some detective. Just the sight of her screwed with his ability to think straight.

In quick order, she pulled out another hoodie, olive drab, and a pair of plain white sneakers. Faster than he'd have thought possible in the small space, she changed and tucked away the spangles and stilettos. But not before he noticed that she wore only a lace cami under her hoodie. It was stretchy and clung to her body, revealing the milk chocolate aureoles of her nipples behind the gauzy material. Lust shot through him like a backdraft, blowing his control all to hell.

Noah tore his gaze away, grinding his teeth. He didn't check her out again until she had pulled out a black knit stocking cap and pulled it down over her head, covering her fountain of curls.

She turned to him. "Better?"

"I don't know. Maybe." He shook his head like a bear with an earache, trying to hold on to his scowl. But it slipped into a curve of exasperation. "Hell. You'd stop traffic wearing nothing."

She cocked a brow at him. "As I recall, you make a pretty bold statement that way yourself."

They both broke into laughter. But it didn't mend the rift. Once the humor died down there didn't seem to be an easy way to continue. They glanced at each other uneasily several times, neither wanting to be the one to break the silence that might have consequences that Noah, at least, was certain he couldn't afford.

Out of sheer desperation, he turned on the radio to fill the vacuum. After a few moments of "I'm to Blame" blaring in accusation at him, he switched to a jazz station where the lack of lyrics wouldn't blast his shortcomings in his face.

Carly pulled her feet up on the seat, wrapped her arms about her legs, and leaned her chin on her knees. Tucked up like that, she looked younger, and fragile, and vulnerable. Part of that had to be that she wore no makeup. Her skin was perfect without any artifice. That stunned him. No false eyelashes or goopy mascara or sticky lipstick for Carly. She was dressed down, as he'd asked.

So, her original getup had been a tease. He wished he'd been in the mood to enjoy her sense of humor. All he could be grateful for now was not having to talk while he watched for signs that the tail he'd lost might have found him again.

He'd gone home to change and feed Harley after the Speedway job, risking being picked up again by a determined tracker. But at least he'd been on his home ground, with all the resources that implied. He was prepared to hunker down until morning, when he planned to confront Durvan with his theory. Then his cell rang.

Carly's phone call had scared the crap out of him. She was poking around in things that could get her hurt, or worse. Still, if he didn't hear her out, she would continue without telling him. That much he'd learned about her. Nothing stopped this determined woman. Not even the threat of being burned up.

Protecting her sat uppermost in his mind. That's why he'd agreed to see her. At least this way, he could be with her for a while without feeling that he was breaking his promise to himself not to further involve her in his personal life.

Except that, now that she was here, he knew it was mostly a lie. He wanted her, to be with her, in every way possible. And some he'd be making up in his head as he went along. One touch and he combusted around her. Like a teenager with his first hard crush. Only he wasn't inexperienced and nervous. He knew exactly what he wanted and how to get it with a woman. And, he wanted it only from Carly.

He glanced at her. She wasn't only beautiful, she was smart, and tough, and loyal. She didn't have to be here with him. Ninety-nine out of a hundred people would have run from the situation. Hell, women and men opted out of relationships every day for much less reason. Not that they were in a relationship. One night of screwing didn't make a relationship.

"Is your son okay?"

He jumped inwardly. "Yeah. Fine. With my parents in south Texas until this blows over."

"You're lucky to have parents for backup."

"Uh-huh." Damn. She'd asked about his family. What had he told her about Andy? He couldn't remember.

He wondered fleetingly if Andy would like her.

His hands tightened on the wheel as he glanced in the rearview mirror.

He'd never considered introducing Andy to a woman he was seeing. He didn't even talk about his son with the women he dated. This thing with Carly was—he didn't know. What he did know for certain, being with her felt good, selfish bastard that he was.

But he had to have ground rules around her. When she touched him, all his critical thinking disappeared into his pants. And he needed to concentrate, on protecting himself and his very precious cargo.

After fifteen minutes of silent musing, Carly straightened up and looked around, surprised to find they were deep on the southwest side of town. "Where are we going?"

"Somewhere we're not likely to be recognized. But first, I've got to eat something. You hungry?"

Harley, who'd been dozing in the backseat, sat up and barked several times. Clearly he understood "eat" and "hungry."

"Guess that's a yes." Noah swerved to cross three lanes of highway traffic to take an exit ramp at the last instant.

Carly reached for the dashboard to halt her sudden sway and turned big eyes on him. "You cut that close."

"Yeah, well, Harley only saw the golden arches when it was almost too late."

Ten drive-thru minutes later, they were back on I-20 West in a truck cab smelling of burgers and French fries, an order of chicken nuggets, three cherry turnovers, and one child's cheese sandwich.

Biting into the golden warmth of toasted bread and cheese, Carly watched him exit I-20 West onto 377 South. Then she saw a mileage sign. "Granbury?"

"Maybe." He glanced at her. "You good with that?"

"As long as the food lasts, I'm good." Carly reached over and grabbed two fries from his bag.

He gave her body a quick sweep. "I thought models had to watch their weight."

She snorted. "Ex-model. I eat like a horse."

He drove on, devouring two burgers in under two minutes. The food helped settle him. He'd skipped breakfast. The one expensive roasted turkey leg he'd bought at the auto show had been eaten mostly by Harley. He grabbed for his cup and took a swallow of the scalding brew without a flinch. Mainlining coffee for that jolt of wakefulness was something every first responder was familiar with.

He glanced over at his suspiciously quiet partner. Carly was feeding him pieces of chicken nuggets, and bouncing her head in time to the music on the radio. She looked ridiculously cute in that knit cap, and happy. Too bad. Time to get real.

He reached over and turned off the radio.

She glanced over at him in surprise.

"You wanted to talk. So talk."

CHAPTER NINETEEN

Carly fed Harley the last of the nuggets. "All gone, boy. Sorry."

She wiped her hands on a napkin and then looked at Noah. "I want to help you solve this case."

He shook his head. "Absolutely not. I'm a professional investigator. I work alone."

"And you're doing a superior job."

He slanted her a dark look from beneath lowered brows. "What's that supposed to mean?"

"Do you even have a statement from me, the only eyewitness?"

He hunched a shoulder. "You wouldn't talk to me."

"That's right. The professional arson investigator couldn't even wheedle the truth out of a sympathetic witness. At this rate you'll have the case solved in no time."

"Not helpful, Carly."

"No." She said the word softly as she reached for another French fry. She swirled it through the ketchup and held it out as a peace offering. "Sorry."

He gave her a sharp-eyed look before he grabbed the fry with his teeth.

She watched him chew before asking, "What do you want to know?"

"I want to know the events of the night of the fire. Every detail you recall. Nothing's too small."

Carly gave her version of the events in sequence, even the phone calls from her aunt, and her inclination not to investigate the barking dog even after she noticed the door was ajar.

Noah listened in silence, stopping her only for clarification. "You're sure the fire hadn't started when you entered?"

She pulled the knit cap off and tossed her head, bringing the cascade of blonde curls to life. "I'm not brave enough to have gone in after a fire started. I was trying to free Harley when I heard a sound like the pilot on a hot water heater come on. And then there were little flames along the baseboard. I was in total denial for a moment."

He glanced at her. "What changed your mind?"

"Fire." She said the word softly. "There was a real fuckin' fire."

He nodded. "Why didn't you just get the hell out and call for help?"

She looked at him with a puzzled expression. "I tried. But there was Harley, and you. I had to help."

Noah recalled the jelly belly feeling he'd felt the first time he went into a burning house to save a civilian. And he'd been fully prepared in turnout gear.

He glanced at her. She, too, was staring straight ahead, remembering things best forgotten. Time to change the subject.

"What prompted your call today?"

She turned her head, looking almost surprised to see

him. "Okay, but first you should know Investigator Durvan came to see me this morning." She snagged another fry and offered it. He took it like a fish took bait. "He said he needed to tie up a few loose ends."

An uneasy sensation moved in Noah's gut. "What were they?"

"All the same questions he asked the first time, about the night of the fire."

"What questions did he press you on?"

"That's just it." She reached for the final fry. "He didn't seem to know what to make of my answers."

"He admitted that?"

"Not exactly." She dragged the fry back and forth through the ketchup. "I once made a living projecting emotions through attitude and body language. Believe me. Investigator Durvan isn't sure about squat." She popped the fry into her mouth.

Noah smirked. He could just imagine Durvan's reaction to being told his give-nothing-away attitude had been breached by a former lingerie model.

"Did he ask about me?"

"You mean, if I helped you start the fire?"

Noah did a double take. "He asked you that?" Durvan had pressed him with that question in the hospital. But he thought he'd dropped that line of questioning.

Carly's generous mouth flattened into a thin line. "We had a moment. He tried to bring up some old mess about my husband's death. I questioned his ability to conduct an impartial investigation."

"How did Durvan respond?"

She reached for a cherry pie. "I might have also mentioned that if he was going to pursue that line of investigation, I might have to get my side of the story out to the press first."

"Well hell, Carly."

She slid the warm fried pie out of its cardboard sleeve and took a bite. "He pushed. I don't like being pushed."

He grinned. "Point goes to Carly Harrington-Reese."

She shrugged and offered him some of her pie. "After he left, I had a lot of questions of my own. That's why I called. Too many things don't make sense."

Noah took a bite, all but finishing her offering. "For instance?"

She looked at the rim of crust left between her fingers, then shrugged and popped it in her mouth. "Why did the arsonist choose that store? There's no easy access. It's not a standalone or even a corner store like Flawless . . . was." He saw her frown, then watched it pass.

"There's a restaurant across the street and a pizza place on the other end of the strip. Parking often spills over into our lot. People would be around at night who might notice something shady going on. Why not choose a place where the arsonist had all the time in the world to start the fire and make certain it took?"

He slid her a funny look. "Did you come up with any answers?"

She twisted toward him in her seatbelt, animated by his interest. "It must be time-related. He had a window of opportunity, not long, to get you from wherever—where did he pick you up?"

"I don't know. But let's say it was outside The Collective Brewing Project over on Vickery. That's the last place I remember."

"That's only a five-or six-minute drive from the fire." She reached out and brushed her thumb down the side of his mouth. "Cherry filling." Without seeming to think about it, she licked her thumb clean.

Noah's body jerked as if she'd applied her tongue to his own. What the hell had she said? Oh yeah. "That's coincidence, at best."

He saw her reach for the second pie. He was hungry all right, but not for pie. "I've got more. I talked with Mr. Wise, my landlord, this afternoon."

"Where was that?"

"In the parking lot behind Flawless. I went to check on the restoration work. He said he was doing the same. I asked him about footage from the cameras in the parking lot." She took a big bite of the fried pie before turning a smug expression his way. Her lips were now shiny red with cherry filling. "Guess what?"

"There isn't any footage." God help him. He wanted to pull over and lick her mouth clean.

Her expression deflated. "How did you know?"

"If Durvan had me on security footage I'd be behind bars."

"No." She paused to lick her own lips free of filling. Watching her was torture. "Then we'd know who forced you into the store."

He slanted her a grin. "You really believe me."

"Don't change the subject." She pointed to his shoulder holster. "How did he get the drop on you?"

"I'm not always armed. But what makes you think it was a he?"

"Okay, *she*. I know how easy it is to distract a man." She reached out playfully and ran her fingers up his thigh until he grabbed them to stop their progress.

She chuckled and pulled free. "But, honestly, I've hauled your unconscious weight around. Getting you in and out of a vehicle, and into that store without causing attention? My bet is on your attacker being a *he*. But how did he render you unconscious?"

Noah scowled. "I was roofied. They found evidence of it in my blood. I could have been walking and talking for a short time without having any memory of it."

Her mouth fell open. "Isn't that proof you couldn't have started the fire?"

"Unfortunately, no." He explained Durvan's theory about drugging himself to avoid the pain of dying in the fire.

She shivered. "But that's insane."

"Many professionals think people who attempt suicide are at least momentarily unbalanced. But you were telling me about this guy Wise."

"Right." She cast a long look at the remaining half of the pie before handing it over to him. "Wise is too cheap to have his cameras monitored. He says the cameras and signage are deterrent enough. But, what if someone knew he didn't have them monitored? And knew the store was empty. That would be additional reasons to choose that place."

"Who would know about the phony cameras?"

"No that many. The tenants, though I don't remember being told about them. And whoever installed them."

Noah thought long and hard about what she'd said. It was dusk now. The bright red orange glow on the western horizon rendered the rolling terrain of upper Hill Country in soft charcoal black silhouettes. "You've got a theory, Carly, and are trying to find facts that fit it. That's not how a detective works. We discover facts and then develop a theory from the actual hard evidence."

The rebuke hurt, he could tell, but she shook it off. He liked her better with every second. "Are you a regular at the Brewery?"

"No. A going-away party was being held there for one of our guys who's moving."

"Did invites go out?"

"Nothing that formal. A few text messages with the date and time made the rounds of the firefighters, and a few other friends."

She nodded thoughtfully. "So then, the arsonist might have heard about the party before deciding to act. He would have set things up ahead of time, knowing when and where to find you." She gasped. "Oh, Noah. What if it's someone you know?"

He glanced at her with knowing eyes. "That's been a given from the first. Hell of a thing."

"Yes." Her voice was small as she reached across the console to again lay her hand on his thigh. This time there was no attempt at playfulness. This was a touch of sympathy. He'd take it. "What about other possibilities? Any enemies? People you've arrested?"

He reached for her hand and curled his thicker fingers over her slender ones. "Already checked them out. All but one is still in prison. He got out last year and promptly left the state."

"What about unsolved arson cases? Maybe there's someone you're looking for who's afraid you're close to catching him."

"You're scaring me, Carly."

"What does that mean?"

"It means you think too well for my peace of mind."

She smiled. "I'm catching your train of thought?"

She was derailing it—with her touch, her interest, her intensity—but she couldn't know that.

"What if I went back and asked Mr. Wise—*ow!*"

He'd gripped her hand hard. "Dammit, Carly. We're dealing with a killer. Get that through your gorgeous head. He could be a colleague, or even a casual acquaintance. He could be the last person I'd suspect. Now do you understand why you need to stay away from me? I can't trust anyone."

"You can trust me." She squeezed back, added her second hand as reinforcement.

Muttering a curse, Noah flipped on his turn signal, and

jerked the wheel right, sending them fishtailing off the highway onto a two-lane country road and out into the darkness of the spring night.

Carly yelped and grabbed the console with both hands a few minutes later, as they bounced off the blacktop and onto the gravel shoulder. Harley barked loudly in protest, pushing his nuzzle forward over Noah's shoulder.

"Harley. Down." At the sound of his handler's voice, Harley subsided back onto the backseat. But his vocal mutterings were eloquent in their protest of Noah's driving.

Noah braked, slowing the truck to a stop on the edge of the road.

Carly turned an angry face to him. "What the hell do you—?"

Before she could finish her protest, Noah put the car in park, unsnapped his seatbelt, and surged across the console to pin her between his body and the door.

"I'm done talking, Carly."

He slid one hand behind her head and released her seatbelt with the other. She only had time to catch a breath before he covered her mouth with his.

CHAPTER TWENTY

It had been humming in the air between them. Carly had been fighting her own feelings so hard she hadn't registered Noah's fierce hunger. Or maybe he was just better at masking his feelings when it counted. But now the pretense was over. The simmering heat between them burst into full flame when his mouth covered hers.

There wasn't a lot of space with the console dividing the front but Noah seemed to have decided that the lack of space was the console's problem, not his. He sprawled across it to get to his goal. How he managed it, she couldn't guess. But it really didn't matter.

She closed her eyes as the kiss went on and on, the better to just feel. The heat of his mouth seeped into her. The muscular rasp of his tongue tangled wetly with hers, tasting of French fries and cherry pie. It was a full body contact kiss, no urgency greater than the need to be lip to lip. It took her a moment to realize she was only touching him with her mouth. It seemed so much, so intimate, but ultimately not enough.

Her arms slid around his torso, careful not to touch the weapon holstered under his left arm and then she was holding handfuls of his shirt, trying if possible to get closer. The heat of his body lit fires along her nerve endings, making her shiver with desire.

Harley, feeling no doubt left out, was the first to voice a complaint. He jumped forward into the space between the front seats and landed all ninety pounds of his furry weight on Noah's back, whining as if he thought he was needed to referee whatever game the two humans in the front seat were playing.

Noah broke the kiss to say sharply, "Harley, down."

Reluctantly, the shepherd backed off and subsided onto the backseat.

"Stay."

Ears twitching, Harley rested his muzzle on his forepaws. But the high-pitched whining continued for a few more seconds.

Breathing hard, Noah looked back at Carly. He didn't kiss her again, but he didn't release her either. As he eased back across to his side, he brought her with him until they embraced across the console. There was no caress to his touch, or even encouragement. He seemed focused on containment. Of his feelings, or hers?

"I shouldn't have done that. But I needed to know if what I'm feeling is real. That you're not just some fantasy I dreamed up because my life is so screwed over I can't see my way clear."

His gaze fixed on hers, he took her hand and laid her palm flat against his shirtfront over his heart. "You feel that?"

She nodded. "That's just hormones racing because you're about to get lucky." Carly prayed her voice sounded lighter than the heavy hammering of her own heart in response. "Don't look so grim. It's just sex."

"That's not what your mouth says." His gaze focused on the fullness of her lower lip. "It says I matter to you."

"All that in a kiss?" She meant to sound skeptical. She sounded uncertain, and astonished. He was right. She'd never been about casual sex. One-night stands began and ended with her first three experimentations with no-strings encounters. They gave her too little of what she hoped for, and nothing worth repeating. But where was her self-possession when it came to Noah? Burned up in the consuming heat of his kiss.

He was staring at her hard, but his expression said he was still fighting the raw lust between them. "Carly, I—"

"You're right. Getting together was such a bad idea. On every level." Her voice shook from the combustibility of her feelings as she prepared to release him.

She dragged her hand down his shirtfront, intending to pull away from the warmth of his body beneath. Instead, her fingers found his belt buckle and curled into it to hold on to him. "Does it have to have words? Can't it just be?" There it was in her voice again, a sound desperate and breathless.

He brushed his thumb across her lower lip. He was so close she could see herself reflected in his gaze. "So what do we do?"

She turned a hand palm up and held it before him. "There's a saying, if you love someone set them free."

Noah cupped her hand in his, and stared into her palm. "I'm not sure which half of that sentence scares me more. I do know I don't want you to set me free. Not until we've had a few meals, played Frisbee in the park with Harley, seen a few movies—ones you'll hate or I'll hate but we'll watch because the other picked it, argued over . . . I don't care what."

"You want normal?" That was the scariest idea yet.

"Yeah. Normal. Whatever the hell that is."

He hadn't mentioned the first part of her sentence. *If you love someone . . .* Too soon, much too soon. Why had she said those words aloud? She usually kept things at bay that scared her, even when doing them.

Time to change up the rhythm.

She ran a finger back and forth along the top curve of his belt buckle. In the light from the dashboard she saw that it was made of heavy German silver with a raised gold rope edging, chased silver scrollwork, and the star of Texas in gold at the center. She hadn't seen it before. But then she hadn't seen much of him—well, not dressed, anyway.

"You like it? It was my grandfather's." His voice held pride of family and tradition.

"Hm." That's when it hit her. Noah was a for-real cowboy. She didn't date cowboys. Not country boys nor urban cowboys, or poseurs.

A Texan by birth, she'd never had a thing for men who wore big-brimmed hats and wouldn't take them off even inside restaurants and movie theaters. That was rude. Everybody worth spit in Texas owned at least one pair of boots. But she avoided men who wore boots that looked more like trophies than footwear.

Her gaze skimmed down his denim-clad legs, though she had to drag them past his package, to where his legs disappeared in to the darkness beneath the steering wheel.

She couldn't see his feet. But did it matter?

Her gaze rose with a question. He held her look for a beat and the heat in the space between them expanded.

Oh lord, they weren't going to stop. He was going to kiss her again and she was going to let him. In a minute, they'd be snatching each other naked, and enjoying every second of it.

The glaring headlights of a passing car followed by the sustained blare of a horn broke the moment.

Carly blinked, trying to pull back from the sexual lure

of the man before her. He'd just told her that he thought the man who wanted him dead could be a colleague, perhaps someone he thought of as a friend. What kind of man made enemies like that? What sort of man was Noah? Really. Up to now she'd been operating on instinct . . . and lust. There was one way to find out in a hurry.

"Tell me about your ex-wife."

He blinked. "Now?"

"Now." Let her be a Miss Sugar Mill of Texas runner-up, maybe. Or a barrel-rider sorority girl. Something so far from her experience that the disconnect between them would be glaringly apparent even to him.

Noah moved back behind the wheel, but he held on to her hand. "Her name was Jillian Tilson. We met through mutual friends. She was fun. The life of the party. Not the most beautiful woman in the room, but no man could take his eyes off her." He gave his head a tiny shake. "I was just an average guy. Not much for partying. But after she'd flirted with everybody in the room that night she chose me. I couldn't believe my luck. And she stuck."

"She sounds like a dream girlfriend."

"Yeah. Only the kind of dream varied with her moods. Nobody had higher days. Or darker nights." He began drawing gentle circles on her palm with his thumb. "A few months into our relationship, I asked her how she saw us. I never believed she'd stay yet, against my better judgment, I was falling hard. She surprised the hell out of me by proposing. She said I was a rock to her river."

"You channeled her energy and evened her out."

Noah's thumb stilled. "How do you know that?"

Carly nodded. "My husband said he was attracted to my American industriousness and earnestness. He was French and didn't take life seriously. So you married."

Noah nodded, his thumb skimming her palm. "Most folks don't like the unpredictability in daily life of being a first responder's spouse. Jillian said she liked that she could never be sure when I'd turn up, or even if. She thrived on the adrenaline of knowing I was risking my life every time I went out the door. She said it made her crave me."

He looked up curiously at Carly. She shrugged, not sure she wanted to put into words what she was feeling. It felt unsafe.

"It worked for two years. But then we started fighting. About everything. She never wanted children. She even made it a condition of marriage."

Surprised washed through Carly. She might not know many things about Noah, but she did know, without a doubt, that he was a family man. "You thought she'd change her mind."

He nodded. "Sounds lame when you say it. But, yeah." He expression sobered and his thumb stilled in the well of her palm. "Then Jillian turned up pregnant."

A little chill ran over Carly's skin. "What happened?"

"I was over the moon. Thrilled. She reacted like I had raped her. Said I'd betrayed our relationship. And then she walked out."

He took a deep breath that shuddered through his body, as if the ugly memory was still alive, somewhere deep. "She was gone four days. I assumed she'd had an abortion. But she hadn't. She told me if I wanted a baby so badly she'd have it. But she wanted out of the marriage after the birth."

Carly held her breath, unable to think of a thing to say.

"She played her part. God, she was the best pregnant woman ever. Never complained, looked radiant all nine months. Had every one of our friends convinced I was the luckiest bastard on the planet. And then Andy was born."

A softness came into Noah's face that Carly hadn't seen before. "Andy was beautiful, even covered in afterbirth. They handed him to me in the delivery room and he peed all over my shirt. I knew then I'd never let go. Do whatever it took to keep my son safe."

He reached up with their joined hands and rubbed his forehead. "Can we talk about the rest of this some other time?"

"Okay." Carly tried to pull her hand away but he held on, closing his fingers around hers. "Your turn."

Carly took a breath. Fair was fair. "Arnaud was a top fashion photographer in Europe. He was known for telling a story with his photographs. Sometimes in a single frame. His specialty was tasteful eroticism, posing nudes where the merchandise seemed a beautiful afterthought. Female and male models threw themselves at him. Having him do a shoot with you could make a career."

She watched Noah's expression go remote. "The ones he took of you are exceptional."

"That happened later. First time I was hired to be in his photos, I refused to undress for him because he wouldn't explain why I needed to be naked. I lost the gig. It was a big job. My agent was furious, and dropped me. Said I was unprofessional. You have to understand. No one said no to Arnaud. A few months later, we ran into one another on another assignment. He said my refusal intrigued him, and he had a proposal for me." Her mouth curved up when Noah snorted his opinion of that. "Not that kind. Strictly business. He became my agent."

He proposed using me in a spread intended for French *Vogue*. They said no. I was an unknown, and the labels were unimpressed. But Arnaud knew the value of his work. He offered to forego his fee if the spread failed. It was a huge success." She smiled, remembering a happier time. After that, he used me in shoots that I hadn't been booked for until he was hired. The lingerie modeling was a natural progression from that first series. I knew I could trust him not to take advantage."

Noah watched her quietly. "You fell in love with him."

"Oh yes. He was ten years older, and very worldly. I felt protected. When Arnaud was working he was happy, focused, intense. He didn't like downtime. When he had it, he went looking for stimulation."

"Drugs."

"Yes. It isn't uncommon in that world."

"What about you?"

"I had two wisdom teeth out at sixteen. They gave me a codeine-based painkiller. It made me feel like my heart was going to burst through my chest. Since then, I resist anything stronger than aspirin."

He held her eyes, steady and without apology. "I had to ask."

"You're a cop."

"Why did you marry him?"

"I didn't, at first. I told him I couldn't marry an addict. So, he went into a clinic in Switzerland and then spent six months staying clean. When we married, we agreed to leave the fashion world because it offered too much temptation. But sober, Arnaud struggled." In embarrassment, she heard her voice break.

Noah reached out and cupped her chin. "What happened?"

"A relapse. So trite." Her free hand waved the thought away. "It had been a year and we were running out of money when I was offered a weeklong job in Sweden. He encouraged me to take it." She smiled, but it was only the tightening of muscles. "While I was gone he ran into some old friends. The coroner said it was common for relapsed addicts to forget their tolerance for drugs had reset to lower doses."

Noah gave her hand a gentle tug. It was all the invitation she needed. She climbed across the console, letting him pull her into his lap. He turned her so that her back was to his chest. His hands on her asked nothing, just offered the warmth and strength and protection of his body enfolding her.

They sat that way for several minutes before he spoke. His lips were against her ear, so he whispered. But his tone was matter-of-fact now, the pain gone to ground.

"The day of Andy's six-week check-up, Jillian announced that she wanted a divorce. That's when things got ugly. Even though she made no secret of the fact that she didn't want to be a mother, she demanded a massive settlement in order to waive custody. Everything I had was the price of keeping Andy. I emptied my bank accounts, my retirement plans. Sold my house, my car, turned everything I could get my hands on into cash. It all went to her so she'd sign away her parental rights. Best money I ever spent."

"Oh, Noah." Carly leaned back into him, trying to hug him from the inside of his embrace. That's why he lived with his parents. Why he was so protective of Andy. Why he was the last person on earth to opt out of life.

"There's something else. I think I'd have handled the rest just fine with Andy. Folks divorce all the time. But about eleven months ago Jillian died of alcohol poisoning. She'd gone back to partying the way she had when we met. She mixed a bunch of pills and booze and went to bed. Never woke up. How do you tell your son his mother died like that?"

Carly reached back and touched his face. "I don't know what to say."

She felt his shoulders rise and fall. "I've been pissed as all get-out ever since. Mostly for Andy's sake. Haven't known how to get past it. Yet you don't sound bitter at all about what you've been through. How do you do that?"

"I was angry at first. I felt betrayed by Arnaud. Then felt inadequate. Sometimes I berated myself for leaving him, knowing he was weak. Then I wondered if he'd encouraged me to leave. If I'd been his jailor, even if I didn't realize it. I'd become restless, too."

She listened for a few beats to Noah's heart, pumping a slow even rhythm. He had the powerful gift of silence. It encouraged her to share her own long-withheld secret. "We were playing house. Pretending that we were okay. But it wasn't real. Arnaud wanted that high more than he wanted me, and it killed him."

Noah brushed his lips against her neck. "It wasn't your call. Addiction is a nasty relentless disease. He and Jillian were casualties."

Carly nestled back again him, noticing for the first time that night had fallen, the world around them grown dark and silent, but for the distant sounds of traffic on the highway behind them. Above them the sky was deep purple and salted with stars. Thankfully, it was too early for mosquitoes. Little flashes of lightning, too faint to be seen earlier, flickered on the northwestern horizon. The earlier winds had calmed, as if the air was holding its breath. Storm coming in? Seems like she'd heard something about the possibility.

She sat forward, feeling the cool rush as their bodies separated. "We should probably go back to town."

"No." His fingers closed over her shoulders. "We can't leave like this."

"No." Carly agreed. "We shouldn't."

She was turning in his arms, sure at last of what she wanted.

This kiss was different. It was long and leisurely, thorough and arousing, soothing and flavored with the promise of even more pleasure to come. Shivers of anticipation shimmied through her as his hands moved leisurely over and then under her hoodie. He caressed her thoroughly, as if there was nothing waiting for them on the other side of these moments. No need to impatiently drag clothing aside. For eager fingers to hurriedly explore. They had . . . now.

When they pulled a little apart, she could see his face was flushed with desire and both their breaths came a little fast.

"Have you ever made love under the stars? In the back of a pickup?"

Carly laughed. "Here? Now?"

"Somewhere nearby. As soon as I can find a safe quiet place."

"You're serious?"

"You've never done it in a pickup truck." He sounded surprised.

"With my parents having careers in foreign service, we moved a lot. Not many opportunities for moonlit trysts with cowboys."

He gave her a look that singed her eyebrows. "You're in for a treat, darlin'."

He drove several miles down the road, then crossed railroad tracks into an open field. He parked and cut the lights. "Wait here."

He jumped out and opened the door for Harley. "Go. Do your business," she heard him say. Harley scrambled out into the tall grass and took off, quickly becoming a shadow that was swallowed up in the dark.

Noah jumped up in the back of the truck and unlocked his father's toolbox. "Aha!" He pulled out a bedroll and knocked on the back window to get Carly's attention. "Come on back. We've got everything we need."

By the time Carly climbed out of the cab and walked back to the back, he had let the tailgate down and spread the unzipped bedroll on the truck bed. He hunkered down and offered her a hand. "I got a nice cozy place for us."

Carly allowed herself to be pulled up beside him. He was grinning like a kid as he knelt beside her on the bedroll. "You okay with this?"

She smiled back, infected by his joy. "All that's missing are a couple of longnecks."

"We don't need beer to kick off this party." He touched her face, his fingers alighting along the crests of her cheekbones as his thumbs framed the corners of her mouth. She could barely see him in the dark, but it didn't stop her knowing exactly what was on his mind. She could feel it in the tension of his fingertips.

"Do you know how beautiful you are? Really, just so damn pretty."

She smiled and felt his thumbs slide over her lips. Instead of answering, she parted her lips and licked the tip of one thumb.

He hissed a breath that sent a sizzling heat surging through her body. God, he was in trouble. Deep trouble. And he was going deeper.

"Do that again." His voice had gone all husky and dark.

She darted her tongue against first one and then the other of his thumbs and then she caught one in her teeth, tonguing the tip until she heard him murmur, "Damn, Carly. You got me sprung."

Laughing lightly, she reached down. Sure enough, the bulge in his jeans was hard enough to drive nails. "I suppose we're going to have to do something about that."

"You could try that tongue trick on other parts."

"There's an idea." She leaned forward and kissed him, intending it to be a quick preamble to the main event. Whatever salacious half-formed idea she'd be assembling disappeared in the wet warm pleasure of his mouth. Time for naughty thoughts later. Kissing Noah was too good a time to skimp over.

Somehow when the series of dizzying kisses ended, they were lying side by side. Her hoodie was open and her cami had been pushed up to expose her breasts. He dipped his head to lick one stiff peak. "Delicious," he murmured.

She located that belt buckle for the second time and unhooked it. He sucked in a breath to make it easier for her to lower his zipper. She plunged her hands inside the open vee of denim and into his shorts, then circled her hand around to his rear. The fine hair on his ass tickled her palms, but she was on a mission. The firm hard curves of his masculine cheeks filled her hands as she pushed jeans and shorts down his hips to expose her prize. He lifted a little to help her, but as the fabric bunched at his thighs he said against her ear, "We might want to stay mostly intact. In case we need to make a quick getaway.

"Really?" Carly hadn't thought a second past getting her hands on his johnson.

He laughed as he rolled her onto her back and moved over her. "We push clothing up and down but not off. Okay?"

Since she was holding the hot swollen object of her search in both hands, Carly could only smile in agreement. "What about tongue tricks?"

He immediately rolled off her, bringing her over on top this time. She didn't waste time with niceties. The thought that they might get interrupted, though there was not a sound in the night beyond Harley's snuffling around in the dark, made her move with urgent intent. She half sat up and leaned over him, hands directing his erection at the best angle for her mouth.

She licked him once, twice, and a third time before he whispered, "Damn."

Feeling every bit of pride at the power she held over him in that moment, she settled in for long sweeps of her tongue that left him wet and glistening.

His hand slid through her hair, fingers clutching her curls, holding her in place. "If I die here tonight, it's your fault."

She laughed and took him in her mouth, stretching to encompass as much of him as she could without choking.

It didn't last long. She felt him tensing, his hand flexing tighter and tighter in her hair until finally he was pulling her off. "Wait. Wait. I want . . ."

She knew exactly what he wanted. She wanted it, too. It was making her weak with need, and oh so hot she could barely think.

He eased her back into his arms, breathing harshly. "That was . . . wild."

She smiled, tucking her head against his shoulder. "I never liked that much before. But with you . . ."

"Damn, Carly. Just when I think . . ." His arms tightened around her until she thought she wouldn't be able to breathe. "That makes this night pretty damned perfect. Best ever."

She smiled against the warm skin of his neck. "You haven't come yet."

"Oh, I will. Just—" He was sucking in air like it was about to be a scarce commodity. He needed just a little more control, just enough to make it all the way.

After a moment, he unbuttoned her jeans and shimmied them and her panties down her legs. And then his fingers were splayed over her lower belly, moving lower until they delved into her cleft. His touch was sure, certain, finding all the places, catching every possible rhythm of pleasure until she was shivering uncontrollably.

With deft moves, he put on a condom then rolled over and entered her. Not moving yet, he just staring at her with a secret smile. "You're so wet." His voice was hushed. "So smooth and silky."

He pressed his forehead into her neck as his lips sucked her collarbone. She stuck her tongue into the shell of his ear. As she did so she felt his cock twitch within her and knew he would not lie still for long.

Still, she was curious. "Is it good for you?"

He chuckled, the vibrations tickling her neck. "You're

asking the man you're holding between your sweet thighs the wrong question."

"What's the right question?"

"That would be, what's your pleasure, darlin'? Fast? Or slow?" He bucked his hips into hers for emphasis.

Carly smiled. "As Tina Turner would say, first do it easy, then do it rough."

"Yes, ma'am." He shifted her head so that he could kiss her, long hard kisses that showed her just how he was about to work her lower down. He moved then, setting the pace in an easy muscular easing in and out of her body. Sensations quivered through her, setting off fireworks behind her closed lids as she held onto him for dear life.

Suddenly the pace changed. He came into her with hard quick urgency that would not allow her to catch her breath. She curled fingers on his rigid biceps and responded with her own body to the demand of his. When she came she arched against him, holding him inside as the waves of pleasure rippled along his shaft. His harsh breath was in her ear and then she could feel his body convulse as he climaxed deep within her.

Carly smiled at the sky and let a feeling of complete peace overtake her. A sliver of silver-white moon hung above his left shoulder. Over his right, she watched lightning run in rivulets of pink-white light through the shoulders of clouds boiling up on the horizon. A spring night in Texas. And it contained everything she'd remembered. The reasons she'd come home. Beauty. Suspense. Vast openness where dreams could run wild. And at the center, the held breath of anticipation for the storm ahead.

After a while Noah leaned in again, this time forehead to forehead and just held her as he whispered so softly Carly wondered if he meant only for himself to hear the words.

"I wish I'd met you first."

CHAPTER TWENTY-ONE

The storm rolled into Fort Worth just after nine p.m. Like a battalion breaking through enemy defenses, straight-line winds battered the city with fifty-to sixty-mile-per-hour gusts. Lightning ran horizontal zigzags through cloud canyons, silvering the underbellies of the deep purple sky monsters. Thunder rolled continuously, punctuated now and then by a sudden crack and boom that shook the walls of homes and businesses when a flash grounded nearby.

He almost missed the taxi pulling up before the apartment building. The first rain splattered against windows and windshield like miniature water balloons. Thick drops that fell individually quickly came faster and faster until they merged into a pounding waterfall, deluging streets and the parking lot in which he sat.

But there was no mistaking the shock of blonde curls emerging from the backseat. Long legs, pert ass—this he recognized. She ran quickly for the shelter of her apartment building, a large purse held over her head as she disappeared into the stairwell.

"Fuckin' bitch."

She'd gotten out somehow, away from his surveillance. All that while he'd sat in his vehicle drinking a Big Gulp and eating Hostess Ho Hos, waiting for Glover to show up, he was certain Carly Reese had been inside. Every reason to think so. Her car was in the parking lot when he arrived. So he'd assumed she was home, waiting for lover boy. Now he knew she hadn't been home to lure Glover here. Perhaps had met him somewhere else.

Anger whip-snaked through him, searing him from the inside. Was Glover on to him?

He'd tailed Glover from the Speedway, certain he hadn't been detected. Not even sure when he'd lost him on I-35W, he thought he'd simply missed seeing Glover exit. So he'd rounded back, weaving in and out of neighborhoods for an hour until finally he thought it was safe to roll past Glover's house.

Sure enough, the prick arrived with that flea-bit hound he called an explosives K9. So he'd hung back, waiting half an hour until Glover reentered his truck and drove two blocks away before gunning his own vehicle and headed out. No need to follow the bastard. He knew he was headed for Carly's place. How did he know? Glover had changed clothes.

"Damn straight, I'd make a great detective."

Once he made the FWFD, he planned to work his way up to arson investigator in no time. He still had time. By then Glover would be an embarrassing footnote with the FWFD.

But the prick never showed.

The rain suddenly stopped, as if shut off at the tap. Thunder rumbled louder, guttural and predatory. And then hail began to fall. Tiny pellets of ice at first, tap-dancing their way down the street, the sound ominous for those with experience of Texas spring storms. And then the pattern changed. Stones the size of marbles began to hammer down, bouncing like popping corn off every surface.

"Fuck it."

He turned on his engine, swearing up a blue steak. Darlene would clobber him if her car turned up pitted by hail when he was supposed to be in Austin on business. Of course, Austin had hailstorms too. But it would be just his luck they weren't having one tonight.

In the distance sirens sluggishly came to life, sounding like disturbed sleepers prodded to crank up to full volume. He knew what that meant. Tornados.

He rolled down a window, uncaring that he was instantly drenched, and swung his head in one direction and then the other, trying to spot the telltale swirl of a twister in the darkness. But a low wall of cloud had swooped in, obscuring the brilliant lightning and the tops of nearby downtown buildings just as residents would be desperate to spot disaster spinning down from overhead.

He drew in his head and rolled up the window, cursing God and every living thing as he wiped his face on a sleeve.

His heart beat to the heavy rhythm of unfairness, pumping up grievance after grievance until he could barely breathe.

He'd wasted three hours, certain he'd corner Glover.

He slammed his hand against the steering wheel, uncaring for the pain it caused. He needed release. Revenge.

Glover had slipped past him again. He didn't know what to do next.

As long as Glover was free, he needed to know what the bastard was doing, who he suspected, who he watched.

"Why the fuck couldn't the police department do their job?" He'd all but drawn them a map with a big X over Glover's face as the arsonist no one had caught.

Looked like he was going to have to be more graphic. He still had a couple of tricks up his sleeve, like the WeMo in the backseat. That asshole Glover used fingerprint ID on his phone. Once Glover had passed out, he used the bastard's right thumb to open the phone, set up the WeMo account, and send the suicide note.

He grinned as he remembered his own cleverness. He was still in charge. Hell yeah.

He shoved the car into gear and put his foot on the gas.

As he turned out of the parking lot on Vickery, the hail intensified, filling the rain-drenched streets with a fine layer of ice. Even the grass on the curb was disappearing under the onslaught. Not that he gave a crap about the weather. If Glover wasn't with Carly, he might be back home by now. Storms put every first responder in the area on high alert. Glover would want to be near his gear.

He switched on his scanner, eager to hear about a fire, any fire.

But first he was going to pay Glover a little visit.

Across town four policemen and Inspector Merle Durvan were serving a warrant at the home of Shiloh Glover, also listed as the official residence of Noah Eastland Glover. A crap time for a search, but the law didn't stand on ceremony when homicide was involved. And they were well within the 6 a.m. to 10 p.m. search time.

After finding no one at home, Merle had waited for an hour, enough time for the weather to turn ugly and his men to be drenched. But he didn't want a mistake to invalidate a good search and retrieval.

Maybe Glover had driven by and seen them, though they had parked a block away in an unmarked van. If that were so, they couldn't leave without getting at least part of what they'd come for. It wasn't often a judge gave authority for a second warrant on the same weekend. But new evidence had come to light, directing them to look in other directions.

After the emergency sirens revved up, Durvan gave the order to enter the premises by any means necessary. They needed to get in and out before all hell broke loose.

Once inside, Durvan was like an old maid aunt, dropping a tarp on the entry floor and directing the other officers to wipe their wet feet before continuing inside. Noah might be about to be disgraced, but his father had earned respect.

"Inventory everything you take. I don't want any screwups." Durvan pulled on plastic gloves. "And, for god's sakes, don't wreck anything unnecessarily. Glover senior is a retired cop."

They had what they came for within two minutes. But Durvan took his time writing up the inventory, hoping that the storm would bring Noah home. One of the officers was getting antsy. A tornado had been sited over White Settlement, where he lived. Emergency vehicle sirens of every type could be heard far and near. It was a bad night, for a lot of people. But not as bad as it was going to get for Noah Glover.

In addition to the search warrant itself, Durvan held an order to arrest.

They were ready to leave when Durvan heard a truck pull into the drive. He approached the door with a smile.

Noah walked in as casually as a man can who's shedding water like he'd been dipped in a stream. His hands were up in the position of surrender. But Durvan had an officer pat him down anyway.

Noah smirked, thinking how much he'd rather still be lying between Carly's soft thighs. As the man's hand slid up his inseam, he jerked. "Careful. You owe me dinner over that move."

Durvan stepped up to him, beefy face tight with anger. "You think this is a joke, Glover?"

Noah met his gaze with a hard stare that spared his old friend nothing. "Not even a little."

The corner of Durvan's mustache twitched. "Where have you been?"

Noah lowered his hands and crossed his arms. "You and I both know I'm not going to tell you about that."

Durvan's expression hardened. "We'll see. I've got probable cause. You're under arrest, you son of a bitch."

Cursing his lack of vision, he wiped repeatedly at the fogged-up windshield. Darlene's crap car didn't have a working defroster. Giving up, he rolled down the driver's side window. Wind and rain shoved their way in past his face, but he didn't notice. A big fat grin spread across his dripping features at the sight unfolding down the block.

And to think he almost missed it.

Across the street, under the glare of the porch lights, Noah Glover was being escorted out of his house, a policeman on either side. It wasn't until he was being turned to be tucked into the rear seat of a patrol car that light glinted off the pair of cuffs circling his wrists.

He sat there a long time after the police cars had one by one pulled away from the curb. The worst of the storm had blown on through. He held a lighter, the only thing his jerk-off of a father had ever given him. But, for the first time in months, he didn't feel like lighting so much as a firecracker.

A calm had settled over him. The work, the struggle, the soul-grinding disappointment of his life had been lifted away. Noah Glover was under arrest.

CHAPTER TWENTY-TWO

Noah sat in his sister's Mercedes staring straight ahead. "Thanks for bailing me out."

Sandra nodded. "It's bad, isn't it?"

Noah was silent for a moment. It was bad.

There'd been questions, so many questions he'd lost count. Not a big deal, in and of itself. He knew the drill. Yet before, he had always been on the other side of an interrogation.

Leave the suspect in a room for a while, long enough to wonder what the arresting officer had on him. Let him grow restless, angry, reckless, whatever his emotionally volatile trigger was. Then, when the suspect was vulnerable, irritable, hungry, thirsty, maybe jonesing for a hit of something illegal, or bloodshot-eyes tired, begin the interview.

When Durvan had finally sauntered in, in a dry shirt and looking as if he'd had a cat nap Noah didn't allow himself, the look in his mentor's eyes told him it was worse than he'd imagined. They had evidence.

Just how much and what kind had been parceled out in

a slow drip of information over two hours, interspersed with dozens of rephrased questions that all revolved around when did he start setting fires.

God Almighty. They thought he was an arsonist.

He glanced over at his sister, who was watching him like a bomb that might go off.

"Don't look at me like that. I'm okay. But the charges have been revved up a notch." Or nine.

"What does that mean?"

"They matched gasoline used in my so-called suicide attempt to the service station near my house."

"How did they do that?"

"With a gas chromatograph. Every service station's tanks have a signature mixture. It's an accumulation of gasoline residues from tankers, ground-water seepage, degrading tanks, and things in the ground that come in with the ground water. We use it fairly often to locate an arsonist."

"Durvan did this to you?"

He glanced at Sandra and kept talking because she looked close to tears or dismemberment of his superior, neither of which he wanted to handle just now.

"It's standard procedure if we get samples of the accelerant used in an arson case. Gasoline is cheap, available, and no one thinks twice when someone comes in with a tank and carts away a couple of gallons. When we suspect arson, I collect samples from all the service stations within a four-block area. If the samples from the fires match just one station, I know where my suspect is getting his fuel. Caught one guy recently because he'd been seen on a bike pedaling away from a fire. I went and checked out the station's video for the day after the next suspect fire in the area. Bingo, guy on bike filled a gas tank. His face was visible. Showed it around and had him in custody within two days."

"Can't Durvan do something like that to prove you're innocent?"

"It's not just the one fire anymore. One of the arson cases I've been working for months came up as a match."

"You've going to have to explain that."

"Okay. But could we leave the precinct parking lot? I recognize that reporter." He pointed to the woman coming across the lot toward them at a fast clip, recorder already in hand.

Sandra's eyes narrowed. "No problem."

She started her engine and waved at the woman. Then she moved her car right into the path of the reporter, as if she planned pull up alongside her. When they were even, the woman leaning slightly forward with a smile of anticipation, Sandra flipped her the bird and pressed her pedal, sending the Mercedes sailing past.

Noah shook his head but kept silent.

Sandra drove several blocks, hit the drive-thru lane of a fast food place to buy two large coffees and then entered the interstate going west through town before she spoke again. "Explain."

Noah sipped the black coffee in gratitude. He hadn't slept much and his brain processes were getting dicey. "When the lab tested the tank from the house, they got matches to the samples of gasoline from other arson fires as well. It's routine. We have unsolved arson fires backlogged all the time for lack of evidence. Sandra, they have me, the gasoline, and six unsolved arson fires all linked."

Sandra scoffed. "So what? All of what you're telling me is circumstantial at best. Hundreds of people use that station daily. It's coincidence that the fires match."

Noah frowned. He was forgetting something. He gulped coffee. Oh yeah. He'd skipped over the most important part. "The gasoline matches are only to the fires I've been investigating for the past six months."

"What are you saying? Durvan now thinks you're a serial arsonist?"

Hard as it had been for him to sit and hear it, that's what the department now thought. "Durvan thinks I chose those particular fires to investigate to keep them from being solved," he added for confirmation before Sandra's could ask, "because I set them."

"That's ridiculous. You *fight* fires." But her voice was hollow now, disturbed by this new evidence. "What does that mean?"

"It means someone's been after me longer than I've realized."

She frowned as she stared ahead, her lawyer game face in place. "Still circumstantial."

"There's more, Sandra. The last arson was a homicide. A homeless man died in the blaze."

Her head swiveled toward him. "Oh, Noah."

"Yeah. Durvan's been looking for motivation for my suicide attempt. Something beyond Bailey's and Jillian's deaths. He thinks he's got it now. The homeless guy's death is what tipped the balance toward suicide for me. Guilt over causing the death of that poor bastard."

"That's why bail was set so high."

"Yeah. But the charges haven't been introduced, or I might not have gotten out, fearing flight risk. They are still pulling the final indictment together. That's why they went back into the house. So far, all I've been charged with is the arson last Friday night."

He looked over at Sandra, who gripped the wheel so tight her knuckles were white with the tension. "I didn't do this."

"You don't have to say that."

"Yes. I do. It could get worse. The way it's going, there's

probably more stuff I don't know about yet waiting to bite me in the ass."

"What are you going to do?

"Work the case until I'm formally arraigned. I've been one dumb sum' bitch not to pick up on something before now. This isn't a simple crime of passion. It's been a slow build to an execution."

"You're going to need help. I can move to Fort Worth, at least until you are formally arraigned. Run interference with the press."

"No. I want you to stand back from this. You have a reputation to think of."

"Then at least let me get you an attorney. You need someone with criminal experience."

Noah nodded slowly. "I won't argue with that."

"There's more, isn't there?"

Noah nodded, hating to lay it on his sister's shoulders. But he needed to think clearly, and no one thought more clearly than Sandra Glover. Except maybe a certain woman with Happy Hair. Carly had tried to make him see a pattern last night. He wished now he'd listened better. But dammit, they absolutely couldn't have further contact now.

"They found footage from a surveillance camera two blocks away from where the fire took place Friday night. They showed it to me. It's grainy and wasn't meant to show action that far away. But it shows what looks like me and Harley in the parking lot and then entering the back of that store half an hour before the fire."

"Jesus."

He nodded. Something about the tape was bothering him, but they wouldn't play it a second time when he asked. "I'd sure like a look at the footage again."

"I'll get Angel on it."

Noah turned a questioning gaze on her. "Angel?"

"Angel Gutierrez. Private eye."

He smiled for the first time in hours. First-rate thinker, his sister. "Okay. I'll bite. On Gutierrez. But only if you promise to go back to Abilene and stay there until I call. He's to deal only with me."

"You can trust him. He's the best."

"One more thing. Carly Harrington-Reese had nothing to do with this. I want to keep her clear of the whole business. So I need you to get a message to her."

Sandra tossed her head, anger breaking through her nerves. "You've just told me you're about to be arraigned for homicide, and you're worried about a woman?"

Noah gave his sister a considering look. "Carly saved my life. Without her, you and Dad and Mom and Andy would have buried me today."

Sandra gasped but didn't argue. "What do you want me to tell her?"

CHAPTER TWENTY-THREE

"MODEL" CITIZEN SAVES SUSPECTED SUICIDE
  CITY ARSON DETECTIVE CHARGED IN ARSON FIRE

The headlines arrayed on her aunt's kitchen table made it hard for Carly to breathe. She'd already seen the local morning news on several channels before she turned them off in frustration and anger. But seeing the words in print had more impact. Nothing she read or didn't read, saw or didn't see, would change the immediate and disastrous fact: Noah had been arrested for arson.

According to all the sources, other charges were pending.

She did wish that she hadn't been identified as the woman who'd saved Noah Glover's life. That made for a whole other source of calls and texts from friends who wanted to know if she was okay. The trouble was, she wasn't quite sure how she felt, other than annoyed as hell. Especially since one headline referred to her past, as if it had anything to do with the fact she'd saved a man's life.

Luckily, Noah's sister had called to warn her that Noah

had been arrested—and made bail—and that the story was about to go public in a big way.

Even as she packed her bags to leave her apartment, Carly fielded and turned down half a dozen requests to be interviewed by local media. How they knew where to find her she couldn't figure out, until one reporter reminded her that her phone number and address were on the statement she'd made to the police. Someone had leaked it. That fact sent her to her aunt's home, where she'd spent the night.

The media weren't being as aggressive at a local judge's residence. They'd stayed behind her gate once Jarius's police cruiser came up the drive.

"Look at this." Fredda Wiley pointed to an article lower down the page in Section B of the *Fort Worth Star Telegram*. " 'According to one source who asked not to be identified, Glover has had a difficult year. First with the death of a firefighter friend killed when a wall of a building collapsed in a fire. And then the death of his ex-wife.' "

"What?" Carly snatched the paper from her aunt. She scanned the article so quickly it took her three times before her eyes would adjust so that the words made sense. *Jillian Tilson, the former Mrs. Noah Glover and recently divorced for the second time, died of a drug overdose eleven months ago. She was reported to have been despondent over the break-up of her second marriage and was abusing prescription painkillers as a result.*"

"Did you know about this?" Aunt Fredda was watching her closely.

Carly shook her head. "I know he's divorced. And that he has custody of his son, Andy. I don't know the details." She felt bad lying to her aunt. But this was something Noah hadn't been able to tell his own son. It felt wrong to share his confidence. But now it was spread over the media, as if it had any relevance. Poor Noah. No wonder he'd tried to protect his family by urging them to leave town.

Fredda took the paper back and finished reading the piece. "I'd be despondent, too, if someone took my child from me. However, there must have been extenuating circumstances with the wife to award custody to the father."

"His ex didn't want to be a mother. She walked out on them when Andy was two months old and never came back."

Fredda lifted her reading glasses to her brow. "I thought you didn't know the details?"

Carly shrugged. "I know he didn't do what he's accused of."

Aunt Fredda leaned toward her. "I understand you like the man, Carly. But don't confuse attraction with reality. There are some serious charges laid out here."

Carly folded her arms, annoyance breaking through her natural respect for her relative. "Haven't you said before that you have a sixth sense about many of the young people who come before you in court?"

"Yes, but I don't usually have feelings *for* the people who come before me."

"I need some air."

Before her aunt could detain her, Carly turned and walked to the back door only to see that the crowd of half a dozen media people parked before the closed gate of her aunt's property hadn't budged.

She turned back and nearly plowed into Jarius. He had arrived after midnight and gone straight up to his old room to sleep. She sometimes wondered if he actually lived at his apartment. He was shaved, showered, and dressed in his police uniform complete with utility belt, gun, and radio. In other words, ready for duty.

She looked up at him. "I need to get out of here. Now."

He evaluated her expression for a moment, and then her attire. She wore a crisp white shirt with the collar up and sleeves scrunched up, jean shorts with rolled hems, and sandals. "You're kinda casual, cuz. Sure you want to face the horde looking like that?"

She stuck a finger in his chest. "The point, *cuz,* would be that you get me out of here without the horde knowing about it.

"Right." He grinned. "Let me grab a protein bar, then I'll bring the cruiser under the *porte cochere* and you can slip in."

A few minutes later Carly was crouched down in the front passenger seat of the police cruiser, half hidden by Jarius's laptop as he drove through the gates of his mother's property. He didn't slow for the reporters. In fact, he gunned the big engine of his cruiser as they turned onto the last thirty yards of the drive.

Only when they were leaving the neighborhood did Carly sit up. "Thanks."

Jarius nodded. He looked every inch a police officer behind the wheel. Solid, capable, dependable. He slanted her a curious look. "You holding up okay?"

"Maybe. It would be easier if I had something to do."

"What about Flawless?"

"There is no Flawless."

"Aren't you going to reopen?"

"I've lost my merchandise. The interior, a lot of which I did myself, painting and papering, is destroyed."

"I get that. But you had a whole lot of women's dreams pinned to your success. What about what you owe them?"

"I know you're not trying to preach about responsibility to me."

"I'm just saying. You made some promises. People believed in you. One little setback and, what? I never thought of you as a quitter."

That stung. "You're the second person to accuse me of that this week. I didn't like it any better the first time."

"So then, do something about it."

She rubbed her forehead. "Easy for you to say. You haven't had my week, or my life."

"Why do you do that? You push me away anytime the talk gets personal."

"I'm sorry. I'm just worried."

"About Glover." Jarius's generous mouth crimped in the middle. "You seem to have a thing for men in trouble. First the Frenchman junkie and now a suicide risk."

She slanted him a hostile glance. "Do you really want to compare our private lives?"

"At least my business wasn't on every "Extra"-type tabloid program for a week. But seriously, Carly. There's nothing you can do about Glover for a while. Maybe months. Trials take their own time."

"He didn't do it."

"That's what they all say." He shot her a jackpot smile. "I'm a cop. That makes me a cynical bastard. Stay away from Glover."

"Now you sound like him."

"Glover told you that? Huh. Maybe's he got some sense after all. He didn't do you any favors by getting all up in your life."

"What makes you think . . . ?"

"Like I always say, you can't play a playa. He's got you tied up in knots. Bet you even think you're in love."

She sighed, stretching her legs out before her. "Did you ever meet someone and you think, 'This is important. Big. Huge. Got to go with it'?"

"All the time. It's usually the booty that speaks to me."

Carly laughed. "You're impossible."

"Maybe. But I see life for what it is. The booty is a powerful thing."

"And when that's not enough?"

"Girl, you're scaring me. Look your cousin Jarius in the eye and hear me good. You can't be in love with a man you met three days ago. You might be sexed up, jammed up, and cross-eyed crazy about what's in the man's shorts, but you can't be in love."

"Okay."

"Why do I think you're not listening to me?"

"Can you drop me off at my apartment?"

"So you can run the gauntlet of reporters?"

"No, so I can get on with my life. All the merchandise I was able to salvage is covering nearly every surface in the space. I need to make calls to the craftswomen and see what we can save."

When he had dropped her off, Carly quickly made her way up to her apartment, simply ignoring the eager young man slouching in the hallway. "I'm calling security about you," she called over her shoulder as she entered her door and then slammed it in the guy's face.

Two hours later, she had made contact with all her clients who lived within a hundred miles and made arrangements for them to come into town on Thursday for a meeting. Only Indija refused to say she'd be there.

And just maybe she'd been hasty about asking to be let out of her lease. Jarius was right. She shouldn't give up without a fight. She picked up the phone and called Mr. Wise.

"Well, now, I was already showing the space to another client." Wise sounded smug about his new deal. "The cupcake baker thinks she could make good use of the extra space in that corner shop. She's willing to pay more for the space, too."

Carly was ready. "Since you haven't signed any agreement and I certainly haven't, we still have an active contract, Mr. Wise. You can't legally negotiate for another tenant. You really don't want me down at the better business bureau complaining about shady tactics by Wise

Developers by negating my lease. And me, the heroine of today's page one. Without Flawless to keep me busy, I'll have plenty of time to complain—every place I can think of."

"You want to come work for me? I could use a negotiator like you."

"We'll just reinstate our present agreement, providing you start professionally monitoring your security cameras at my location. Think of it this way, it'll be cheaper than what you'd have had to pay my relatives if I were dead. Did I mention my aunt's a local judge?"

"Sure, sure, whatever. Only don't do me any more favors. I can't afford them." He took a deep breath. "And about the fire. I'm sorry that happened to you. But why didn't you tell me?"

"The authorities asked me not to speak to anyone until they had done their investigations."

"From the sound of it, you risked your life for the last person who'd be grateful."

"There was the dog." Carly hung up before he could reply. For a moment she sat staring out her window, wondering how Noah was. He was free, so he was okay. Just the thought of him sitting in a cell made her stomach queasy.

She would stay away from him, because that was what was best for him at the moment. This was no time for her to make his life harder. The only way she could help was to get on with her life so she didn't worry. Too much.

But not contacting Noah wasn't the same as not thinking about him. Hardly a moment went by without Carly remembering a moment or two of the last time they'd been together.

Their love making had been interrupted by a particularly close lightning strike that made the hair on both their

arms and heads stand on end. It must have happened to
Harley, too, because he howled in sudden surprise, then ran
in circles until Noah subdued him.

Her mouth softened in a smile, remembering Noah's
scramble to pull up jeans and leap off the truck bed at the
same time. They were getting rained on by the time he
turned to the truck cab, with Harley in tow.

Strange. She'd never thought anything in her life could
make fodder for lyrics for of a country and western song.
But last night there'd been the guy, the sky, the truck, and
the dog. It didn't get much more Texas than that. No longnecks needed.

She looked around her apartment, overloaded with
items from Flawless. She needed to find a place for her
vendors' meeting. Churches and community centers usually had space for rent. And then she needed to hit Costco
for lots of plastic bins in which to store things until then.

It was in the papers. And all over the local news channels.
He'd bought the paper, which he rarely did, and recorded
all the local channels at the same time to make certain he
didn't miss a single word about Noah Glover being arrested. This was better than the Cowboys winning the
Super Bowl. This was payback. It felt better than sex.

Now he knew why Noah hadn't died in the fire. He
hadn't fucked up after all. Pure bad luck had screwed up
his plan. And that hot chick.

There it was in print. The owner of the women's boutique Flawless had been in her store and heard something
that prompted her to call 911.

Carly Harrington-Reese. She had not only been on the
premises that night, she'd saved Glover's life.

He'd read all about her online this morning. Looked
at her nasty pics again too. He remembered pilfering
the catalogues of scantily clad women that had come in

the mail for his mom when he was in junior high. Those women striking provocative poses were the closest thing to porn he could get his hands on. Whacking off to them was his first real thrill.

Carly could have and probably had had any man she ever wanted. Famous men. Actors and shit. But it was well known that uptown women liked to go slumming. Glover must have been fucking her crossways. That's why they were sneaking around together.

But Glover had been eliminated.

He sat back with a silly grin on his face, flicking his lighter up and closed, entranced by the flame.

Carly must be a total freak, like the women in the porn he preferred. Darlene could never be like that. For all her love of liquor and a little weed, she stopped him whenever he wanted to try something different. Said she wasn't no whore.

He'd bet Carly slept in satin sheets.

He was getting a hard-on. But not now. Now he had to be cool. But soon, *fire*.

CHAPTER TWENTY-FOUR

"I can salvage most of the feather headbands and collars." Joi Caruthers had spread out her feather creations on one of the newspaper-covered banquet tables set up in the church basement. "They'll need to be refluffed and re-strung on dry leather."

Carly looked up from where she was seated at the table, her fingers posed over her laptop keyboard. "How soon can you deliver two dozen?"

"Let's see." Joi nervously pushed a long strip of straight dirty-blonde hair back from her plump pleasant face. "I'm busy with an order for a dance troop over in Dallas. But Spirit and her friends are about to be on spring break. I could maybe get them to help."

"That would be great. I'll try to think of some way to reward them if they do a good fast job." Carly smiled encouragingly at her client. "Thank you, Joi."

Joi was very talented but she was also painfully shy. It wasn't just the wheelchair that confined her spirit. Something long ago had stamped "damaged goods" on her features. A single mother, she made and sold whatever she could think of to keep a trailer around her and her thirteen-year-old daughter, Spirit.

Carly tapped down the empathy welling up. Joi didn't need sympathy. She needed a livelihood.

Carly glanced over to where several of the other women who'd made it to the meeting were still sorting and gathering their crafts from the plastic bins. Most of them had never met. So far, the meeting wasn't going well. They seemed uncertain of why they were there, tentative, and wary of one another. Pots of coffee and mounds of sugary donuts hadn't made a dent in the frosty atmosphere. Her artists weren't gelling.

Two women kept glancing at Carly as they rummaged and murmured back and forth. Those sounds weren't encouraging. So far, only eight of the fifteen craft persons who'd said they could make it had arrived. If anyone else came, they'd be almost an hour late.

Footsteps and raucous laughter sounded in the hall a few seconds before the double doors to the church basement were shoved open. Through them came five young women dressed in painted-on leggings or butt-skimming shorts, hair in various lengths and shades and architectural shapes, and enough jewelry to choke a zoo's worth of elephants. They were dressed for maximum effect and trailing lots of attitude. Indija had arrived, entourage in tow.

Carly sighed and stood up as they approached. She recognized insecurity masquerading as overwhelming force. She just wasn't certain how to defuse either. If the look on Indija's face was any indication, that might not be possible.

Carly didn't get to speak before Indija interrupted, her black eyes bright with mischief. "What you got going on here? I thought you were running a business." She flicked her gaze around the room to include everyone. "Looks like a rummage sale up in here."

Carly sighed. Indija was throwing shade. "Glad you're here, Indija." *Sort of.*

"This is Kamiska." Indija pointed a stiletto-like gold fingernail at the young woman to her right. "She's at the art institute, too. Designs clothes and does nail art."

Kamiska held up a hand of manicured nails. They were stunning, a French manicure using black polish with silver tips. Then she held up her other hand where the colors had been reversed. "Can't sell that in your shop."

"But it's gorgeous work," Carly answered, impressed. "Do you work in a salon? I'd love to come by."

Kamiska rolled a shoulder in irritation. "I only do custom work."

Indija took the moment to move in closer to Joi, as if sensing a weakness. Carly held her position but readied herself to stop a bully.

Indija gazed over Joi's shoulder. "That's pretty." She pointed at a feather necklace. "But can you do something street?"

Joi looked from Indija to Carly, her expression puzzled. 'I'm not sure what you mean?"

"This is faux Native American rip-off Boho chic. Pretty but weak."

Joi jerked as if she'd been struck, but Indija didn't seem to notice. She went on speaking.

"But you got potential." Indija grabbed up a necklace to which long iridescent black and purple feathers had been attached, creating a fringelike bib. "You made this?"

Joi nodded but pushed deeper into her chair as if expecting another assault.

Indija held it up and studied it. "Reminds me of grackle feathers. Those rackety birds are everywhere you look in the summer. Loud, rude, struttin' around in parking lots and people's yards like they own it all. Crap that white mess all over your car and don't care. That's *street*."

Joi smiled tentatively. "So my necklace is street?"

"Not yet. But watch this."

Indija opened the necklace, but instead of putting it around her neck, she whipped it behind her and pulled it around her waist so that the feathers trailed down over her skimpy shorts. She began strutting around, the bounce of her rear making the feathers dance with her movements.

The other artists who'd come closer to watch the exchange laughed and clapped. Indija's friends were more vocal.

"Now I know that's right."

"That's so sexy."

Indija struck a pose near Joi. "You got to sell your merchandise. Pretty isn't enough. I'd name your line 'Tail Feathers.' This baby should be 'Street Grackle.'"

"Wait 'til I hit the club wearing one of those." Kamiska stood up and shook her generous behind. "Talk about shaking a tail feather. I'll need an extra large, all right?"

Another of Indija's girl pack stepped up. "Could you do a necklace—Oh! I know what you should call them. *Butt*laces. I want a buttlace made of blue jay feathers. Blue jays are the original gangsters at my mother's bird feeders. Definitely street."

Joi looked stricken. "I'm sorry but I can't do blue jay feathers. They're protected under the Migratory Bird Treaty Act. So are cardinals and grackles and almost every other local bird, except mallard ducks. Even if I found the feathers, I'd be in trouble if I used or tried to sell them."

Indija frowned at Joi. "Then where do you get your feathers?"

Joi paled at the sound of Indija's sharp tone. "I buy legally on line, when I can afford it. Most times, I search them out. My uncle Bernie and his friends raise domesticated chickens for show at stock shows. Their feathers are legal. Some have gorgeous plumage." She pointed to the necklace Indija still wore around her waist. "Those are from his Black Breasted Red Phoenix Rooster. Of course, I got to clean them good. Birds carry parasites such as mites and lice and diseases, too."

"Eeek!" Kamiska dropped the necklace she'd been admiring and stepped back.

"It's okay. I work them real good. First with mothballs and then soak them in a fifty/fifty mixture of Isopropyl alcohol and hydrogen peroxide. Then I wash and dry them with a hair dryer."

"Girl, your face is pink. Bet that's the most words you spoke all week." Indija offered her a small smile as Joi went scarlet.

"My granddaddy raises pheasants for restaurants over by Sherman." One of the women who'd collected her batik purses approached Joi. "I could get you feathers."

"Me too." Kamiska leaned down next to Joi. "My cousin volunteers part-time in the bird area at the zoo. She's always bringing home something weird, an ostrich or a parrot feather. She says they molt. Anyway, if you could get my buttlace ready by Saturday, I'll supply you regularly with all sorts of exotic feathers."

Joi beamed. "I'll have to check on which ones I can legally own. But that would be nice."

Carly sat back with a big smile as she listened to her artists toss around other ideas for Joi's next collection.

One hour, two empty coffee urns, and several empty donuts boxes later, there were no strangers among the group of local artists. They were bartering and sharing expertise. Even better, three women had volunteered to help Carly repaint and paper Flawless.

Carly caught up with Indija as she was about to leave. "Got a minute?"

Indija looked at her friends. "Hit you later."

When they were alone, Carly put on her all-business

face. "You've got a rare creative gift, Indija. You look at one thing and see the possibilities of turning it into something else. But do you have to jackhammer your ideas into people?"

Indija rolled her eyes. "Made them listen."

"Perhaps. I'd like to offer you a job, as my creative assistant." Carly held up a hand. "But I'm not convinced you can handle it."

"What do you mean? I just gave a person work. That Joi person was about to bolt and never come back."

"You intimidated her. And, for the record, you expanded Joi's collection, not changed it. That's the kind of imaginative thinking I can use from a creative director. But if you work for me, you'll have to work with every personality type. Your job would be to help keep Flawless's offerings unique by challenging our artists to continually be better than they already are."

"I can do that."

"But will they let you? You know how you feel when someone disses your work?" The face Indija made said it all. "Pull that feeling out before you sit down at the table with whomever you're working with from now on."

Indija shrugged carelessly, but Carly could see her already thinking of things she might do. "Anything else?"

"Yes. You can't be late. Ever. I don't do diva. Been one and am so over it. If you're late even one time, I'll find someone else."

Indija's mouth twisted. "You said my talent is rare."

"Not rare enough for me to deal with cheap grief from you. Don't test me. I don't want to lose you. And trust me, you don't want to lose me. Meet me at Flawless at nine a.m. tomorrow."

Indija struck an impatient pose. "You really save a man from a fire?"

Carly folded her arms and cocked a hip, giving attitude

to attitude. "I really did. Is there anything else important you want to talk about?"

"How much I get paid?"

"Let's see what you can do."

Carly climbed the stairs to her apartment feeling energized by the morning. Things were back on track with Flawless. It would be weeks, maybe more than a month, before she could reschedule the grand opening. But there seemed a future now, one stronger for the interaction of the women she was trying to help. She should have remembered sooner. Better to teach a person to fish than simply bring them fish.

"Hey there, Ms. Reese. Just the person I want to talk to."

Carly jolted to a halt with her foot on the top stair. Standing by her door was the CowTown Fire and Water Disaster guy. He wore his usual coveralls, and his cap, twisted around backward, covered his dark blond hair. "Cody, what are you doing here?"

"I come to talk to you. About some business," he added as she continued to frown. "You got a minute? Because I'd surely like to get busy."

"Get busy on what?"

He made a gun with his hand, forefinger pointed at his head, and made a loud *bang* sound as he dropped his thumb like a hammer. "I got so many ideas going in my head I forget to start at the beginning sometime. I was chatting with Mr. Wise earlier and he tells me you've decided to redo your boutique on Magnolia, after all."

"Yes. But I don't see what that has to do with your company."

He held his grin. Today his skin looked rougher, or maybe it was that his face was flushed. He certainly seemed agitated. "I just come to tell you I'm available for any kind of jobs and installations you might need in getting your place fixed up again. Besides this day job, I'm quite a handy man. Ask Mr. Wise. I done all kinds of jobs for him." He pointed to her door. "Why don't we step inside to discuss it?"

"How did you learn my address, Mr. Cody?"

"Didn't I say? Mr. Wise give it to me."

Carly doubted that. When she'd leased the space for Flawless, she was still living at her Aunt Fredda's. But like the reporters that had flocked around, he found out somehow. But she didn't like the idea of being accosted at her front door.

She lifted her chin. "We'll have to talk another time. I have a lot of things to do today. Drop by Flawless after ten a.m. tomorrow. We'll be assessing the damage."

She saw his lids flutter down, as if he didn't want her to look directly into his gaze. "You're right. I should have waited. But to be honest, I just want your business so bad. You see, I read all about you in the papers. You're famous."

His fanboy grin annoyed her. "Not anymore."

"I mean, a real celebrity." He didn't seem to know when he was being shut down. "First you're a supermodel and now you saved a man's life. I guess that makes you practically a superheroine, too. Who knows what you might do next? Make a movie, maybe? You sure are pretty enough."

"That's very flattering." She reached for her phone and pulled it out.

"Now, now, I don't talk to flatter a woman like you. I meant every word."

"Thank you. But I'm pretty much just living my life like the next person these days."

"That's what I was thinking. The day we met, you didn't say a thing about saving a man's life. And it was just hours after. Most folk would have been bragging up a storm about what they'd done. But not you. I guess extraordinary things happen to a person like you every day. Too bad the fella you saved didn't care if he lived."

"That's not been proven, Mr. Cody." Carly heard the chill in her voice but, really, this man had no business here. "How did you get up to my floor?"

"One of your neighbors was kind enough to let me through the security gate. Saw me standing there waiting. Guess he took one look at my van and attire, and figured I'd be pretty easy to pick out if something wasn't on the up and up."

The fact that he had a ready answer annoyed Carly. "Like I said, another time."

He took a step forward. "I won't take above half a minute of your time."

"Mr. Cody—"

"Uh-oh. I don't want to make you mad." He began backing away. "Not my intention at all. I'm just so damned impressed. I don't suppose you'd let me take you out to dinner, just to show how much I admire you."

"I don't date strangers."

"*Hoo-whee*. That look of yours just about froze my privates off. Must be another of your supermodel superpowers. I can see how you might need it. Looking so beautiful and all. You must get hit on more than a nail in a hammer factory."

Carly's hauteur expression collapsed into a smile. "Really, Cody, you're too much."

He grinned right back at her. "Now see. I made you smile. That just makes my day. I can go back to work a happy man."

Carly relented. Maybe she was being needlessly rude. "What sort of side work do you do?"

"Almost anything. Electrical, ductwork, paneling, insulation, flooring. You name it. I can even put in a security system for you. I did that for Mr. Wise."

That caught her attention. "You put in the cameras in the parking lot at Magnolia?"

"I did. And over at some of the other Wise properties."

"By yourself?"

"It's not rocket science. Why don't we make a list of what you need and I'll give you a good deal? A cut-rate deal for the heroine of the hour. Seems like the least I can do."

Carly glanced at her phone for the time, mostly as a reason to offer an excuse. "I'm sorry, but I'm expecting a business appointment to arrive in ten minutes."

"My dinner invitation still stands. I'll take you anywhere you want to go. How about Bonnell's? The chef's been on the Food Network and everything."

"Thank you, but no."

"Okay. Then at least meet me for a drink after your meeting. Say five o'clock? Six? Seven?" He kept adding times as she shook her head.

Carly took a breath. She was tempted to talk to him, if only to learn more about the things Cody did for Mr. Wise, like those cameras. Mr. Wise had said only he and the person who installed his cameras knew they didn't work. Maybe Cody had talked to someone about that job, someone who wanted to know more than he should.

"I can spare thirty minutes after seven o'clock." She thought fast of a place close by where there wouldn't be a menu to slow them down. "Do you know The Usual?"

"The usual what?"

"It's the name of a bar on Magnolia, not far from Flawless."

"That'll do. You can give me directions when I pick you up."

"Use your GPS. I'll meet you there. It's not a date. I'll have only have thirty minutes to give you, Cody."

He grinned. "Yes, ma'am. Best thirty minutes of my year so far, guaranteed."

Even as she watched him leave, she had the nagging suspicion that she'd made a mistake in encouraging him. Despite his *aw shucks* act, he didn't seem like the type of man who would politely take no for an answer. Maybe she could ask Jarius to drop by the bar at seven thirty, just to give her an out.

"Don't be a wuss, Carly. You've dealt with rock stars." Smiling at a particularly sticky memory, she turned and unlocked her door.

At the very least she might be able to pick up a bit of information from Cody that could help Noah. Maybe Cody knew someone who was a firefighter. Noah said the fires he'd been accused of setting were started by a professional who knew how not to leave personal evidence.

The thought of Noah made her stomach feel funny. The intensity of the man completely destroyed her usually cool facade. He didn't do calculated, or cunning. He was out there, all relevant emotions present when properly motivated. They didn't have sex. They burned each other's guard walls to the ground. What was left was potent, precious, and scary as hell.

She was feeling again. Feeling more than ever before. Arnaud had been affectionate but aloof. Love for him had been a sensory pleasure, like a good wine, or a good high. Noah was a boots-on-the-ground, ready-for-action male. He didn't pretend about what he wanted. And he gave back in full, stunningly hard pleasure.

There weren't words for that. It was rare, but it was real. She knew that now. And wanted more. But she couldn't depend on it. Not until Noah was free to make his own feelings known.

"You fell for a cowboy, Carly. Who would have guessed?"

She put her things down and looked around her apartment. Absent the stacks of boxes she carted to the church, it looked like home. But suddenly, that wasn't enough. She needed to do something. Anything. She hadn't been able to do a thing for Noah since he was arrested. The suspense of not knowing what was going to happen next was killing her. So she was going to have a drink with a restoration guy.

But she wasn't going to take any chances. She pulled out her phone and called Wise. Two minutes later she felt a little better. Wise confirmed that Cody had done work for him and gave the younger man a glowing endorsement. At least now she felt better meeting a practical stranger. After all, it was just for a drink in a public place.

CHAPTER TWENTY-FIVE

"Beer run. Your turn." Mike Wayne leaned back out of the refrigerator and waved the last bottle of Blue Moon at Noah, who sat at the kitchen table.

Mike had showed up the evening after Noah made bail, and announced he was spending his four days off with Noah. Noah suspected that Durvan had sent him to keep tabs on his suspect. But Noah was too glad to have company of any kind to turn him down. It was a better offer than dealing with Sandra, who'd offered to do the same. Mike, at least, wouldn't want to "talk about it."

Mike had bunked out on the sleeper sofa in the TV room, refusing to mess up a bedroom. He was living out of a duffle bag, neat as the Marine he'd once been.

They'd watched every kind of sport over the last three days while the defense attorney that Sandra had found for Noah went to work, trying to find out what the district attorney had in mind for additional charges. So far, the district attorney's office was being very closed mouth. Not a good sign.

"You want steak or barbecue tonight?"

Noah looked up from the computer he'd borrowed from his sister. To keep from going stir crazy, he'd been making lists and checking every detail that ran through his mind about the night of the fire. "I don't care what we eat. As long as it's hot and there's plenty of it. You do the beer run."

Mike hung his hands over the back of a kitchen chair. "The press hasn't been around all day. Why don't you hit the shower and we'll go out for a change?"

Noah scratched his three-day-old growth of beard. "You trying to tell me I stink?"

"Okay. You stink. Going to seed before my eyes. Have some pride, dude. They come to arrest your ass again, you don't want to look like the Unabomber in your photo shots."

Gallows humor. They'd traded a lot in that the past few days. One way to manage the eight-hundred-pound gorilla they weren't discussing.

The doorbell rang. Harley, who'd been dozing at Noah's feet, sat up and barked, but he didn't move away from his handler's side.

"I'll get it, sweetheart." Mike's voice had gone falsetto, mimicking a housewife. He'd been running interference of every kind for Noah—answering the door, answering the phone, picking up take-out, or ordering meals to be delivered. Mike could veg out better than anybody he'd ever known.

Mike was back within a minute with a lumpy padded envelop. "Special delivery. Had to sign for it. You expecting something?"

"No." Noah took the package. The return address was for A. Gutierrez, his sister Sandra's private investigator friend.

He tore it open. Inside was a DVD marked: Westside Conservatory Senior Living Center and Well Care Facility security camera.

Noah looked up at Mike, cop face in place. "Are you here as my friend or as Durvan's watchdog?"

Mike laughed. "I'm offended by the question."

Noah's expression didn't change. "Because if you're here in an official capacity, I have to ask you to leave the room."

Mike crossed his beefy arms, a frown furrowing his brow. "If I'm here as a friend?"

"Then I could use another pair of eyes."

Mike considered Noah's request, then gave his head a slight shake. "I was tired of earning a regular paycheck anyway."

As Noah shoved the disc into the computer, Mike pulled up a chair.

The beginning of the footage was the same that Noah had been shown by Durvan during his interrogation. Noah pointed near the top of the screen. "Watch for a truck to pull up here. It'll be in the parking lot that's on the next block."

After two minutes a truck came into view, the same uneven light and slightly out-of-focus images seen from a distance.

"That's your truck?"

Noah nodded. "Looks like it. Watch closely."

The truck pulled up before the back of a building, nose-in so that the driver's door faced the camera. The security lights in the parking lot came on, giving them a better view than expected. Still, the distance made the images indistinct. A man got out on the driver's side and opened the rear door. Out hopped a German Shepherd, his actions indicating that he might be barking.

"That's what was bothering me." Noah looked over at Mike. "You ever see me release Harley from the truck without first putting him on a leash?"

Mike shrugged.

Noah refocused on the computer screen. "See that? Harley doesn't want to be leashed by that guy."

"You're going to have to do better than that."

After a moment of struggling, Harley was on the leash and following the man around the front end of the truck where they disappeared into the shadows on the other side. The back door to the store where the fire took place was blocked by the way the truck was parked.

Noah sat forward. "This is where the footage I was shown during interrogation stopped. So this is where things should get interesting."

For a good five minutes the video ran without anything happening but the occasional car driving past on the street between the camera and the faraway parking lot. After a few minutes, the security lights in the parking lot died, leaving the truck little more than a shape in the dark.

Noah wiped a hand down his face. "Damn, I was hoping there'd be more activity around the truck."

"Like what?"

"Hold on." Noah touched the image of his truck. "The interior light didn't come on when the guy got out of the truck on the driver's side, did it?"

"So?"

Noah ran the video back to the place where the man got out. "There's no light inside the cabin with the opening of either door. If someone else is in the truck, we can't tell. I'll bet a month's pay I'm in there passed out on the passenger side."

Mike gave him a strange look. "Dude, admit it. So far, all you've got on video is a big yawn." He yawned for emphasis. "I'm calling in two rib dinner orders at The Railhead."

"Wait. Look at this." The security lights had come on again, showing a man climbing into the vehicle. This time the man was wearing what looked like coveralls. "What am *I* wearing, and where's Harley? I wouldn't leave Harley behind in a building."

Mike looked down at the dog sprawled at Noah's feet. He'd never seen Harley more than a couple of feet away from his handler at any time. "Maybe you let him in on the other side first. Like you said, we can't tell squat about what's happening on the other side."

Noah paused the video. "Harley and I have a routine. We exit and enter the same way, every time. Driver's side, both of us. And what about the coveralls? That's not me, Mike."

"Then who is it?"

"That's the million-dollar question." Noah hit Play. "I need you to pay close attention for the next twenty minutes. It's vital that you see this for yourself."

Mike sighed and subsided into his chair. "You're buying the beer plus two pounds of ribs and a pound of sliced brisket."

The truck left the lot.

After six more minutes of boring footage, a car pulled up near where the truck had parked, and a woman got out. In the glare of the activated security lights she had no distinct features. But it was plain to see she was young and slim, wearing jeans, heels, and a skintight top.

Mike leaned forward. "Now that's the first interesting thing on here."

Noah didn't respond, just watched intently as Carly unlocked the back door to Flawless. Her timeline said she'd been in her store less than five minutes the first time she thought she heard a dog and gone out the front door to check. That they couldn't see on this footage. Ten minutes more passed before she exited the rear door of Flawless.

She was carrying an armload of things to her car. They saw her pause and turn her head, as if listening. Then she put her things in the car and closed it. She stood there a few more seconds then crossed back toward the building into the shadowy area where the door to the next-door store was, where Noah lay unconscious inside.

"Did you see that?"

Mike yawned and pulled out his phone to place an order. "Man, I haven't seen anything interesting, besides the woman, in forever."

"Exactly. If I drove the truck off to park it somewhere else, how did I get back in the building for Carly to find me?"

It took Mike three seconds to process Noah's words. Then he leaned forward. "Let me order some food before I die. Then I need you to play that part again. Starting from when the truck leaves."

Noah played that section three more times, both men watching for images of a shadow or silhouette that could be a figure returning. There weren't any.

Mike shook his head. "Durvan showed the unit the first part of the video before your arrest. He didn't say anything about this."

"That's because he can't place me in the building and still explain the truck being driven away. He's got loose ends."

"That's a hell of a loose end."

The two men stared at each other.

Finally, Mike sprawled back in his chair, its front two feet rising off the floor. "I guess I never did think you did it. I just couldn't figure out another way it could have happened."

Noah nodded. Durvan must be sweating bullets over his not-so-neatly tied-up case. "You want to talk about the case now?" They'd agreed the first day that all subjects pertaining to Noah's arrest were off limits.

"Get in my truck. You can explain your theory while we pick up our food."

"What's with you and food? You got a tapeworm?"

"It takes fuel to keep this body in prime condition. Speaking of bodies, you can buy me a car air freshener. Man, you need to hit the shower before someone calls the board of health."

Noah grinned. "Harley goes too."

Mike glanced down at Harley, who had perked up at "food." "Scratch the air freshener. You're paying for my truck to get detailed this weekend. Can't have dog hair all over my date."

As they drove to The Railhead, Noah explained what seemed the most likely scenario. "The light in the truck cab was out for a reason. No one would be able to easily identify who was driving, and if there was a passenger. The video doesn't show the passenger side of the truck. I could have been out cold when the arsonist dragged me into that store. Everything to start the fire must have already been in place. He just needed to add the body. He probably put on the coveralls to keep from leaving incriminating evidence. The bastard's smart."

Mike nodded. "Yeah, man. It makes a kind of sense. But who is it?"

"That's how you help me. Who do you remember being at The Collective Brewing Project that night? Maybe not at the party but in the place. Other firefighters. Police. Friends. Anyone."

Mike rubbed the back of his neck. "I didn't stay long. I had to work the next day, like you. There was that one dude I ran into on my way out. John Wayne somebody."

"You mean J.W.?"

"Maybe. He's a wannabe firefighter. Plays volunteer over in Edgecliff Village."

"Yeah. That's him. Did you talk to him?"

"No. Guys like him chap my ass. Thinking they're somehow better than us professionals because they operate without all our equipment or specialty training. They have to improvise. Think on their feet." Mike was making quotation marks with his fingers. "But who do they call when it gets too hot for amateur night?"

"If J.W. wasn't at the party, what was he doing at that bar?"

"Trying to talk to you." Mike pulled into the drive-thru lane of the BBQ place. "At least, he asked me if you'd come in yet."

Noah had gone still. Harley, smelling the rise in his handler's pheromones, snuggled his big head in closer to Noah's, rubbing his snout along Noah's jaw. "You might have told me sooner that someone was looking for me that night."

Mike spared him a quick glance. "We're talking about J.W. Why would he want to burn you up, man?"

Noah shrugged. "I'm clutching at straws. You got any other candidates?"

"No."

"Me either." That didn't mean Noah was ready to jump to the conclusion that because he'd been looking for Noah that meant J.W. was the person who wanted him dead. First of all, they were on friendly terms. Besides, there was no motive.

Even so, the cop in him reverted to investigative procedure. When one didn't have a suspect, one didn't rule out anyone.

Noah cycled through what he knew about J.W. They'd been together when J.W. was taking some classes on firefighting that Noah had taught two years ago. He'd made an effort to be friendly whenever they bumped into each other after that. Which, now that he thought of it, was fairly often. The guy liked to hang out with professionals because he had dreams of being a professional firefighter. Everyone who ever talked to J.W. knew that.

That's why Noah had made the call a couple of months back after J.W. missed making the Fort Worth Fire Department newest class of recruits. He thought the turndown might go easier coming from an acquaintance. He'd even made suggestions about trying his luck in a smaller metropolitan area. Even offered to write the guy a recommendation. Thinking of J.W. as his enemy didn't make sense. Especially in light of the other evidence.

"You still got to explain those other fires." Mike looked over at Noah as he passed him their order. Obviously, Mike was spooky good at reading his mind.

Noah shrugged, drawing in the deep mouth-watering smells of warm slow-cooked beef and ribs wafting from the bag. "Without the suicide, the rest becomes circumstantial, at best. I need to talk to Durvan."

Mike snorted. "You start trying to tear his case apart, Durvan's going to double down on you."

Noah nodded. "I would, too. He's close. But I'm going to snatch my freedom out of the gap in his case. Which means we need to talk. Tonight."

Mike smiled. "This could get interesting. Let me make the call to set it up."

Noah nodded.

One minute later Mike disconnected. "Durvan says if you want to come in and make a statement tomorrow morning, he'll be in the office. Bring your A game."

Noah nodded, feeling the tiniest bit of light at the end of his tunnel. "Guess I'll take that shower after all."

CHAPTER TWENTY-SIX

Carly was running late, half-hoping Cody had not been able to find the place or been scared away. Not that meeting Cody anywhere else was a better idea. More than likely she was just clutching at straws in order to feel that she was doing something, anything, to help Noah. That thought made her finally push open the door to the bar.

The Usual was the kind of place a stranger might pass by and never notice. The building showed Magnolia Avenue a windowless pale-brick front with a single small door set in the middle. It had an industrial speakeasy vibe and a modern hipster atmosphere with handcrafted cocktails.

She let her gaze roam the softly lit open area. The bar to the right was cluttered with upscale professionals and artsy regulars who liked to watch the bartenders create classic and spur-of-the-moment requests. Her focus moved quickly from there to the sparsely arranged tables and chairs and on to cozy sitting nooks with sofas or comfy chairs. Radiohead played on the jukebox. It took a few seconds for her to realize she was already staring at the man she'd come to meet.

Cody sat at a table near the back, a beer can in hand. He'd changed from coveralls into a plaid shirt and jeans. Even from a distance she could see colorful tats on his forearms where he'd rolled his sleeves back to the elbow. His hair, uncovered for a change, had been washed and blow-dried and fell in a straight flop above one eye. He'd made an effort, which she appreciated. But it wasn't going to do him any good.

She moved toward his table, glad she'd dressed down in baggy jeans and an oversized top that enveloped her figure. No need to give him the wrong impression. She'd even covered her hair with a fedora and wore sunglasses, in hopes of not being recognized. For the past few days local media had been showing pictures from her modeling days.

"I see you found a drink."

Cody held up the can. "Something they call imperial lager. It's not Bud but it's beer."

She noticed he didn't stand up. But when she reached to pull out a chair, he was up in flash. "Let me. My mamma taught me better than that."

The waitress made her way over with a menu. Carly shook her head. "I'm sorry but I have less time than I thought."

"One drink?" Cody looked hurt. Not a good way to get information from him.

"Okay." She glanced down. "I'll have a Don't Ask, Don't Tell."

Cody scrunched up his face. "What the heck is that?"

"Vodka and ginger beer and a few other things." The waitress smiled at Cody before turning away.

"I made a short list." Carly pulled a notepad from the depths of her purse. "Basically, I need new insulation and the wall boards replaced. Wiring checked for safety, and new fixtures hung. The painted concrete floor seems to have survived. Other things, like the painting and wall-papering, I did myself the first time. I plan to do that part again, with the help of some friends, once the basics are done. How much of the basics list do you think is something you can do?"

"Let's see." Cody leaned forward, managing to touch her hands with his fingertips. She casually pulled her hand away reaching up to adjust an earring. "It seems like a lot of work for one man. Especially since I have a very short timetable. I'm getting a bid from the company that did the original interior work."

Cody looked over the list then leaned back and gave her a grin that didn't quite reach his pale gray eyes. "You don't think I'm capable."

"I think, Cody, that one man, however talented, has only so much time to give to a side job like this. You do have a day job."

He sipped his beer from the can, ignoring the frosty lager glass sitting before him. "I work the hours I want. Besides, I can get help if I need it."

"Other CowTown people?" Carly looked over as the next jukebox choice began. Mile Davis's "So What" from *Kind of Blue*. The waitress set her drink down.

"No. I'll get help from my other job. Some folk like to call my second job more of a hobby." His eyes narrowed. "What would you think, I wonder?"

Carly picked up the martini glass. "What sort of job is it Cody?"

Cody leaned forward suddenly, eyes bright. "Were you scared, being caught up in that fire?"

Her cocktail splashed over the rim onto her hand.

"Oh, did I upset you?" Cody pushed a couple of cocktail napkins at her.

"Yes, you did." Carly put her glass down and dabbed at the wet spot on the table, her drink untasted. "Why would you bring that up?"

"Because I know something about being in fires. In fact, I know a lot about firefighting in general. That guy you saved, the one trying to kill himself? He used to be a firefighter. But I guess he lost his nerve, went into investigation. Decided instead to chase people who start them because he couldn't take the heat."

Carly reached for her glass and took a tiny sip. She didn't want to discuss Noah with anyone. "So you're a Fort Worth firefighter, too?"

Something flashed in those gray eyes, a shrewdness that Cody had totally seemed to lack in their previous encounters. "I work for the Edgecliff Village Volunteer Firefighters." His gaze dared her to tease him about not being a "real" firefighter.

Humor was the last thing on Carly's mind as this new knowledge of Cody sank in. "I know Edgecliff Village is still a separate town within the Fort Worth city limits. Even so, I'm amazed there are still volunteer services within the DFW Metroplex."

"We're a dying breed. White Settlement just went with the Fort Worth department."

Carly chose her words carefully. "Firefighting is a dangerous job."

He watched her for a moment, before leaning forward again. "Yes, Carly, it is. Let me show you how dangerous."

He laid his left arm on the table and shucked his sleeve up to his armpit so that she could see the tattoo there. NO FEAR in rich stenciling. A stylized cross floated above the words. All of it lay in a field of bright red and gold flames. It took her a second to realize that the compelling colorful design had been inked over roughed, damaged skin.

He must have seen the realization dawn in her face, for he nodded and pulled down his sleeve. "Struck by burning debris while I was serving in the navy as a Damage Controlman. We're responsible for emergency, fire, and rescue. Ventilation system caught fire on board. First in, it almost cost me my sorry ass. Second-degree burns. "He patted his arm. "After that, nothing scares me."

Nothing scares me. The words formed a mental picture in Carly's head. Cody knew all about fires, how to fight them, and also how they started. Was it possible?

"You must know Noah Glover, since you're a fire-fighter too?"

"We've met." The reserve in his voice put Carly on edge. "You know him well?"

She shook her head and reached for her drink to have something to do besides stare at the man across from her. "Never saw him before the fire."

"Too bad he's not the man everyone thought he was."

"Oh?" Carly glanced across the table, trying to reconcile the Cody she thought she knew with the details she was learning about the man sitting across from her.

"Noah, now, he was everybody's fair-haired boy these last few years. Making arson investigator so young. Teaching classes over at Tarrant County College Fire Service Training Center. But being special can become a burden, I suppose." He grinned suddenly. It made him appear older and more worldly. "Folk like me will never have that problem."

"Oh, I don't know." Carly toyed with the base of her stem glass, more troubled than she wanted to admit to herself. "Tell me about the last fire you fought."

His eyes narrowed. "You don't want to hear about that."

"I do. I admire anyone who does what you do."

He reared back and signaled for another beer. "All right. About a week ago I was out . . ."

Carly heard him talking, but the words weren't getting through the tangle of her own thoughts.

Was it possible? Could Cody be the man who'd tried to kill Noah? Surely not. She was building air castles that would collapse under the weight of any kind of sensible reasoning. If Noah and Cody were known to each other, wouldn't Noah have suspected him?

Also, why would Cody go out of his way to make himself known to her if he was the one who started the fire? She was the party who spoiled his plans.

Cody didn't know you were the Good Samaritan until Noah was arrested and the story made the media.

The words sounded so clearly in her thoughts, Carly jerked, thinking she'd spoken them aloud.

"You okay?" Cody reached out and touched her arm. "I guess I've been too frank. I forget some stories aren't for delicate ears."

"It's okay." Carly slipped free of his touch to reach for her drink, but her hand shook.

Cody reached out again, this time patting her hand. "Maybe you better go slow on that drink. You seem a little tipsy."

Carly nodded. "You know, you're right. I shouldn't finish it." She pushed it away. "Anyway, I need to go."

"Not yet. I'll order us some food from Holy Frijoles next door. This place allows food to be brought in since they don't serve it here. Can't have you driving on an empty stomach."

Carly stood up, trying to think. "Maybe you're right. I need to find the Ladies, and then we'll see." She turned and headed for the restrooms without looking back.

She needed to speak with Noah. Now, before Cody left. If she was way off-base, he would tell her.

At the moment, she was pretty sure Cody thought she was every kind of an idiot. Not that it mattered, unless she was right about him.

Suddenly, she really did need the Ladies.

The disappointment of her call going immediately to

Noah's answering service rolled through her middle. Nothing to be done about that.

"Noah. You know who this is." She spoke softly, still inside the toilet stall. "I've got information about a man named Cody. Works for CowTown Fire and Water. He's also a firefighter. Says he knows you. We're here at The Usual. I'll explain why when you call me back. No wait, I'll call you back."

She returned to find the table full of butcher paper on which an assortment of delicious-smelling food could be seen.

Cody popped up from his seat, looking as proud as if he'd made it all. "Look at all I got us. I bought a little of everything."

"It looks good." She sat tentatively. "But I should have told you, I'm a vegetarian."

"See, I know that." He grinned. "That's why I ordered fried squash blossom, and *huarache* with the fried mesa, green or red salsa, onions, potato, cilantro, and queso. No meat. Did I do good?"

Carly stared at the food then looked up at him, her expression cold. "Have you been stalking me, Cody?"

"What kind a question is that?" He looked stunned, glancing around to see if they were drawing attention. Luckily, the tables were far enough apart for them to be eavesdropped on. "I read one little old article about a woman in *People* magazine. It said you were one of them veggie heads."

"I see." Carly willed her pulse to slow. "I appreciate your thoughtfulness. But let me repay you for my portion. I, really, can't eat a thing."

He stared at her, not taking his seat. "I'm really not your type, is that it? Ordinary sum' bitch like me can't measure up, no matter how nice I am."

His statement embarrassed her. "No, that's not it. I told you earlier. I'm very busy."

"Yeah." His thin mouth curved down at the edges as he sat. "You go on then." He picked up the list she'd shown him. "Don't worry. I'll still do your job, and for a fair price too. Unlike you, I don't have a reputation to worry about."

She'd been approached countless times by men who thought she'd date them just to prove that she didn't think she was too good for them. They were disappointed. She was too good for anyone who'd accept a pity date on a dare.

But in Cody's case, she decided to give in, only because she didn't want him to suspect she was on to him. If, in fact, she really was on to anything.

"One bite. The squash blossoms really do look good."

"I ordered you another of them fancy drinks." He pointed to the full glass where her half-drunk one had been.

Alarm zipped up her spine. *Noah was roofied.* By this man?

She smiled, feeling her knees begin to quiver beneath the table, and pushed the drink away. "Oh no. You just accused me of being tipsy. I'm going to eat a bite of food to absorb the alcohol I've already drunk. And then I have to go by to see my aunt."

She pulled out her phone and punched in a number. "Hi. Just making sure you're still expecting me. Yes. No more than thirty minutes. I promise, auntie."

She hung up and grabbed a blossom. *Damn.* Noah hadn't picked up that time either.

She gave Cody ten more minutes and had a second squash blossom before she stood up and laid two twenties on the table. "Got to go. My aunt will be calling if I'm even two minutes late. Thanks for a nice—er, evening." Her voice sounded a little strange in her ears. It must be the strain of making small talk to a man she was beginning to suspect had tried to kill Noah.

"I'll walk you out."

"No, finish your dinner." She lifted both hands in protest. "I'm parked just out back. Come by the store tomorrow with your—um, esti-, your calcu—your costs."

She was relieved that he didn't try to follow her out. Something didn't feel right. She would try Noah as soon as she was locked safely in her car. He might agree to meet her somewhere. At the very least, she'd get to hear the soothing sound of his voice.

"You look a little rocky, lady. You need a ride home?"

Someone was speaking to her. She didn't know who. He stood in the shadows.

She was saying no.

She tasted the word, felt it slide like velvet across her tongue.

But the syllable never emerged as sound.

CHAPTER TWENTY-SEVEN

"You hear something buzzing?"

"Like what?" Noah slid the remains of gristle, fat, and bits of pork rib plus two slices of brisket into Harley's bowl.

Mark patted his pocket. "Not mine. Your phone?"

"Don't think so." Noah reached into his pocket. "Damn." He'd been sequestered in his home so long he'd forgotten to grab his phone when they went for food earlier.

"Sounds like the buzz is coming from the sofa."

While Harley wolfed down the offering as though he hadn't already eaten two generous scoops of dog food for dinner, Noah went into the family room.

Sure enough his phone, stuck down between two cushions, was signaling that he had a message. He pulled it out and looked at it. His heart began knocking uncomfortably against his ribs. There were two messages. Both from Carly.

"Family call?" Mark stood in the doorway with two beers from the six-pack they'd bought on the way home. Very few people had the number to Noah's new pay-as-you-go phone.

Noah looked up. "Yeah. Andy. I need to call him back. Turn on the game. I've still got March Madness brackets in play. I'll just be a minute."

Without waiting to see what Mark would do, he headed down the hall to his bedroom. Harley, feeling particularly fond of his handler tonight, followed, licking Noah's fingers for the final tastes of meat.

Noah punched Carly's number without checking her messages. She could tell him what she'd wanted directly.

The phone rang, and rang. Finally, the answering service came on. He swallowed a curse. "Hey, Carly. You called. I was out. I'm back. Call me. Anytime. As soon as you can. Whenever. Call."

He shook his head when he was done. He sounded like a desperate teenager.

"I don't think that call is in your play book, Glover."

Noah turned around slowly, intimidation in every line of his body. "You were sent to spy on me."

Mark stood in the bedroom door, looking anything but guilty at being caught. "It was suggested that I might be able to keep you from doing something dumbass. Like talking to an eyewitness." He did a chin-up at Noah's phone. "Why is Carly Reese calling you?"

"I don't know. She's not answering."

"Did she leave a message?"

Noah looked down. She had. Two, in fact.

Mark's brow shot up his forehead. "Man, what are you up to?"

"It's personal."

Mark shook his head. "You need deniability if Durvan gets wind of this. I'm staying. I can't hear a thing on her end from here. But I can vouch for what you said."

"Prick." Noah said it without heat.

"That's what friends are for." Mark moved to lean a hip against the dresser, prepared to wait Noah out.

Noah pushed Play.

Noah. You know who this is. I've got information about a man named Cody. Works for CowTown Fire and Water. He's also a firefighter. Says he knows you. We're here at The Usual. I'll explain why when you call me back. No wait, I'll call you back.

"What the hell, man!" Mark had jumped up as if the dresser had bit him in the ass.

Noah knew his expression had given him away. It must have turned murderous. He pressed the Speaker button and hit Play again.

This time it was Mark's face that changed from surprise to concern as they both listened to Carly's message. "Who's Cody?"

"J.W. His full name is John Wayne Cody."

Mark mouthed an obscenity, but Noah was pressing Play for the second message, which they listened to together.

Hi. Just making sure you're still expecting me. Yes. No more than thirty minutes. I promise, auntie.

Mark frowned. "What was that one about? Wrong number?"

"No. Distress call. Carly's in trouble."

Noah's voice was flat, but his heart rate was anything but.

He checked the time and calculated the interval between Carly's two calls. She'd called the first time at 7:21, just minutes after they'd left to pick up barbecue. She'd called the second time ten minutes later. That ten-minute gap made his gut tighten. Something had changed. Her voice in the second message was higher pitched, as if fear were squeezing her vocal cords.

He brushed past Mark. "Your theory about J.W. just grew legs."

"Wait up. How is Carly Reese involved in this mess?"

Noah grabbed his wallet and Harley's leash. "I'll tell you on the way."

"Way where?"

"To Carly's apartment."

Noah went to his kitchen and opened an upper cabinet to pull out his pistol and shoulder holster.

Mark was watching him with hard eyes. "You don't want to do that."

"We're police officers, as well as arson investigators. I have a right to be armed." Noah's voice held a challenge.

"Yeah. But you're angry. Firearms and anger are not a good combination."

"I won't shoot him unless I have no other choice."

"Man." Mark wiped his mouth. "What if Cody's packing?"

"I'm a very good shot." Noah finished strapping on, then bent down and rubbed Harley's head, who whined in excitement. To Harley the gun meant "on the job." "It's okay, boy. We're going for a ride."

He leashed Harley then looked up at Mark. "You coming?"

Mark nodded. "I'm driving. Seeing you like this reminds me why I was a firefighter, not a cop. The fire might kill you, but it doesn't shoot back."

On the way out the door, Noah called Carly again. No answer.

He crushed every negative feeling that tried to crawl up and gain a foothold in his consciousness.

Carly wasn't answering. That's all he knew. She might still be with Cody.

He checked his watch. Eight thirty. Doubtful. She might have gone home. Or, she might have decided to go to her aunt's, for safety's sake. That would explain the second message.

He dialed Fredda Wiley as he opened the back door of Mark's truck to let Harley in. "Hello. Mrs. Wiley. Is Carly with you?"

He hung up thirty seconds later with his ears ringing from the dressing down the judge had given him. It started with "No, she's not." It ended with, "If she wanted to speak with you, Mr. Glover, she'd do so. If you have any decency, you'll leave her alone."

Not at her aunt's.

Noah called Carly several more times on the drive. No answer. He decided against leaving a message, or sending a text. If J.W. was with her, he might have possession of her phone. A text message or the sound of Noah's voice would let him know he and Carly were connected. Perhaps even tip him off that she had called.

They made it to Carly's apartment building in record time. On the way, they had passed The Usual and made a turn through the parking lot. No Mazda.

Noah surveyed the parking lot at Carly's apartment. Carly's Mazda was not there, either. He took a second to absorb that fact. It was still early. She could be at the grocery store or even the mall. But he didn't think so.

Noah opened his door. "Stay here with Harley. If she's at home I'll call you."

"No way." Mark opened his own door. "I'm kind of responsible for you now."

He pressed Carly's intercom button. No answer. Noah keyed in her pass code.

Mark didn't say a word but his eyebrows were eloquent in their surprise.

They ascended the stairs like a pair of SWAT team members.

No answer to Carly's doorbell or knocking.

"You got her key, too?"

Noah ignored Mark as he pulled out his phone.

"She's not answering, man."

Noah punched a number. "Wiley? Noah Glover. Do you know where Carly is? Hear me out. She called me twice tonight, and left messages. Said she had some information for me. I'm at her apartment and she's not here or answering her phone. Do you have a key? Right. I'll wait here, in case she comes home."

Fifteen of the longest minutes of Noah's life passed before the pounding of booted feet could be heard on the stairs and then Jarius Wiley appeared in full patrolman gear. "This better be legit. I'm on break early."

Noah did the introductions. Mark and Jarius shook hands.

Jarius was all business. "Before I open my cousin's door. What's this all about?"

Noah debated. "Carly thinks she has a line on the man who started the fire."

"What?" Jarius shook his head. "No, never mind. I believe you. That girl should have been a cop. Save us all a lot of aggravation." He slipped the key into the lock.

Carly's apartment was dark, as though she'd left in the daylight and not been back. The three men quickly checked the small space. Nothing was out of place. There were no dinner dishes, and her bed hadn't been slept in.

Noah turned toward the front door without a word.

"Where are you going?" Jarius's question went unanswered. Noah was already on the stairs.

Both men hurried after him. Mark double-timed it down the stairwell to grab Noah's arm. "What the fuck, Noah."

Noah swung around, body tensed to fight if necessary. "I'm going to pay a visit to J.W."

"Not on my watch. If Carly's really missing, we need to call Durvan back. This is his case."

Noah held his friend's stare. "If J.W. has Carly—"

"Then you'll need the full authority of law enforcement

in apprehending this guy, whoever he is." Jarius loomed above the two men on the lower steps. "This is my cousin we're talking about. I need details. Now."

Noah looked from Jarius to Mark. "Call Durvan. If Durvan doesn't buy my theory—"

Mark and Jarius exchanged glances before Mark said, "You'll have to make him."

"I'm missing basketball for this?" Durvan was dressed in sweat pants and a zip-neck pullover with a mustard drip down the front. Clearly the three men standing in his living room had interrupted an evening in front of the TV.

Noah moved past Mark. "We've got a line on the man who committed the arson fires."

"I believe the arrest warrant had your name on it."

"Jesus, Durvan. Do you have to be a prick on all levels?"

"All I've heard so far is proof you've been tampering with a witness. I told you to stay away from Ms. Reese."

"I explained to you how we met and why before the arrest." Noah glanced down, expecting to see Harley. But his K9 was still in Mark's truck.

Durvan bulldozed ahead, as if Noah hadn't spoken. "You come here with unsubstantiated allegations about a person no one has reported missing, and I'm supposed to accept your version of what's happened to her? Now if that's all you got to say, I'm done. Show yourselves out."

"What about Carly Reese?"

Durvan turned to Jarius, who'd spoken. "You don't know she's missing, Patrolman Wiley. You have no proof she's not at the movies. Or staying over at a girlfriend's. Hell, she could be out on a date with someone less chancy than Glover. If in forty-eight hours you haven't heard from her, you know what to do."

Noah squared off against Durvan, his chest heaving in anger. "If anything happens to Carly, I'm coming after you."

Durvan glowered at him, not giving an inch as he curled thick fingers into fists. "Take your best shot, Glover. Or get the hell outta my house."

Jarius, a little taller and definitely younger than either man, inserted himself into the testosterone-fueled space between them, one hand on the Taser at his belt. "Back off, Glover. This isn't helping Carly."

Noah never took his gaze off Durvan, his expression still carrying the threat of bodily harm. "I've seen the video, Durvan. *All* of it."

Durvan scowled. "What are you talking about?"

"The security video from the retirement home. I saw a man go in and then come out and drive my truck away. Mark saw it, too. And neither of us saw a man come back in the time before Carly Reese arrived. You know I'm innocent."

"The hell you are. Your confessional text. Your fingerprints. Your WeMo app used by your phone the night of the crime. Fuel from your gas tank used as accelerant. That's probable cause."

Noah's blue gaze was iceberg cold. "Explain how I could be unconscious in that store at the same time I drove my truck away."

Durvan looked annoyed. "Answering that is not my job. That's for the DA's office to ponder. You've been arrested and will shortly be arraigned on several counts of arson and possible homicide. I've done my job. You're going down, Glover."

Noah took a step toward Durvan, pressing against Jarius's unyielding rock-hard frame. "You know I didn't commit this crime. What's your deal? Were you scared you'd be accused of going soft one of your own if you didn't arrest me? Meanwhile, you've handed the real criminal a get-out-of-jail-free card."

Durvan shot him a baleful stare. "Prove it."

"That's what Carly was trying to do tonight."

Noah backed up a step from Jarius, letting his rage out through his teeth. "Though God knows I asked her to stay out of this. She went to see a man named J.W. Cody tonight. Something happened that made her call me twice."

He pulled his phone and played the phone messages for the benefit of Durvan and Jarius.

Jarius was dialing Carly before the second message began. He shook his head after a moment.

Noah looked at Durvan. "She's not answering her phone. Even *you* must find that strange."

Durvan stroked his mustache. "Who is this Cody guy?"

Mark answered to give Noah more breathing room. "Volunteer firefighter with Edgecliff Village."

Durvan nodded slowly. "Yeah. I heard of him. Mouthy. Won a couple of citations? Recently missed making the firefighters' final list of candidates."

Mark nodded. "That's him."

Durvan took a moment to process. In the end he turned his stare on Noah. "Why him?"

"I don't know. Yet. But I will figure it out."

Durvan watched his colleague and protégé for several long seconds. "I still don't know why you came to me."

"That would be my call." Mark looked from Noah to Durvan. "Noah wants to go by Cody's place. I thought we should talk with you about that first."

"Damn straight." He turned his attention to Noah again, fury rising in his eyes. "No way you go anywhere near a potential person of interest's place."

Noah folded his arms, relaxing now that he had Durvan's attention. "I don't need your permission. Cody and I go back a ways. A man's allowed to drop by an acquaintance's home. If Carly's there, I'm taking her out."

"And if she isn't there?"

"He's the last person to see her. I have some questions for him."

Durvan frowned. "If you assault the man, you could ruin your case before it's made."

"Then maybe you better come along as chaperone."

"If you're wrong about this—"

"Yeah. But if I'm right?"

"Two minutes to change. Don't anyone move a damn foot out of this room until I return."

J.W. Cody lived on the outskirts of Edgecliff Village, on Hobart, a street of small one-story houses not much bigger than a double-wide with a carport. The neighborhood was tree-lined and the yards, even in the dark, appeared well kept.

The house with Cody's address turned out to be easy to find. It was overgrown with shrubs and trees, the grass losing the battle with taller sturdier spring weeds determined to stand their ground. There was a truck up on cinderblocks in the drive with a faded For Sale sign on the dashboard. No sign of Cody's company van, or the truck Noah remembered him driving.

Durvan rode with Mark and Noah. Jarius, reluctantly, had had to abandon them for an emergency call on his police radio. He'd left with the words, "You find her or you don't, you call me."

Durvan had agreed that Noah would approach the door on his own. He was the only one with anything close to a plausible reason to come knocking.

Noah checked the time. 9:15. He blew out a breath as

he approached the door. He needed to be loose. He needed to be just dropping by, looking for a mutual friend who said she'd been with Cody earlier. And now couldn't be found. How Cody responded to that would tell him what he needed to know.

The second knock on the door caught the attention of a man walking his Weimaraner on a leash. "He's not home. Haven't seen his truck in two days."

"This is Cody's place, right?"

The man nodded.

Noah stepped back off the porch toward him. "Why are you keeping tabs on him?"

"He owes me twenty dollars." Neighbors, bless them. "You?"

"Yeah. He's got something of mine, too."

The man nodded. "Good luck." He moved on.

Noah walked back to Mark's truck and hopped in. "Drive around the corner. I'm going to double back and check the rear, make sure Cody's not hiding in there."

As they drove around the corner, Noah spotted a gravel city utility easement threading between the backyards of houses facing Hobart and the next street.

"Stop here." He got out with Harley on the leash. His excuse if he was seen—walking Harley.

Durvan pushed his head through the window, looking like a bulldog with a mustache. "Don't do something stupid, Glover."

"Right."

Noah hurried down the gravel lane into the darkness, fairly certain that the easement wouldn't be blocked by debris. Some of the houses had fenced yards. Behind them dogs barked. In one he heard the splash of what sounded like a fountain. He heard TV sets, children, and adults talking. He listened but discounted them as not relevant as he counted houses back to the middle of the block and Cody's residence.

He kept a tight leash on Harley who, in his work harness, knew he was to keep quiet. Bomb dogs were careful by nature. Almost delicate in their actions in sniffing out their targets. No one wanted an excitable dog who might knock over a device, setting off the explosion his or her handler was working to prevent. A positive find meant sitting down. Harley's reaction to a big positive was to lie down, ears pricked forward, as if pointing out the direction.

There was only a three-foot high-cheap wooden fence around the back of Cody's house. A half-hearted attempt to set a boundary. Noah opened the gate and ducked under an over-hanging branch as he moved toward the back door.

He knocked and listened. Nothing. He tried the door. Locked. In the shrouded darkness he couldn't see much. After another knock, he chanced it and opened his phone, letting the meager light play over the door. It wouldn't be hard to force. Breaking and entering. Compared to arson and manslaughter charges, that didn't seem so bad.

He looked down at Harley. "I smell gas. Do you smell gas?"

He was in before he allowed himself to think hard. The kitchen smelled of stale pizza and something much worse. Spoiled eggs? Cabbage?

Harley sneezed twice.

"Yeah. Disgusting." Chances were, Cody hadn't been home in at least three days. Smells like that would have driven all but the sickest jerk-off to do a little cleaning.

Noah held his breath and hurried into the main room. The light of his phone wasn't cutting it. He'd have to take a chance. He found a switch in the hallway and flipped it. There were three rooms off that hall. A bedroom at either end and a bathroom into which he stared. It was clean. He went toward the back bedroom.

There was a double bed made up with a chenille spread. A small floor lamp and a cheap desk with one drawer made of pressed board. Noah opened the drawer with a hand covered with the tail of his shirt.

The drawer was stuffed full of newspaper clippings. Several fell out. They were about Noah. He picked up a few more, uncaring that he was leaving prints now. Every article was about him. Photos of every honor he'd received or stories about when he'd closed an arson case.

He stuffed them back in and pushed the drawer closed.

He and Harley moved quickly to the front room. The blinds were drawn but he knew he was taking a chance opening his phone for light. This time he didn't have to open or touch a thing.

He switched off the light and hurried through the back door, wedging it tightly so it wouldn't be immediately apparent that it had been jimmied.

He forced himself to walk back down the easement. Harley trotted along, wanting a quicker pace too.

Durvan was leaning against the truck, parked at the end of the gravel road. Mark was still behind the wheel.

"He's not here. And there's no sign of Carly having been here either. No signs of a struggle."

Durvan nodded. "We're done."

"Don't think so. You might want to have a look at this."

Durvan looked down at the phone Noah thrust at him. He'd pulled up photos—of photos. Two were shots of Noah and his son out at Fort Woof. Two were of him with Carly, taking in the shadow of her apartment building. In one they were kissing.

Durvan looked up. "What's this about?"

"Those photos are taped over the bed in the front bedroom of Cody's house."

Durvan stared at the pictures again, his squint all but swallowing up his eyes by the time he was done. When he again looked up at Noah, the focused gaze of a hunter on the scent had appeared. "Looks like we got us a new person of interest."

CHAPTER TWENTY-EIGHT

Carly came awake sluggishly. One drink. She'd had one drink she didn't finish because she wanted to get away from—

Jarred by the memory of Cody, her eyes flew open. The world beyond her gaze was black. She blinked several times. Each time her lashes touched and caught briefly against something. Covering. Over her eyes. The sensation carried a memory. She'd once done a photo spread with Arnaud where the models were blindfolded and told to grope around a set filled with designer bags, shoes, and other accessories until they touched something. They were to freeze in positions of surprise, delight, or awe—even though they had no idea what prompted those happy reactions.

But this time there was no groping possible.

Her hands were tied. Behind her back.

She opened her mouth to—No. She couldn't open it.

Her mouth was taped shut.

Pure terror shot through her at the realization. For several seconds she twisted and bucked, trying in a blind panic to disentangle herself from whatever bound her mouth, hands, and feet. All she managed to do was fall off the edge of something onto a hard floor. The fall knocked the breath out of her.

For several seconds her heart pounded in her ears while she was certain she was about to suffocate. Breathing through her nostrils didn't seem to bring in enough oxygen. Tears started behind her blindfold.

She fought the sudden roll of her stomach. If she were sick, she knew she'd choke to death.

You're alive. You're alive, Carly Harrington-Reese. Live. Live. Live.

The words rang clearly if silently in her head. If someone—Cody?—had wanted her dead, she wouldn't be breathing. Someone had left her alive. Her job? Stay alive.

She lay on the floor so long she couldn't guess how much time passed before the roaring in her ears ceased. Gradually her senses came back. She smelled old wood and dust and the faint musk of a dead animal. Beneath her cheek there was a fine silt of grime. She was inside. In a place that hadn't been cleaned in a long time. No point in imagining what shared the darkness with her.

A sneeze wracked her body, bending her in on herself. *Oh please Oh please. No more sneezes.* Her nose would fill and then she'd be choking again.

She held her breath. It worked for hiccups. She didn't know about sneezes. But she had few options. Seconds passed. No more sneezes.

After a few moments more, she realized she wasn't injured. She could flex her fingers. Wiggle her toes. Bend her knees toward her chest. Move her head from side to side. She needed to sit. Sitting would make her feel better than lying there like a sack of bagged potatoes.

It took a little maneuvering. But she'd always been flexible. Once on her back, she was able to do an awkward sit-up. Using her heels, she pushed herself backward until she came up against the object she'd fallen off of. Cold metal pressed across her back and upper arms. Above the metal lay something soft. A quilt? She remembered now the squeal of springs as she'd fallen. A cot frame?

She leaned her head back against it to rest. Figuring out how to untie herself was going to take time. A thrill of fear fluttered through her dodgy stomach. How much time did she have? Was Cody coming back? Or had he abandoned her? Abandonment was preferable. With time, she would get loose. She absolutely believed it.

She ignored the icy feel of the room. It wasn't a cold night. But her fingers tingled from a lack of blood flow in them. She flexed them over and over, forcing blood through her veins. Then she did the same with her feet, then pushed and pulled her knees back and forth on the floor until she was breathing a bit hard. Now what?

Get your mouth clear, Carly.

In her struggle to sit, she realized that whatever was taped over her mouth had become gummy from the heat of her breath. It moved now as she strained to open her mouth. She vaguely remembered hearing something about being able to eat duct tape off one's face. A trick at a party? Or a YouTube video? Her head was full of so many semi-useless things.

She pushed her tongue between her lips and tried to stretch her mouth. It hurt as the tape pulled at the sensitive skin of her lips and cheeks. But doing something felt better than doing nothing. She pulled her mouth wide again and again, each time pushing with her tongue until, little miracle, a side came loose. She tried to rub her mouth on her shoulder but didn't get much friction because of her arms being tied behind her.

Patience, Carly. It's working.

After another minute she had an end in her mouth and

she chewed frantically, until she was panting. She paused to just breathe. She wasn't a mouth breather but not being able to have the alternative had horrified her. After several deep slow breaths, she went back to work, finally chewing it all off.

Uncovering her eyes wasn't going to be that easy. She realized as she worked the tape over her mouth that her eyes were sticky, too. And that when she moved her head, it felt wrapped all the way around by a tight band. No way was duct tape going to come out of her hair with a struggle. That thought revved her anxiety.

"You did good, Carly. Don't crap out on yourself now."

Her voice! The sound of it was the most heartening thing so far. Talking to herself was soothing.

"Think, girl. What next?"

Sounds of a distant vehicle snagged her attention. Not hard to hear in darkness without sounds. Except there were some. Scratchings at the baseboards and just outside that she'd refused to acknowledge. The faint bark of a hound. But not engines. No appliances humming, like a refrigerator. Nothing moving in her space, until now. The truck was coming closer.

The irrational thumping of her heart was as foolish as the hope her blindfold and bindings would suddenly dissolve. Anyone coming here probably wasn't anyone she wanted to see.

The panic she'd been pushing away came back roaring louder than the truck engine sounding much closer. She was at the mercy of whoever drove that truck. Only crazy people abducted other people. Crazy men abducted women for horrible reasons.

The truck engine died. The crunch of footsteps neared, and then boot heels rang on concrete outside. The sound of a key in the lock scraped along her nerve endings. And then somewhere in the distance a door creaked open.

"Sweet baby Jesus, protect me." She couldn't help it, she cringed.

Mistake! He'd fucking let his dick take charge.

He paced the entry of the unfinished house, the heels of his boots clacking on the tile entry, despite the booties he wore.

For a few minutes in the bar, when Carly had looked at him with those big eyes while he was talking about fighting fires, he thought, *I'm in there.* Knew where the night was headed. Women were like moths to a fireman's flame.

The pocket of his hazmat suit crackled as he reached for his phone to check the time. She'd be coming around soon. Unless he dosed her again.

Lots of women liked men with dangerous jobs. They thought it made a man a better lover because all of the testosterone it took to brave the danger. Screw the women who fought fires.

"Penis envy" was how one older firefighter had explained the phenomenon to him when he first came on the job.

Whatever. Women wanting a penis? That was just sicko.

Something changed Carly's mind about him. Was it his burn scars? He was proud of his tats. She'd seemed fascinated.

Maybe he'd talked too much. That story about a burned-up body. Yeah. Should have kept his trap shut over that. Darlene hated those stories. But some women liked gore.

The wariness in Carly's gaze as she tried to disengage hit him like a kick in the gut. Ice pick to his ego, the way she'd tried to leave. Twice.

He hadn't taken a single deep breath until she returned from the restroom. He'd paced just outside the Ladies door until he got a funny look from the waitress.

The food he'd brought with him and hidden underneath the table was cool by the time she returned. But he was prepared. Just a little bit of sugar to help the medicine go down.

He'd already planned their evening. How he'd do it, and where.

Construction in a new neighborhood off Village Parkway, just north of Alta Mesa, had ceased when the builder came up short on money. A single half-built house was the only structure in the two-block area. New construction tucked into the vee between I-35W and I-20 was vulnerable to thieves who could jump off either highway, loot and jump back on, carrying away copper tubing, wiring, paneling, brick, rebar, whatever could sell quickly.

CowTown had sent him to check on the cleanup following damage from thieves. The isolated house met all his requirements. Always on the lookout for potential sources, he'd made a copy of the key, just in case.

He thought of it when Carly agreed to meet him. He'd set up the cot in the house that afternoon. Brought alcohol to wipe anything they touched down. Careful planning.

He'd brought her here to do the dirty and then he planned to have her back in her car and parked in her apartment parking lot before the glory juice wore off.

She'd wake up not knowing what had happened. His word against hers that he was the man who'd fucked her. She deserved it. Saving and then screwing his nemesis.

And who'd believe she'd been raped? A model? Not like she hadn't done it hundreds of times. With hundreds of men. He'd be just one more. But, he'd have the secret knowledge that he'd screwed Glover's bitch and left her without an idea who her assailant was.

But then she'd started talking as he drove her to their destination, rambling on about needing to talk with Glover, how she found the man who'd tried to kill him.

That's when the plan took a radical turn.

"Fucking bitch!" She'd found him out, somehow. She

wouldn't answer any direct questions but she was getting worked up. So he'd had to tie her up, using the electrical tape from his backseat. Getting her in the house was easy after that.

But then he found he couldn't get it up.

He didn't rape her. She was supposed to like it. A comatose woman couldn't get him off.

The heat was rising in his blood, that boiling pressure that needed release. But he wasn't going to make any more mistakes.

So he'd left her while he went somewhere to think. Two hours later, he had squat. Now he was back, to make certain she hadn't been found. But that possibility would disappear with the sunrise.

"Shit!" The universe was against him.

What to do? What to do? He slapped both sides of his head with the palms of his hands as he paced. Got to be a way out.

He took out his lighter and began flicking it, watching the flame with hypnotic fascination. He waved his hand over the flame, feeling the heat curl and sting his palm. Even as he hissed in a breath in reaction, he knew the pain wasn't going to be enough. He needed a fire.

He looked around. The shell of the house he was standing in, with unfinished wallboard and open insulation in the attic, would make a helluva blaze. Light up the night sky like a Roman candle.

But he wasn't a killer.

"Fuck." He pressed his burnt palm into his mouth, licking at the pain like an animal would.

The first death was Glover's fault. Glover deserved to die for making him so enraged he'd forgotten his protocol for setting the fire that accidently killed that poor homeless fart. Always before he'd been meticulous. That was why Glover couldn't catch him. But the game had to end. He pocketed his lighter.

If only Noah had gone up in smoke. A just death for a death.

Carly was a whole different matter. He couldn't kill her. But he couldn't let her go either.

But maybe he could make what happen to her look like Glover's fault.

He paused. If she died in a fire, just like all the others they thought Glover set, in every detail, the police might conclude that Glover had killed the only eyewitness to his suicide attempt.

"Won't work." He spoke aloud to keep from spooking himself. He needed to think it through.

What could she know that would make Glover look guiltier?

Pillow talk. Glover had bragged to her that he'd gotten away with arson before he was arrested. Now she was a liability.

No. He needed something less complicated.

Easier if she simply disappeared. A corpse found in a fire without ID could take weeks, months to identify. Glover might already be convicted.

Of course, the disappearance of a celebrity would draw lots of attention. If and when they did identify her, Glover would naturally be a suspect.

He smiled. He had photos of them together. Taken with his cell phone.

He could send them to the police, anonymously. After a couple of weeks. Nudge the arson investigators. They might not be able to pin it on Glover, but it would look bad that the woman who saved him had disappeared. And they would have picture proof that he'd been witness tampering before his arrest.

Witness fucking, more like. At least he had them kissing.

The great solid mass of indecision resting on his chest began to lift.

He'd needed to cover his own tracks for the evening.

No one had seen him follow her. He very conspicuously went out the front door five minutes after Carly left by the backdoor. He'd thought he might have to follow her home. But there she was, sitting behind the wheel of her car, looking lost. A whisper in the dark. That's all it took. And he was behind her wheel.

He'd have Darleen swear he was home from eight o'clock on. She'd say anything if he got her that new motocross bike she wanted. Like a maggot in her head, she couldn't stop droning on about it every time they watched a competition. He'd be able to buy a hot bike somewhere. He knew a guy.

Alibi done.

Now he just needed to make a few arrangements.

He walked into the family room where he'd left Carly on a folding cot. For a second his heart stopped. She wasn't there.

He whirled around, afraid to use a light of any kind that might alert someone that the vacant house wasn't empty tonight.

He walked the perimeter of the room, letting the light from beyond the windows direct his search.

He found her in the kitchen pantry. She scooted herself into it and tried to close the door.

"Stay away from me." Her voice was coarse with fear.

He wasn't angry. He was grateful she was still there.

Even so, he hauled her back to the cot and dosed her a second time. Taping her mouth shut so that she had to swallow. She fought him, stronger than he would have thought possible for a tied-up drugged-up woman.

When she finally passed out, he stripped her, no interest in sex now that he had a blaze to plan. He gathered up everything, even her jewelry and shoes. Nothing must be left to make identifying the body easier. He carried it all to his truck and backed it away slowly from the house so as not to draw attention. Coming back after he'd parked on another street, he used an old broom to scatter his tire tracks. Then the impressions of his booties in the dirt of the yard. His handyman truck contained everything he'd needed so far.

Carly's Mazda was another matter. He'd driven her here and then taken her Mazda and parked it in her own lot, just after midnight. Come morning, if anyone was looking for her, they'd find her car and think she'd come home sometime during the night.

If he had time, tomorrow, he'd use her passkey to check out her place and return all her clothing, jewelry, even handbag and phone. But for now, his schedule was too tight for those details.

The night was so quiet he could hear himself breathing as he drove out of the neighborhood with his lights off.

Three hours. That's about all the time he'd get to set his plan in motion before the sun rose and the roofie wore off. He didn't want her to suffer. He was not a cruel man. Or a killer. He had no choice.

Three hours to plan the last best fire of his career.

CHAPTER TWENTY-NINE

Four men in the room at the Fire Investigation building stared at the whiteboard containing every detail they could cram on it about the fires Noah had been investigating. After hours of discussion and argument, they had zilch. The tension had already spilled over twice into shouting matches. Now the room hummed with the buzz of overhead lighting and frustration.

Eight hours had passed without any sight or sign of Carly. They were monitoring dispatches about every fire in the county. There'd been a kitchen fire in a bucket-of-chicken type place just after midnight. An apartment blaze started when a child decided to make a volcano for school, without informing her parents first. And a collapsed building on the north side. Nothing, so far, that sounded like the work of an arsonist.

No one dared say what they all wondered. Was Carly Harrington-Reese dead?

"No reason to think so," Durvan had said repeatedly at the beginning of the gathering. "Maybe a hostage situation." The photos in Cody's house had finally convinced

Durvan that Noah could be right about Cody being a suspect in his arson case. "Arson is one thing. But this Cody person has to know there's no going back from murder."

The last time he said it, Noah had slammed out of the room and was gone an hour. The discussion had not come up since he'd returned.

Durvan came into the room now, brisk and businesslike. "Been on the phone with the police. The BOLO out on both Cody's CowTown van and the truck registered in his name haven't yielded anything yet. Neither vehicle has been sighted."

"J.W.'s probably gone to ground until he decides what to do." Jack Burnett, the arson investigator on call overnight, had joined Noah, Mark, and Durvan in their search for Cody.

"Or, he could be halfway to Mexico."

All three men glanced in Noah's direction, but he seemed not to be listening to them.

Mark shook his head as Durvan was about to head over to Noah. "While you were checking that, I called Cody's boss to ask where he's supposed to be working come daylight. He wasn't on emergency night shift tonight. The job Cody's scheduled to work today doesn't start until eight."

It was a little before seven. Sunrise no more than a pale promise on the eastern horizon.

"I'll ask that they have an officer there to see if he shows up."

"There's got to be something we missed in those other fires." Mark smacked his desktop. "We're looking at old clues in light of new information. Why can't we come up with something?"

"There's only so much the FWPD is willing to do for us. Or the DA's office. As far as we know officially, Cody hasn't done a thing wrong. Not being at home isn't a crime. Neither is collecting newspaper articles, or even taking pictures in public places." He glanced in Noah's direction. "Carly isn't missing as much as not accounted for, since we have no proof otherwise."

"Wish we could get a warrant to search J.W.'s house. Those pictures would be enough to make Carly's absence a high priority."

Durvan grimaced. "We can't know about them because it would add breaking and entering to Glover's list of crimes. Move on."

Mark glanced up at the board. "Isn't there always a pattern for an arsonist? That's what you teach us. We know the methods change for arsonists as they get better. But the motivation stays the same. What's motivating Cody?"

Durvan shrugged. "We don't have time right now to go through Cody's life to see if he was having a bad day or can account for his location each of the days we caught those suspect fires."

Mark nodded. "There might even be some we missed. Still listed as undetermined because none of them were high-risk or high-cost fires."

"Until the homeless man." Durvan stroked his mustache. "Could have been an accident. But Cody doesn't strike me as the kind of arsonist to make mistakes. My bet is on it being intentional, but why? It was out of character. What set him off? Good news? Bad news?"

"The need to be recognized? Vanity?"

Noah's voice came from the back of the room where he'd been hunkered down listening and evaluating. But it had taken every bit of his firefighter training to sit and go methodically through this drill.

He was by nature even-tempered, not easily rattled. The best firefighters had the ability to maintain their composure while multitasking, thinking on their feet in the face of life-and-death emergencies. But his skill set was being tested to the max as the hours ticked by and nothing could be found of either Carly or J.W.

Noah gritted his teeth. He had nothing but the faith that Carly was okay to hold this all together. Any other thought wasn't tolerable. The worst-case scenario seldom occurred. If and when it did, there'd be time enough to deal with the incredible fear banked down behind his heart.

Right now, Carly being alive was the only reason for him to be sitting here wearing out his enamel. He'd been husbanding his energy, going down deep. It would be light in less than an hour. When the sun cleared the horizon, he was going to tear Fort Worth apart and find Carly.

He stood and came forward slowly. "Mark mentioned a pattern. Arsonists usually work an area, for the sake of convenience."

He moved before the large map of Fort Worth posted on another wall with the fire precincts clearly marked. The sites of active arson investigations were pinpointed on the map, alike colored pins used to show which had been linked.

He'd stared at the six orange pins that represented some of the arson fires he'd been investigating. These were the ones he had now been accused of starting. They'd never stood out before. Six among a dozen more he knew were arson but had no leads on. They weren't high priority. Nothing of true value had been damaged. In most cases, the houses had been derelict so long the city couldn't find the legal owners. The locations weren't clustered by convenience, neighborhood, access to highways, none of the things that usually led to an eventual suspect and arrest. These six fires were almost uniformly spaced around the city, which made them impossible to connect together until the source of the gasoline had been found to be identical to the gasoline in his lawn mower tank. That's all he had. What had he missed?

Noah pointed to the middle of the circle of orange pinpoints. "The only thing these fires have in common is that they—Fuck!"

He stared at the place where his finger was jammed against the map. It was his block, practically on top of his house. "He made my house his bull's-eye. That's it!"

"Let me see that." Durvan, Mark, and Jack moved in together behind him.

"Damn if you're not right. The fires are spaced just about equally distant from your street." Durvan smiled for the first time. "Good catch, Glover."

Noah removed his finger. "There's more. There's a fire in an almost perfect ring around the city, except for—"

"—Edgecliff Village." Mark looked embarrassed to have beaten Noah to speech. "Sorry."

Jack smiled. "You know what they say. Don't shit where you eat."

Noah took a deep breath. "My fake suicide was a one-off. Up until then Cody was trying to frame me for arson. Because I didn't know that, I didn't notice the pattern."

Crissie, who'd come in to work the desk, appeared in the doorway. "We just got a call. There's a grass fire in Edgecliff Village. But it's bordering on Fort Worth proper so FWDP is sending out a crew."

"Who called it in?"

She looked at her notes. "An Edgecliff Village firefighter volunteer."

"J.W. Cody," Noah and Mark said together.

Crissie frowned. "How did you know?"

CHAPTER THIRTY

The sun was rising by the time Noah and Mark sighted the distant plumes of smoke from the grass fire that was their destination. Durvan was right behind in his own vehicle. They needed his truck to carry their equipment. The early rays illuminating the smoke showed the deeper gray was turning whitish closer to the ground as water and other flame retardants were applied at the base fire.

Unfortunately, they were wedged in with rush-hour traffic streaming up and down Village Parkway, along with school buses turning in and out of neighborhoods to pick up students. The snarl was further complicated by rubber-neckers with nothing better to do.

Cursing under his breath, Noah pressed the floorboard on the passenger side with his right boot. He hated being a passenger! More than that, he hated not being in command. Every minute of delay was eating up his self-control.

Harley, in the backseat, began to vocalize softly. The pheromones pouring off his handler were disturbingly intense. Noah might look a study of coolness in his slouch, but Mark and Harley knew their travel companion was anything but.

Noah reached back a hand and stroked his partner. "It's okay, Harley. It's just taking us too damn long." Useless anxiety wasn't doing the job for either of them. Hold back, control emotion, and wait for the opportunity. That was practically his job description.

"Easy, bro." Make flicked a glance Noah's way. "This is our first solid lead. It's going to get us what we want."

Noah didn't answer. Nothing to say. Carly was out there, somewhere. He knew it. He had to find her. Fast.

The thing he couldn't keep from eating at him was *why*. Why had Carly put herself in jeopardy by talking with Cody? Why did she feel the need to do anything at all? For him? The idea scared the living hell out of him.

He wasn't accustomed to anyone taking care of him. That was *his* job. He'd always shouldered it just fine. Would be doing so now, if she hadn't disappeared.

This was why he didn't want her involved in the case. God knows he'd said that to her often enough.

Guilt ripped at his calm. He knew this was his fault. In spite of what he'd said, what he'd done told a very different story.

He'd wanted to be with her. Wanted to touch her. Wanted to dive into her silken heat. Pump long and hard into her, offering pleasure even as he took it from her. He still wanted her. Just thinking about it was enough to make him curse his own weakness. But he also wanted to talk to her. She challenged him, didn't sit in awe or expect him to have all the answers. They'd operated from the first as if they knew each other by heart. Shortcuts. Shorthand. They didn't play games. It was easy and exhilarating with Carly. She made him feel . . . so many things he'd thought he'd lost.

He wanted her. Wanted to be with her. Wanting to know

that she was in the world and happy. But now her life was in jeopardy. His fault. His to correct.

"Selfish prick!"

"Huh?"

Noah ignored Mark's questioning look. He would never expose Carly's confidence, her generosity to him, by ever telling a soul about them. Mark, Durvan, and the rest might speculate from here to doomsday but they'd never get a word out of him.

Something raw and ugly whip-snaked through Noah. If that asshole Cody had hurt Carly—

Finally, police intervention in the form of traffic control rerouted most of the commuters to other streets and they were allowed through to the blocked-off area after showing their FWFD credentials.

Two engines plus a grass wagon and water tank were on-site. Fire had burned halfway across a field between two new housing projects. Fires like this were often easy to contain and put out by an attack "from the black," that is, approaching it from the rear over already-burned ground. That way, there was nothing to catch fire behind the crew that might box them in. But a brisk March wind was frustrating efforts to contain the blaze this morning. Burned patches of grasses, flame links pushed by the wind, could be seen farther afield than where the main fire spread on a rolling lip of yellow flames. Blackened ground was still smoking heavily, sending up a gray veil that obscured the neighborhood in the direct path of the flames.

Once out of Mark's truck, Noah pulled out his fire gear. The set he kept in his truck had been impounded with the truck. Luckily the department provided two sets for its members, so that one would always be clean and ready to use.

A stiff breeze dragged at his gear as he stomped into his boots, and pulled up his pants and suspenders in one move. His bunker jacket was bulky and hot, so he stashed it under his arm to carry if and until it was required. His gloves were stashed in a pocket. He dumped his helmet on his head and grabbed Harley's leash.

Durvan and Mark were dressed likewise as the three men crossed over to the fireman in charge. The acrid sting of smoke and ash swirled around them as the fire sucked up more and more oxygen for fuel.

"Damn wind. But we're getting it knocked down." The Edgecliff Village fire captain came up to share his progress when he recognized Durvan. He offered his hand. "Fire chief sent for you guys to go in to search for cause?"

"No, this is an unofficial visit." Durvan's look was stern all the same. "Looking for one of your men. J.W. Cody. Need to speak with him."

"He's here somewhere." The fire captain looked around, scanning the line of men working the margins of the grass fire. Dressed in bunker suits, helmets, and other gear, it was nearly impossible to tell one man from another. "There." He pointed at the far end of the blaze. "Working the edge by the road in the reflector vest."

"You hold on to Harley." Noah tossed his leash to Mark.

"Whoa!" the fire captain called as Noah headed in Cody's direction. "We've got an uncontrolled burn on-going. I can't have unauthorized men in the field."

Durvan stepped in between them and pointed. "Looks like you've got maybe a hundred yards before the edge of the blaze meets that far fence line. This wind will eat up that distance in no time. You got the first row of houses behind that fence on alert to be evacuated?"

"We're on it." The fire captain began shouting orders into his radio, giving Noah the chance to make his way toward Cody.

Noah walked right up to Cody, who was using a back-pack foam sprayer, and grabbed him by the arm to swing him around.

"Where's Carly?"

Cody spun around with a look of surprise. "What the—? Glover? What the hell are you doing here?"

"Not the right answer." Noah hit him like a freight train, knocking both men to the ground.

As the two men grappled on the still smoking ash, other firefighters came running to pull them apart. But not before Noah had wrenched Cody's helmet off and thumped him with his fist a couple of times, demanding, "Where is she? Where?"

Regaining his feet with the help of two of his fellow firefighters, Cody pulled off a heavy hair glove and wiped at the blood on his face. "What the hell, Glover? You been drinking?"

Durvan and Mark had Noah by the arms, but Noah was angry enough to make holding him back a test. "Where's Carly?"

"Who? Oh, you mean Ms. Reese. Haven't seen her since yesterday when she gave me a list of work she wanted done on her store. I got it somewhere back in my truck." He bent to pick up his helmet. "Now I got to get back to the fire."

As Cody turned away, Noah shook free of his friends. "I know it was you who tried to kill me."

He took a step toward the man though both Durvan and Mark flanked him, ready to intervene again. He looked back at them and they paused at the expression on his face. It was a cop's face. He was back in control. He'd released just enough of his rage to master the rest. There'd be no more brawling.

He turned the full force of his personality into the stare he focused on the man. "It's over, J.W. We've got video of you last Friday night, coming out of the store where you left me and Harley to die. You drove off in my truck."

Cody scowled. "That's a lie."

Noah took another measured step closer. "You forgot

about the security cameras in other nearby parking lots. The senior citizens apartments, for instance. I know you started those other fires, too. The one that killed the homeless man is going to send you to prison."

"You've lost it, Glover." Cody was still smiling, certain he was Teflon-coated against all accusations.

Noah's voice lowered to a snarl. "I've been to your place. I saw the pictures. "

He was hammering J.W. with everything he had. Looking for a crack in the man's facade. They were so close again he could smell the man's stale breath despite the choking smoke of the nearby blaze. "You've been stalking Carly. Where is she?"

He saw uncertainty, finally, in J.W.'s blink and kept bringing it. "You want me in prison? I'll definitely be going there—for your murder—if you don't tell me where Carly is. Now."

"That's enough, Noah." Durvan grabbed Noah's shoulder from the rear.

Noah jerked his head toward his friend with a snarl.

Freed of Noah's menacing gaze, Cody turned to his two colleagues who had come to his aid. "You hear that? This man's threatened to kill me." He turned back to Noah. "I got witnesses you already attacked me."

Harley, who had been sitting tensely by Mark's side, suddenly ran up to Cody, sniffing him. Cody bent over to pet him. "Hey there, boy."

Harley sidestepped, sniffed the man's hand, and then sat and looked back at his handler.

A chill ran down Noah's spine. Harley had just *alerted* on J.W. That meant the man had recently handled explosive materials of some sort.

Noah grabbed him by the front of his jacket. "What's on your hands, Cody?"

"I don't have any idea what you mean." Cody flicked a

heavy glove at Harley as the dog tried again to catch the vital scent. "Get off me." Cody swung away. "I'm going back to work."

"Not today." Durvan stepped out and said, "I'm placing you in protective custody until this matter is settled."

"You can't do that. You don't have any jurisdiction in Edgecliff Village."

"So sue me." Durvan produced handcuffs and cuffed Cody. He pulled Cody over to where two Edgecliff police officers were keeping gawkers away and spoke to them.

Cody was shouting and swearing, threatening to sue Noah, the FWFD, the city, and anything else he could think of. But it was the voice of a scared man.

Mark looked at Noah. "Now what?"

"Harley signed on J.W. That means he's recently been around explosive chemicals."

Mark's face went grim. "You think he's made an explosive device?"

Noah nodded. "He's hoping to get rid of Carly in a way it will take a long time for forensics to identify. Come on." He headed toward the rear of the fire where volunteers had parked the vehicles.

Just to be certain Harley's actions hadn't been precipitated by his fight with J.W., Noah led his K9 past several other vehicles first, allowing Harley to sniff them thoroughly. Working him quickly so that he wouldn't accidently sign to Harley which vehicle he was concerned around, they wound their way back and forth between cars and trucks and vans.

Harley kept stopping to sneeze, clearing his air passages of the burn smell that permeated the air. But the second they approached J.W.'s van, Harley started stepping high, tail going rigid as he sniffed the door on the driver's side. When he reached the door handle, he sat, hard and alert.

He didn't have the right to search the vehicle without

probable cause, but that didn't mean Noah couldn't look inside through the window. He pulled his flashlight and aimed it inside the van. Between the seats in the back he saw a jug of all-purpose fertilizer. He stopped breathing. Ammonium nitrate.

"Damn," Mark said softly when he had looked in.

"Yeah." Noah barely had breath for sound. He pulled a treat from his pocket for Harley, and then a second one, praising his dog highly though he felt sick inside.

"What'd you boys find?" Durvan jogged up minus J.W., now being held by local police.

As Mark explained, Noah turned inward and mentally threw away everything they had been concentrating on during the night. None of it now applied. The facts now were these.

Carly was missing.

J.W. had taken her.

He must have decided she had figured out he was the arsonist.

He needed to get rid of her.

More than a fire this time, he needed more damage more quickly.

He didn't have time to make an elaborate plan like he did for Noah's suicide.

The grass fire had been called in by J.W. More than likely, he had started it for a reason. Distraction.

Distraction from what? Another fire.

Noah remembered Carly's question about the Friday night fire. And it gave him a watery gut feeling.

Why not choose a place where the perpetrator had all the time in the world to set the fire and make certain it took?

What better place than in his own community?

Edgecliff Village was small. If J.W. wanted to distract

the local fire department, it must be because the fire he'd set for Carly was nearby.

Heart thumping at low heavy strokes, Noah looked up. The prevailing winds whipping up from the southwest were driving the fire northeast, into a populated neighborhood. Evacuation would take the attention of every first responder, diverting attention from any other fire, especially one deemed less important.

Noah turned to face the opposite direction of the fire, upwind. For two hundred yards there was nothing but scrub brush and grass. Beyond that, the field gave way to a cleared area where the streets of a new housing development had been paved. No housing to see yet. Just a single, half-finished structure sat isolated in the middle of the second block. Someone's dream house that had yet to be realized.

Noah shivered in response to an adrenaline rush. Could Carly be in there, close enough for J.W. to watch her burn, but using his involvement in the brush fire as his alibi?

Harley had followed his handler's gaze, something dogs alone among domesticated animals do. He lifted his snout, sniffing the breeze moving directly past the house to the south and into the field where they stood. After a few seconds, he began to whine and tug at the leash, wanting to head in the direction of the structure.

Noah bent down and stroked his K9, the beginnings of a smile on his grim face. "Is that where Carly is, Harley? Do you smell her on the breeze? Or is it the explosive?"

He reached up and released Harley's leash.

The German Shepherd took off like a furry dart across the field.

Noah stood up, fear suddenly crawling up through his glacial calm. Carly and a bomb. J.W. had left her to die.

Just as quickly as it reared up, the fear died. He'd worked the puzzle pieces and won.

"Got you, you bastard!"

And now he was going to get Carly.

Noah outlined the bare bones of his theory to his colleagues as they ran back to their vehicles.

Mark thought it was a long shot.

Durvan called it a Hail Mary pass without even the hope of a receiver. "That's just plain nuts. J.W.'s gotta be smarter than that."

Noah didn't waste his breath arguing. His full focus was on Carly. If she was there in that house, then she had very little time left. The grass fire would be controlled soon. He could hear the sirens of additional FWFD apparatus rolling toward them bringing reinforcements in the way of firefighters and resources. J.W. must have wanted the explosive fire to start in the thick of things.

It took less than three minutes before they were pulled up before the house. Harley was there before them, barking and clawing at the front door.

Noah called him back.

Harley came racing back to his handler, tail flying and tongue lolling in happiness. He'd done good, and he knew it.

"Good Harley. Best damn dog in the business!" Noah crowed in a high excited voice, stopping to give praise that would have no meaning for Harley later. Dogs lived in the *now*. So he loved on his dog and fed him two more treats, using precious seconds that counted. Without Harley, he wouldn't be here.

"New construction," Durvan said when he'd exited his truck and stood surveying the house. "No brick to hold in the heat, but no protection against the updraft a fire inside would create. Harley thinks there's an explosive device inside. I'm calling in the bomb squad."

Noah wasn't responding. He had turned to the task of donning the rest of his equipment, making certain every piece fit and lay flat, the many layers of protection against flames essential for safety. He didn't fight fires anymore, but he did go into active burn sites that were deemed suspicious in order to collect evidence before it was destroyed. The drill had been with him so long it was muscle memory, eliminating every other thought.

"Here." Durvan tossed him a helmet shield and breathing apparatus from the back of his own truck. "You might need extra gear. But I wish you'd wait until we can get a truck over here and get a hose line started."

Noah shook his head. "There's no fire. They won't spare a truck when they are fighting to save occupied houses. I'm going in now."

"Then take this." Durvan handed him a backpack full of flame retardant with a short hose and wand attached. "Don't be a fool. If it's not doing the job, come out."

No one said what they all knew. They hadn't brought bomb squad gear with them. Noah was taking what the other men thought was an unnecessary risk, without knowing for certain a person was inside. But there was no way to know that without first entering.

"I'll take the door." Mark had suited up and was holding an ax, the kind used to break through doors and rooftops.

Noah eyed him closely. "You're sure you want to do this?"

"Bomb squad on the way." Durvan was shouting from the open door of his truck. "ETA fifteen minutes."

"Too long."

Mark nodded. "Let's go get her."

With Harley tucked safely away in Mark's truck, they approached.

Mark hit the doorframe with the ax, splintering wood and shattering what was probably a very expensive door.

The explosion, buffered by the half-open door, still managed to force both men back a step. But Noah kept going, right into the heart of the new conflagration. Carly was in there. He was going to get her out.

The house was filling quickly with smoke. Whatever explosive device J.W. had used was only to ignite the accelerant that saturated the main floor. He could smell the gasoline even through his breathing apparatus. New houses were made of materials that ignited easily and burned quickly. Even without drapes and furnishings, the house would be up in flames within a few moments. As he made his way across the floor, the swoosh of flames appeared all at once, in every room. The smoke gathered quickly as wallboard and laminated wood flooring burned. Where to begin looking?

He braced himself for the worst, and went back to school in his head.

The thing about primary searches is this. You'll be going in for live victims, often before the first hose is full. It's not like in the movies. Flames don't dance around behind and in front of you, backlighting your fellow firefighters like goblins in a Halloween cartoon. The flames don't show you stairs or furnishings, or holes in the flooring. There's only smoke. You can't see shit. But you can feel things. Like heat. Lots of it pressing in everywhere.

So far, that wasn't his problem in an empty shell of a house. There was only a light smoke condition.

It should have made him feel better but it didn't. Poisons from flames were often invisible and could kill before heat ever became a problem.

Noah heard movement behind him, probably Mark coming through the door, but he didn't waste time to check. He headed methodically from the entry with its eight-foot ceiling through to the living room, his *classroom* still functioning.

A primary search begins as close to the fire as possible.

He turned a corner with a curved wall and came to a stop. A mattress lay in the middle of the family room floor. It was in full flame, yellow licks rising three full feet in the air. He couldn't see a body but he didn't waste time evaluating.

Swearing savagely, he hit the blaze with flame retardant.

"Jesus!" Mark's voice came through his radio though he was at Noah's side. He added his efforts to Noah's.

But Noah was moving again. Carly was not lying in the bed that he knew Cody had meant to be her funeral pyre. Heart pounding so loudly he could hardly think, he headed for the bedroom. Go to school, he told himself.

If someone is still alive in here, where would they most likely be?

He came upon a closed door.

You can't see shit. But you'll hear things.

He heard something. At least, he thought he did.

He couldn't say why, but he thought the sound came from there.

He pushed through, aware that the fire was climbing walls behind him.

Nothing in the bedroom.

And then he heard it again. A voice. A woman's scream.

He barreled through the opening into the bathroom.

Carly lay curled on her side in a Jacuzzi tub. She was naked, her hands and ankles strapped by electrical tape. Her mouth was red and raw, and her eyes were uncovered by the bandage strapping her head. He could see her arms and knees were bruised, but all he cared about was that she was screaming. That meant she was breathing. But the fumes had followed him from room and room. She wasn't safe even here.

He bent over the tub to touch her, his heart pounding

so hard he could hardly hear his own voice. "Carly, it's Noah. I got you, baby. You're safe." She jerked under his touch but stopped screaming. "Hold on. I've got you."

He grabbed his radio and shouted. "Found Carly. Extricating."

"Roger." Just as Mark came through the bathroom door a second explosion occurred in the family room.

Both men flinched, but Mark was shouting a reply. "The place is booby-trapped. We need to go now. Get her out of there." Mark pointed to the big square decorative window over the tub. "We're going out that way."

Noah wriggled out of his backpack and stripped off his breathing apparatus then bent and scooped Carly up by the waist. His remaining gear was bulky, impeding his efforts to haul her out. With her hands tied behind her back she couldn't help him. But once she got her to her knees, she was able to get her feet under her and push herself to standing. He leaned in and shoved her up over his shoulder, caveman style, uncaring that she was naked, this once.

As Noah backed away, Mark stepped over the rim into the tub and swung his axe. The window shattered. He swung several more times until he had cleared the frame of glass fragments that might cut them. Then he turned to Noah.

"You two first. I'll get the gear." He stepped back and let Noah climb into the tub and then swing a leg over the windowsill.

Noah didn't stop when his feet hit the packed earth outside. He suspected that a third explosion might bring the house down upon them. With a hand clamped behind her knees to hold Carly in place over his shoulder, he made several long quick strides to put distance between them and house before turning to check for his partner. He sighed in relief as he saw Mark climbing through the window. Then he turned and headed for the street where fire equipment and firefighters were arriving.

Durvan met Noah before he reached the curb with a silver blanket to cover her. Once it was wrapped around her, Durvan tried to take Carly from him. Noah held tight. "I got this." He moved to the far side of the street from the burning house, passing firemen with hoses headed toward the blaze.

Finally, he knelt in the grass and let Carly slide from his shoulder. He caught her to keep her from falling. "Get me a knife or scissors."

Durvan pulled a knife from his pocket and carefully slit the tape binding Carly's wrists and ankles. More slowly, he worked the blade between her hair and the tape so as not to damage her hair or eyes.

All the while she stared up at Noah, and she was smiling. When she was free she reached up and grabbed his neck so hard it surprised him. "I knew you'd come. I knew it!" But the relief was too new. Her voice still held the plea of a prayer.

The realization that he almost didn't make it in time sent a hard shiver through Noah as he pulled her protectively close. "Are you hurt? Did he hurt you in any way?"

She pulled back and shook her head.

But Noah needed verbal confirmation. "Is Cody responsible for this? Just say yes or no."

"Yes." She seemed about to say more but she voice caught and she coughed and half-choked.

He touched her face tenderly. "That's enough. Don't try to speak. The ambulance is here. You're safe, and you're going to be fine." His tone was gentle, his expression mild. Until he glanced up at Durvan, who remained watching them.

"You can arrest that son of Satan for attempted murder now. Carly will testify to it."

Durvan nodded. "With pleasure."

CHAPTER THIRTY-ONE

Two months later

"Come on, Harley. Faster. Faster!" Andy ran ahead of the German Shepherd who was nearly twice his weight.

They were running the obstacle course at Fort Woof. The park at nine o'clock on a Saturday was full of people and their pets. But few dared the embarrassment of trying to get their dogs to show off their physical prowess on the Agility course.

The obstacles were built low enough for even small dogs to enjoy. That meant they were not a taxing effort for Harley. But the dog gamely played along, jumping over low barriers, running through hoops, and ducking into plastic tube tunnels. Boy and dog were having a great time.

Noah stood nearby, his son's windbreaker slung over his shoulder. He grinned as he watched Andy's flushed face and heard his shouts of delight over Harley's performance. He drank in the sights and sounds of his son as if they were pure oxygen.

They came out here every Saturday or Sunday morning that Noah was off. And Noah made certain he did something alone with his son when his days off were in the middle of the week. Recently, he'd picked Andy up from school for a dental appointment. Andy didn't make it back for classes. Instead, they went to see the latest Disney offering at the movies.

"You're spoiling Andy," his father said just yesterday.

He was. And it would have to stop. But not yet. Not when just looking at his son made his heart swell with fatherly pride and the fierce need to protect and teach him how to take care of himself. For times when he wasn't around.

Life had always been precious to Noah, but never more than in the past two months.

He nearly died.

Carly nearly died.

He wondered how she was dealing with it all.

He hadn't seen her since the night he'd spent with her in the hospital right after the fire. She was suffering from exposure, and cuts and bruises that, to his amazement, she'd inflicted on herself in her attempts to get away. Not once, but twice. Even bound, she'd managed to push and pull herself like a slug across the family-room floor and into the back bathroom because she remembered being told that lying down in a tub was a safe place from a fire.

But not if he hadn't arrived when he did.

Listening to her ordeal made him want to get J.W. Cody alone for five minutes. Thankfully, the man was beyond his grasp.

Cody had taken a plea bargain after his attorney saw the case the DA's office put together against him. The multiple arsons, manslaughter, plus two attempted murder charges would have put him away for life. Instead, he'd taken fifteen years, no parole.

Andy was beside himself with delight when the course

was run. He approached his dad in a half-run, half-skip lope. "Did you see that, Dad? Harley cleared every obstacle."

"I saw that." Noah bent down and scooped his son up to twirl him around, ending up holding him off the ground upside down by one ankle.

Andy squealed with delight. It was a daily ritual between them.

Two mothers standing nearby with their kids sent him disapproving looks but he only smiled. "He's training to be Spiderman."

When he'd righted his son, he handed Andy Harley's leash to use as they walked back toward the entrance.

"You're a very good teacher, Andy. Maybe we should enter you and Harley in Dog Agility in a couple of years."

"Uh-huh." Andy was frowning now. Noah had learned to go with the sudden switches and unpredictable moments that made up a child's emotional life. But he was often baffled by them.

"What's the matter?"

"Tomorrow's Mother's Day, Dad."

"Yeah." Noah tried to keep his voice neutral.

"Kids at school say I can't celebrate it because I don't have a mom."

Noah's heart contracted as he debated how to answer.

Andy looked up at his dad. "Is it okay that I don't have a mom?"

With a heavy heart, Noah paused and squatted down before his child. "It's okay. Absolutely."

The shadow in his son's eyes, as blue as his father's, remained. "Could I ever get one?"

"What do you have in mind?"

"Angela's mom and dad divorced. But her dad got married again and now she's got two moms. So if you got married, that means I'd get a mom, right?"

Noah's lips twitched. "Sounds like it."

Andy stared at his dad a moment longer and then turned to walk on. "Okay."

Noah had the unreal sensation that he'd just been told by his son that he was falling down on the get-a-wife job. Who knew?

Noah laid a hand on his son's head. "You know we do have someone to celebrate on Mother's Day? GiGi. Grandmothers and even aunts are included in the day."

Andy nodded. "Yeah. I made her a card in art class."

"Whoa. Then you're way ahead of me. I need to buy her a gift." Thanks to Andy, he had a place in mind. "Want to help me choose one?"

Andy looked up with a serious expression. "Nothing for the kitchen, or house, or yard. That's what she told Grampa."

Noah laughed so loud he startled the birds sitting on a power line overhead. "You're already ahead of three fourths of the men in the world when it comes to gift giving for women."

The opening of Flawless was already a success. And it was only an hour old. The banners fluttering in the warm May air had attracted quite a crowd. Added to that, Carly had convinced her local vendors to set up tables both inside and out on the sidewalk, to show potential customers their work in progress. Seeing something being made increased its uniqueness.

Carly stopped by Joi's table. "How's it going?"

"So well! I've had a TCU sorority order ten dozen Tail Feathers to give as mementos to alumni for homecoming next fall. Means I'll be dyeing feathers purple for days."

Carly grinned. Despite the initial enthusiasm for the new word *butt*laces, it was determined at a later theme meeting for Flawless that the word might be a turnoff for some. They elected, unanimously, to go with Tail Feathers.

"We've sold all but two of your headbands and all of the necklaces. I will take as many orders as you can fill."

"I've been working nonstop," Indija said from a nearby table. "This guy from UT Arlington collects rocks and minerals. Says he can hook me up with some hard-to-find crystals and stuff. Look at this." She held up an arm wound with copper wire from her middle finger up to her elbow. Cradled along her arm, three webs of twisted copper held three large soft green spheres. "He called them bubble crystals. They're from Mali."

Carly admired them and moved on to her other suppliers. Every one of them was busy demonstrating. A huge amount of work had gone into the last two months, and lessons were learned. She didn't have to go it alone. It was better to have colleagues. Her vendors were now invested in what she was doing. They felt empowered. And they were going to make a living from doing something they loved. It didn't get better than that.

Kuppy Cakes Bakery, located next door, had opened the weekend before. That dispelled any lasting horror of the fire. In fact, an employee dressed like a decorated cupcake was handing out samples of one of the random cakes on a platter to passersby.

She walked back into her store before realizing that the crowd of ladies and young girls had been joined by two males, one large and one small.

"Noah." Carly couldn't find air.

Feelings she'd been denying were suddenly vying for and clogging up her throat. But she wasn't going to act all weepy grateful he'd shown up after two months. A woman had her pride, even if her eyes were shamelessly taking in his dimensions in lascivious detail. For instance the way his knit shirt didn't hide at all the warm hard musculature beneath. Or those bulges of muscle beneath the short sleeves that she knew personally were strong enough to carry a woman securely out of a fire.

Nothing below the belt buckle, Carly. Have some pride.

She walked up to him, a bigger smile on her face than was strictly necessary. *Behave like yourself, Carly.*

She reached up to place a hand on each of his shoulders and gave him a quick kiss on each cheek, continental style. Damn, he smelled the same. No. Better. "Welcome to Flawless, Investigator Glover."

She saw his pupils expand, eating up the blue, and remembered what that kiss had inspired the last time. Desire plunged through her, going straight to the appropriate lady parts. *Ooh* boy. No time to get flustered. There was a child present.

She looked down at the boy and knew instantly he was Andy. She could have picked him out from a gaggle of kindergarteners. He was a miniature of his dad, from his curly hair, several shades lighter than his father's, to the sky blue eyes that crinkled in the corners when he smiled. In fifteen years or so, ladies would be in serious danger of losing their hearts.

"You must be Andy." She offered him her hand.

Andy took it and shook formally, but he was staring at her.

Noah frowned. "What's the matter, son?"

He looked up at his dad. "How come she kissed you?"

"Ah." Carly squatted down, balancing easily on her heels. "What I did is called a continental kiss. Very popular in Europe, where I once lived. Would you like one?"

Andy shook his head, but he was watching her in a kind of curiosity.

Carly smiled. "There are lots of ways people from other places greet one another. Americans shake hands like we did. Europeans kiss both cheeks. Do you know what the Inuit people of the Arctic do?"

Andy shook his head, brows drawn down in concern.

"They rub noses. Would you like to rub noses?"

"No-*oow*." The word was broken up by a giggle as Andy pressed back against his father's long legs. He was smiling now.

Carly nodded. "Okay. Friends?" She held out her hand again.

Andy took it. "You're funny."

"Thank you. What can I do for you gentlemen today?"

"We need a Mother's Day present. For my GiGi."

"Does she like jewelry? How about a pair of earrings?"

Carly moved over to the table where her personal pieces were displayed. "If she has pierced ears, she might like these." She held up a small pair of sterling silver earrings in the shape of flowers with the tips of the petals rolled back. Inside, the stamens were made of gold.

Andy looked at his dad. "It's not for the kitchen or the garden. Will she like them?"

"Guaranteed." He met Carly's gaze. "Especially when you tell GiGi you met the lady who made them."

Andy looked up at Carly. "You made them?"

"Everything in the store is made by hand. If you're curious, you can go and see what some of the artists are making at their tables. Oh, and there are samples of cupcakes from next door, if that's okay with your dad."

"Dad?"

"Go ahead. But stay in the store. And only one—okay, two cupcakes."

Noah followed Carly to the cash register. It gave him time to appreciate what she was wearing. A sleeveless blouse with the ends tied loosely at her navel and a black miniskirt. Simple. But she made it look elegant. Of course, she wore braided leather sandals with laces crisscrossing back and forth up to her knees. Women's fashion. He'd never understand it. But on her, whatever she wore was sexy as anything ever.

Their fingers brushed as he handed her his credit card. "I've missed you, Carly."

She didn't look up. "I've been around. Every day. For two months."

"I know. I thought maybe you needed time and space to process things."

She looked up. He wasn't certain that was better. He could see the hurt peeking out behind the shade she was throwing. "Did you need it?"

He nodded. "Cody. The hatred. What it did to my family. Getting straight again on the job. It all took time. After my part in your suffering, I wasn't sure you'd want to see my face again."

"Okay." She turned away.

"Wait." He touched her arm. "What does that mean?"

"It means you went two months without getting in touch." There it was. The mistake he'd suspected he was making. But he'd wanted her to have a chance to get over him. What they'd started was too hot not to cool down.

But she hadn't cooled on him, and she was doing a miserable job of hiding it. That hunger she banked back most of the time had leaped to flame in her eyes as she regarded him. And with it, the hope inside him that just maybe he hadn't ruined it all.

"We need to talk."

"Not here." She handed him his card back and began tying a lovely pink bow around the box containing the earrings.

"Then let me come back and take you to dinner when you close."

"I'll be too tired to go out."

She must have seen the disappointment register in his

expression. It softened hers. "You're welcome to come over for dinner tonight. I'm making spicy sweet potato bean burritos."

He'd be there, even if she were serving mud with rocks.

"You came." Carly leaned in and kissed Noah on both cheeks, then added a third kiss, just because, before dancing away into her apartment.

Before she could back completely away, he snagged her at the waist with an arm. "There's been something on my mind all day."

"Oh yeah?" His arm felt so good, and comforting. But she had her pride. She slipped free and moved into her living area.

Noah followed. "You impressed the heck out of Andy. He's asking if we can come by your shop again soon. I got to admit, it's got me a tad worried, since you sell only girly stuff."

"It probably has more to do with Kuppy Cakes next door. I saw him sneak a third." She had walked over to the sofa but didn't move around it to sit.

He moved right in behind her, caging her with his body against the back of the sofa. "So, here's what's on Andy's dad's mind."

His braced his arms on the sofa back, one on either side of her. Very close, but not touching. "I want to know about what other kind of kisses were you going to tell my son about?"

"Oh, you mean like the Inuit kiss?" She turned within the space he allowed and pushed her face up to his and rubbed her nose back and forth along the length of his.

"That's pretty damn erotic," he murmured.

"Yes. It comingles breaths like a mouth kiss and offers the stimulation of nerves we don't think of as sexual."

"Whatever. They called it an eskimo kiss when I was a kid. Of course, it wasn't sexy as you make it."

"Eskimo is a term that has fallen out of favor. But the next time you want an Inuit kiss, you know where to find me."

"Indeed, I do. So, lay that on me again."

When she moved back from the kiss, he was grinning at her. "What else?"

"Butterfly kisses." This time she reached up to frame his face with her fingers and turned her head to the side as she moved in. When her eyelashes touched his cheek, she opened and closed her eyes rapidly. "Butterfly-wing kisses."

"Damn. That went directly to my nether regions." He pulled back with a strange intensity in his face. "Want to try that all over my body?"

She smiled but shrugged. She tapped him on the chest to be released. "If your curiosity is otherwise satisfied, I have to check the oven."

"Why?" He followed her. "What else do you have in your personal bag of kissing erotica?"

She clicked on the oven light and checked her burritos before turning around. He was right there, blocking any easy way around him.

"There is the bee kiss." She angled her head to bring her lips against his neck just below his ear and pursed her lips, making a buzzing sound as she pushed air out between them.

"Damn, Carly. You're going to have me on my knees."

"Not the worst position for a man." She licked then blew into his damp ear, gently grazed his earlobe with her teeth. "Ear kiss."

He sighed like a man under duress. "I'm hoping like hell you aren't done yet."

"I'm just getting started," she whispered, before leaving a tongue trail down his neck.

She lowered her hands from his shoulders and reached to pull his shirt up out of his pants.

He watched her lids at half-mast. "You undress me, and dinner is off the menu."

"Wasn't all that hungry anyway."

She lightly raked her fingers back and forth across the skin of his belly that she'd exposed. "You know that game you play with a baby, blowing on the tummy?" She glanced up at him as she poked a thumb into his belly button. "Belly kiss coming up."

She lowered herself and replaced her thumb with her tongue, flicking it rapidly in and out over his navel.

Noah flung his head back. "That kiss wasn't the only thing that came up. I'm hard as a pipe."

"You're so easy." She snaked back up his body, grazing him everywhere with the impression of her own. "Any more requests?"

"Let's save something for next time."

She gazed him a questioning look. "Next time?"

He ignored the provocation. They both knew this was only the beginning.

This time it was his turn. He settled his hands on her waist. "French kissing has always been popular with me."

She smiled. "That old standby."

"Yeah. Boring as hell, right?" His hands slid up her torso, taking the hem of her shirt with them until his warm calloused hands were holding her naked back. "Let me see if I remember how to do that."

The stroke of his tongue along the seam of her lips was like an injection of lust, direct and mainlined, her body instantly ready for him. And then he proceeded to show her that he hadn't forgotten a thing about how to French kiss, adding a few variations as he went along.

By the time he broke the kiss, she was sagging against him and he was holding on to her for dear life. And somehow their clothes had found the floor.

"Why don't we take this to the bedroom? And you can show me all those kisses again. But on different parts of the body."

She turned off the stove, took his hand to lead him to her bed. And she did exactly what he requested.

And then he improvised, trying out butterfly kisses on her nipples. And bee buzz in the cleft between her thighs.

By the time he slid into her she was panting, and his groans were so loud she was glad her bedroom didn't have a common wall.

"You feel so damn delicious, Carly."

She was feeling him, too. He felt so good inside her she was weeping, and all for him. When they climaxed, her body clamped down on his so hard she could feel every pulse of his ejaculation as he emptied into her.

Noah flung a hand over his eyes, trying to remember how to speak. "Where did you learn all that? No, don't tell me." Other men, sophisticated European decadent lucky ducks who knew how to dazzle women. He'd just have to accept her past.

She crawled up over his chest, her smile the best ever. "You won't believe me."

He grunted.

"Baby-sitting training classes."

"Get out."

"Really. The Inuit kiss, the bee buzz, the butterfly wing, and the tummy blow are all pretty standard ways of making small children laugh. Gentler than tickling, which can sometimes turn into torture."

"How'd you come to turn child's play into adult erotic torture?"

"You asked me to." She smiled and kissed his chin. "No

man ever asked me about playful kisses before. So I improvised."

Noah saw the truth of it in her face. "So, this was all just for me?"

"Don't get a big head."

"Oh, that's not what's getting big—again."

"Men."

"Yes. And glad as hell to be one when you're around."

He rolled her over and under him, framing her face with his fingers. "You're the best thing that's ever happened to me, Carly. You wreck me every time we're together. Every time."

Her expression became serious. "It's not a game for me with you."

"You think I don't know what? This thing between us, I know you feel it too. I'm trying to accept it. I don't deser—"

She cupped her hand over his mouth. "Either accept it, or get out. It's a gift. Gifts are flawless."

He smiled. "Please remind me, every two or three months."

She quirked a brow. "That's a big leap."

"We'll see." He waggled his brows at her. "Want to play Hide the Salami?"

"Vegetarian, remember?"

"Hide the Banana?"

AUTHOR'S NOTE

Dear Readers,

Once again, the K-9 Rescue Series has taken me on an adventure and introduced me to new wonderful people and dogs. This latest installment, *Explosive Forces*, required me to venture into the complicated field of Arson Investigation. My guide was Brad Sims, Arson Investigator with Forth Worth, TX Fire Department's Arson/bomb Squad Division. Brad isn't a dog man, but his knowledge of arson and arsonists proved very valuable to me. He also introduced me to Mike Ikerd, another arson investigator who is partnered with a gorgeous black Lab Explosives Dog named Quigley.

Hope you are enjoying the series. If you missed any books, here's where to look for them all: www.ddayres.com.

See you next year with another.

D. D.

Don't miss the next book in the K-9 Rescue series
by D. D. Ayres!

PHYSICAL FORCES

Coming soon from St. Martin's Paperbacks